Matthew Arnold Stern

Amiga

Black Rose Writing | Texas

This is a work of fiction. Names, characters, businesses, places, events, and
incidents are either the products of the author's imagination or used in a
fictitious manner. Any resemblance to actual persons, living or dead, or
actual events is purely coincidental.

ISBN: 978-1-68433-388-2
PUBLISHED BY BLACK ROSE WRITING
www.blackrosewriting.com

Printed in the United States of America
Suggested Retail Price (SRP) $18.95

Amiga is printed in Calluna

*As a planet-friendly publisher, Black Rose Writing does its best to eliminate
unnecessary waste to reduce paper usage and energy costs, while never compromising
the reading experience. As a result, the final word count vs. page count may not meet
common expectations.

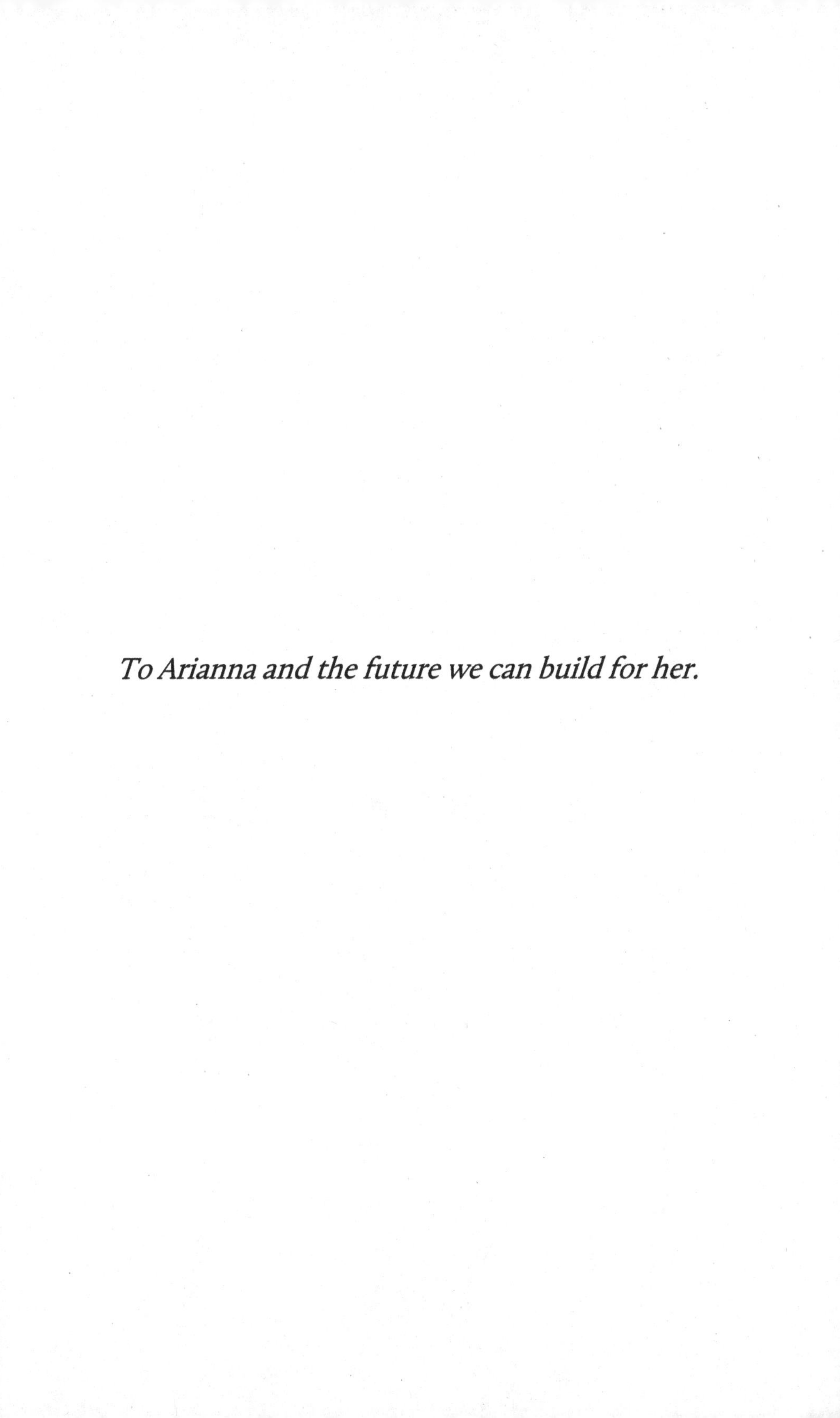

To Arianna and the future we can build for her.

Amiga

CHAPTER ONE
July 1985

He picked up the blue linen paper. "Miss Rodriguez?"

"Laura."

I smiled. My faculty advisor taught me to smile at interviews. After two months of interviewing, I had been in enough beige, aluminum, and glass conference rooms and sat in enough knock-off Herman Miller chairs that smiling started to seem natural.

The offices looked the same. So did the managers who interviewed me. The men, and they were always men, wore ties. Wide, conservative striped, and usually in beige and brown tones. That was the type of tie worn by the man who picked up my resume. He introduced himself as Doug Staley. He was the lead programmer. His tie was crooked and loose. He was probably going to yank it off and toss it in a desk drawer as soon as my interview was finished. He had a wispy blond mustache and wore oversized glasses with thick smudged lenses.

He introduced the other men. Jim Fowler was the manager of the programming department. He also wore a loose beige tie and an ill-fitting brown sports coat. At the end was Steven McGregor, the director of engineering. I could tell he was a director because he wore a proper navy blue suit jacket and a yellow power tie with small navy blue designs. Seated next to me was the HR representative, Louise Stansfield. Her oversized gold loop earrings nearly brushed against the inflated shoulder pads of her aggressively cobalt blue dress.

"It says you have a master's degree in computer science from Cal State Northridge." Doug spoke slowly and methodically.

"Yes. I graduated in May. Magna cum laude." I left that out in my first few interviews. I never felt comfortable about tooting my own horn, even though my faculty advisor gave me tips on how to do it without sounding like bragging.

"I see." Doug didn't look up from the paper. He seemed unimpressed.

I straightened my glasses. "My thesis was on managing local memory when processing high-resolution graphics on modern personal computers. I showed how the Motorola 68000 is the best microprocessor available today for handling such..."

Jim interrupted. "Do you have any work experience?"

"Yes." I kept smiling and sat up straighter. "I worked in the computer lab on campus. I helped students with projects and assisted with upgrading our 3270 terminals to IBM PCs, and..."

"Any professional programming experience?"

"During summers, I worked in the computer department at West Valley Savings and Loan." I turned to Doug and noticed he hadn't looked up from my resume. "I have that listed under work experience."

Jim continued. "What did you do there?"

"I maintained accounting programs developed in COBOL on an IBM System/370 as well as creating an interface with a Diebold TABS 9000 series ATM. By creating the interface in-house, the bank saved thousands over hiring a consultant."

"You assisted a programmer?"

"I wrote the interface myself."

Jim stared at me. I couldn't tell if he was impressed, or if he couldn't believe that a 24-year-old could have created such a complete mission-critical ATM interface herself. Actually, I was 21 when I wrote it. I didn't tell them that, or why I felt so motivated to create a way people could bank without seeing a teller. It might have helped if I mentioned those things because the men didn't seem that interested with anything I've said so far. Doug kept staring at my resume. Steven, who hadn't said anything so far, seemed focused on my breasts.

Doug's eyes moved to the top of the paper, "It says you live in...Reseda? Is that in LA somewhere?"

"Yes, but I'm planning to move to the area if I'm hired. I'm staying with a friend in San Rafael in the meantime."

"You're not looking for a relocation package, are you?" The way Jim asked it, I assumed one wasn't available.

"No," I kept smiling. "I'm excited about moving to Silicon Valley. In the computer industry, that's where the action is."

"It looks like you received an impressive number of awards." Doug said the first positive thing about me in the interview, but he spoke in his flat, methodical voice. "You won a $2,500 scholarship from SHPE. What's that?"

"Society of Hispanic Professional Engineers."

Then Steven blurted out the first thing he said in the interview, "Are you an American citizen?"

My back stiffened. I took a small and silent breath.

"Yes. In fact, my father served in Vietnam. He died in combat."

Doug looked up from my resume. The room fell silent. I may have won my self-respect, but I knew I lost the job.

*** BREAK ***

Louise escorted me out of the conference room. When we were far enough away, she put her arm around my shoulders and pulled me close.

"Laura." Her voice was nasal and condescending. "Let me give you some advice as one working girl to another."

She stopped and let go of me. I turned towards her. She grinned tightly.

"Men like girls who are smart, but not too smart, and certainly not as smart as they are. And men don't like a girl who tells them they're wrong. There aren't too many girls in computer programming, so you should be very careful about how you present yourself. Especially a girl like you, Miss Rodriguez." Her curt tone emphasized the Spanishness of my name.

I stood silently in the hallway. I would walk out of that place without a job or my dignity.

"One other thing." She looked down at my black dress slacks. "Wear a skirt."

*** BREAK ***

They say the Golden Gate Bridge is romantic, but it felt less romantic each time I sat in the mass of cars inching towards those orange Art Deco towers.

I went through all of the interviews in all of the beige conference rooms with beige men. I did everything my faculty advisor told me to do. I checked and rechecked my resume for typos. I focused on my work experience. I treaded the careful boundary between selling myself and bragging. I focused on results from my work experience. What was I missing, besides a penis?

*** BREAK ***

It took me an hour and a half to drive from Silicon Valley through San Francisco traffic. I might as well stayed at home in the Valley and looked for work in Orange County. I was glad I bought a 1984 Honda Civic hatchback before I left college. At least I didn't have to go broke driving to interviews at places that had no intention of hiring me.

I should have felt relieved to pull into the parking lot of the apartment complex after spending way too long in a car. But I knew what was waiting for me when I got to the apartment. I smelled it before I stepped in the door.

I found Tina cross-legged on the floor and leaning against the sofa. She hunched over the bong between her legs like she was fellating herself with a smoke-filled glass dong. She exhaled, adding to the raunchy smelling haze that filled the living room.

"You look stressed. Take a hit."

She raised her bong towards me. I stared at the yellowed water and dark brown resin stains and shook my head.

"I'm fine."

"No, you're not." She set down the bong and reached into a baggie for another pinch.

"Really, I'm fine."

"Suit yourself." She packed the pinch into the bowl.

I turned away from her and headed towards the hallway.

"But seriously, Laura. You should try it. Marijuana is good for you. It's natural. It grows from the earth."

"So does hemlock." I walked down the hall.

*** BREAK ***

I entered her office and closed the door. The hazy stench from the living room followed me there. I opened a window and turned on the ceiling fan.

This had been my bedroom since I started applying for jobs in the Bay Area. Tina and I met in junior high and hung out together in high school. We went to CSUN together as well, but she got tired of living with her parents and the San Fernando Valley in general. She moved to San Rafael. She did some graphic design, maintained databases for different social activist groups and politicians, and produced a talk show on KPFA. She must have managed to piece together a good living. She had an Apple II and a Macintosh, and those were really expensive.

I had to sleep on her sofa. I didn't mind because she was doing me a favor letting me stay here, even if her place smelled like a Grateful Dead concert on 4/20. I also had ready access to the phone. That reminded me that I owed Mom a phone call. I set down my purse, pulled out my wallet, and took out my MCI card.

*** BREAK ***

"Don't be so discouraged, Laura." Even over a long-distance line, her voice sounded like her warm hand caressing the side of my face.

"I didn't think this would be so hard."

"Most worthwhile things are."

"Thanks, Mom." She knew the right things to say. Sometimes.

"And if things don't work out…"

"Mom, I'm not going back to work at the bank."

"But they love your work."

"Mom, they program in COBOL. With punch cards."

"It's a programming job."

"But it's not what I want. There are so many exciting things going on in the computer industry right now. I don't want to be left behind!"

"I know. I just want you to remember that have options. There is a path for you, Laura. You will find it, I'm sure."

*** BREAK ***

Perhaps Mom was right. Perhaps I would find my path. But first, I had to eat. And I couldn't eat in an apartment full of weed odor.

"Hey, Laura?"

Tina's voice had a serious tone. But it was hard for me to talk seriously to someone whose eyes were as red and glazed as hers. Still, I focused on those eyes and listened.

"You know, Clark's coming back from his internship in DC next Thursday, and well, I'd really hate to have to…"

"I understand."

"You do?"

I put my hand on her shoulder, even at the risk of getting a contact high.

*** BREAK ***

It was a bit of a relief that I had to leave Tina's. I felt uncomfortable about imposing on her, especially for as long as I had. It would also feel good to breathe smoke-free air.

As I walked through San Rafael, I wondered if I would miss it. San Rafael was stuffed into whatever flat space they could find between hills, and it spread into the hillsides when they ran out of room. San Francisco felt like that too, and so did most of the other cities in the Bay Area. It didn't feel like home. Home was a flat, expansive valley with streets in a perfect grid. No skyscrapers, no roller coaster-like winding roads carved into hillsides, and no pale men and women staring at your breasts and skin tone and telling you to leave.

Mom was right. I had options. And I had the option of going home. Even if it meant coding with punch cards like it was 1969.

*** BREAK ***

I would miss Golden Dragon. It was a hole-in-the-wall Chinese restaurant on Fourth Street next to some men's clothing store named Schwartz. I'd also miss Mrs. Lee. She and her husband owned the place. He worked in the kitchen while she took orders up front. It was an energetic, noisy place. The chatter of the diners. The clanking of utensils against steel woks.

Mrs. Lee's wrinkled face opened into a smile when she saw me. "The usual?"

"Yes, please."

She wrote Chinese characters on an order ticket. I didn't have to read Chinese to know what it said. "Kung pao chicken, spicy, light on the peanuts. White rice. To go."

"$4.25, please."

I pulled a five out of my wallet. She tore off the perforated slip off the bottom of the ticket with my order number. I handed her the money. She gave me three quarters, which I put in a glass tip jar.

"Thank you." She smiled and handed me the slip. "You're number 58."

I nodded. "Thank you."

I left the counter and threaded through the tightly packed tables to the back of the restaurant. Next to the restrooms and pay phone was a corkboard plastered with ads and announcements. It was San Rafael's local message board. If there was an apartment to rent or someone needing a roommate, I'd find it there.

Mom said I had options. I also had the option to stay in the Bay Area and continue my job search.

I scanned through the collage of photocopied flyers stapled to the corkboard. One had a black-and-white picture of President Reagan with a Hitler mustache that announced a "Punks for Peace" concert. It partially covered an index card with crude hand-drawn letters, "Roommate wanted. Smoker OK." Not for me, especially after breathing pot-infused air for two months. A couple of index cards were in Spanish. I took a couple years of Spanish in high school. I learned enough to buy a pair of gloves in Madrid, but not enough to hold a conversation.

That's when I found it. I straightened my glasses and leaned in close. I had to read it twice to make sure my eyes weren't deceiving me.

Programmer Wanted
Must know 68K assembly language. No experience necessary.

The bottom was fringed into tearable strips of paper with the phone number to call, 415/555-1115.

Was this for real? With the dot-matrix print, it certainly looked like it was created by someone with a computer. But who would advertise a programming job by sticking a flyer on a corkboard? Was this job legitimate? Or was it some sort of scam?

And why was I standing there staring at it?

I knew Motorola 68000 assembly language. I based my master's thesis on it. Whoever was looking for a programmer was obviously developing for a 68000 machine. Probably a Macintosh, but I've seen stories in the computer press of some other companies developing products for it. Perhaps this was a startup, something out of someone's garage. This could be the next HP. Or Apple. Or an underfunded pipe dream that makes people work for free with the promise of stock options, only to fail in three months.

I looked at the phone number dangling at the bottom of the flyer. Do I take it? So far, no one had.

If I took this job, I would have to find somewhere to live. Would this place pay me enough to cover my rent and my other expenses? What if I applied, and they didn't hire me? Could I endure any more rejection? I could just as easily pack up and head back to Reseda, where I knew I had a job and a place to live. No more painful interviews. No more uncertainty.

"58!" Mrs. Lee called.

I stared at the flyer again. I tore off a strip with the phone number.

CHAPTER TWO
October 2016

"Why are they calling the shots?"

"It's ridiculous. We bought them."

Chris and Warren leaned over my cubicle partitions. They were long-timers at MHR Imaging like I was. I started in '96 when I went back to work after Stacy was born. Chris was already there. He was one of the first employees when the company started in Canoga Park. Warren started a few weeks after me. We weathered the dot-com bust of 2000 and watched in horror as 9/11 unfolded on the lunchroom TV. We mourned with Warren when his son was killed in Afghanistan. I probably mourned the most because I knew how it felt when Dad was killed in Vietnam. We survived the Great Recession together. We weren't sure whether we would survive this.

"We all know why."

We turned towards Bob, who just got out of his cubicle and walked to over to mine. I dreaded what he was going to say. Probably something about President Obama. We had to endure his constant talk about how terrible liberals are and how great a president Donald Trump would be. Whenever he'd tell me something he read on Breitbart or heard on Tomi Lahren about how the Democrats would take away our guns and Christianity, I'd smile, say "That's interesting," and walk away. I didn't care about politics. I had bigger things to worry about than Hillary Clinton's stupid emails.

But Bob said something work-related and possibly true.

"They're replacing us all with those punk millennial kids. They're half our age, and they can pay them half as much."

"But they don't have our experience," Chris assured us. "We wrote those graphic libraries from scratch. We had to run them on Pentium II processors with 32 megabytes of RAM on Windows 95. They don't know how to optimize compression or improve retrieval rates."

"They don't have to," Warren argued. "Their smartphones outperform the average PC from five years ago…"

"And they use them to catch stinking Pokémon," Bob grumbled. "It just makes me sick, these tattooed participation-trophy snowflakes thinking they can barge in here and push us aside."

Warren stiffened. "You know, you're talking about our children's generation."

"That's why I'm glad I didn't have kids," Bob replied.

Chris looked at me. "What do you think, Laura?"

I leaned back in my chair and stared at the men hovering outside my cubicle.

"We've been through this before. We've been bought. We've bought others. Executives come and go, org charts get redrawn, and we're still here."

"But for how long?" Bob interjected.

I leaned forward. "Why do you think this is different?"

"Because *we're* different. Let's face it. We're older now. We're dinosaurs to those kids. And they may be the asteroid that makes us extinct."

The concern in Bob's voice concerned me as well.

*** BREAK ***

My concerns about my job gave way to my concerns about Stacy. I knew she had another round of chemo today. I expected her to be sound asleep when I got home. Instead, the house was filled with her laughter. Not the sound of someone who just got a high dosage of powerful drugs.

I stepped into her bedroom. Stacy was in bed, surrounded by her friends from the volleyball team. Michelle hovered her iPhone in front of Stacy as Hailey, Allison, and Gaby peered at the screen.

"Mrs. Hamilton?"

Michelle tapped the iPhone into silence and tried to lower it inconspicuously against her side. Clearly, they were watching something they didn't want me to see. I smiled anyway.

"We took Stacy to her appointment." Gaby sounded almost apologetic.

"That was kind of you," I said. "Thank you."

"But Allison," Michelle nudged the blond-haired woman in the CSUN Matadors Woman's Volleyball t-shirt, "She almost passed out."

"What can I say?" Allison protested. "Needles freak me out!"

"I appreciate all you do for Stacy." I then noticed the half-eaten cookie on the comforter. "You even brought her a snack."

"Uh, Mrs. Hamilton..." Gaby muttered as I stepped towards Stacy's bed.

That was when I noticed the wrapper underneath the cookie. I picked it up and stared at it for a moment. I then looked at Stacy. "I don't remember a Dr. 420 Healthyherb being on our insurance plan."

Stacy and her friends exchanged nervous glances. She then spoke softly, "My friends helped me get a rec today. It's supposed to help with the nausea. It's why I don't feel so sick."

I put the cookie and the wrapper back on her bed and exhaled softly. "At least you're not smoking it."

More nervous glances between Stacy and her friends. Finally, Michelle spoke up. "Mrs. Hamilton, do we have to leave..."

"Of course, not." I smiled to assure them. "In fact, would you all like some pizza for dinner?"

Stacy and her friends' faces brightened.

Then Allison said, "Can we have gluten-free crust?"

*** BREAK ***

Dr. 420 Healthyherb must have helped. Stacy was able to walk her friends to the door. She asked me to stay by her side in case she felt unsteady.

But Gaby was already walking arm-in-arm with her. "Our next home game is against Hawai'i. Can you come?"

"Of course, I..." Then Stacy glanced at me. "I'll try."

I gave them a reassuring smile. "If she's well enough, she'll be there."

I stepped back as Stacy's friends encircled her with hugs.

Michelle clutched her hand, "Stay strong."

Allison kissed her cheek, "You got this, girlfriend."

I bit my lip and then tried to make myself smile.

*** BREAK ***

"It's OK for you to cry." Kevin's deep voice floated from behind me as I sat in our home office.

"If I start, I won't stop."

I realized that I had been staring at a Visual Studio window with an unfinished C# project. I couldn't even think of what I was coding. I lowered my head. Kevin's thick brown forearms wrapped around my shoulders. The soft warmness of his kiss pressed against the back of my head. I lifted my hands from the keyboard. I brought my right arm across my chest and rested it on his bicep. His muscles weren't firm like they were when we started dating, but I needed to feel his warmth on my fingertips.

He reached over and put his hand over mine. "You don't have to be strong."

"I can't be anything else."

"That's my Laura."

I could feel his smile behind me. I allowed myself to smile as well.

"Do you want to go to bed?" His voice softened.

I exhaled and glanced at the screen. "I've got to finish this. We have a code review tomorrow."

Kevin leaned over and kissed my cheek. "Don't stay up too long."

"I'll try not to."

He let go of my shoulders. I turned to him and kissed his lips. "Good night. Love you."

"I love you too."

I kept my eyes fixed on him as he stood up and headed towards the office door. He gave me one of his broad bright smiles before he headed towards the bedroom. I turned back to my laptop, but my hands couldn't get back to the keyboard. They covered my face, and I exhaled hard into them.

CHAPTER THREE
July 1985

I brought only one skirt to the Bay Area, and I hated it. I hated skirts in general and the pantyhose that went with them, along with the constant need to cross my legs, adjust the hem, and wonder if the guy was listening to me or staring at my shins. I wanted to ace this interview, so I had no other choice but to wear it. Fortunately, it was a conservative plain navy blue one that went just below the knees. It paired well with most of my dress blouses. At least the ones that weren't wrinkled. I chose a light blue one. I gave it and the skirt a quick sniff to make sure Tina's pot stench didn't soak into the fibers. Getting a job was hard enough without having prospective bosses think I'm a stoner.

Then the makeup. I hated it as much as the skirt. I had to smear all sorts of crap on my face and still make it look natural. I had to put on mascara and eyeliner, even though they would be barely noticeable behind the lenses of my glasses. And lipstick. I picked a brownish tone because I didn't want my lips to distract from the words I had to say.

Men are lucky. They can throw on clothes without much thought. We had to think of everything. I even had to make sure my bra wouldn't be visible through my blouse. At least we didn't have to wear something as stupid and useless as a tie.

I added one final touch, my grandma's pearls. Grandpa bought them for her when he returned home from World War II. She gave them to Mom before she died. I knew how precious they were to Mom, so I was grateful that she let me borrow them for my interviews. "Maybe they'll give you luck," she told me.

They haven't so far, but today might be the day.

*** BREAK ***

I drove up Irwin Street, a one-way road that extended from the Fourth Street offramp from the northbound 101. I found an empty curb on the left. It looked like a residential district. Nothing looked like an office building. I had to think twice before I got out of the car. It seemed like a safe neighborhood, but I made sure I locked the door and checked the handle.

I double checked the address that Darryl, the man I spoke to on the phone, gave me. He said it was 27643 Irwin Street. It was an old two-story house with dark redwood siding and faded forest green trim around the windows and eaves. It didn't have much of a yard. Just a small patch of grass in front of the porch with an oak tree in the center. One of its roots pushed up the sidewalk.

A path of stepping stones led from the driveway that ran next to the house to the well-worn steps up the porch. I had to tread carefully with my heels, another women's fashion trend I hated, and clacked up the steps. I found myself confronted with a screen door with a faded wood frame and a tear in the screen. Next to the door was a doorbell with the brass worn off. I stared at it for a moment. What was I getting myself into? Was this even a real business?

But I told Darryl I would be there at ten o'clock, and it was ten o'clock. I pressed the doorbell. A loud buzz came from the other side of the door.

After a moment, the front door opened. A man's face peered from behind the torn screen.

"Come in."

I grabbed the black iron handle and pulled the door open. He wasn't dressed as if he was about to interview me. For starters, he didn't wear a tie. He wore a short-sleeve dress shirt with light blue stripes. His brown dress slacks were tight around his hips but loose around his legs. His dark blond hair seemed thin and wispy, but well combed. Shadows covered his eyes. He seemed well proportioned in his shoulders, arms, and legs, but his gut looked like what a man would be if he were six months pregnant.

I smiled, just as my faculty advisor reminded me, and extended my hand. "We spoke on the phone, I'm..."

"I know who you are. Come in." He stepped away from the door without shaking my hand.

I tried to maintain my smile. "You must be..."

"Darryl Posner."

I followed him into the front of the house. A stairway was immediately in front of the entrance. Next to the stairway was a marble pillar with a small brass figurine. The house seemed dark, and specks of dust floated in the air.

"It's a lovely place you have here." I felt my muscles tighten.

I followed him through an entryway into what seemed to be a living room. But it looked like a living room from 50 or 60 years ago. Everything seemed antique. A plush velvet sofa and matching chair in oak trim. A glass table with ornate gold-colored iron trim. Floor lamps with velvet shades with gold fringes. Even the technology in the room seemed old. A large cabinet TV from the sixties sat against the wall. It probably had vacuum tubes, if it even worked. Another cabinet contained a record player that probably only played 78s. On top of it was a radio in a cathedral case and a cloth-covered speaker. It only had AM. They probably listened to the Pearl Harbor attack on that radio. The only tech that seemed to work was the grandfather clock with its pendulum swinging in a glass case.

The room looked like it belonged in a museum. It certainly didn't look like the location of a computer company.

I didn't know what to do. I stood in the middle of that room watching Darryl walk towards the sofa.

"You asked about the programming job."

"Um, yes?"

He turned towards me. "You can program a computer?"

"Yes?"

He sat down on the sofa. "You're hired."

"But...don't you want to hear about my qualifications? I know 68000..."

"I don't know anything about that stuff. My brother put that on there." He crossed his ankles. "You want the job, or don't you?"

I realized I had been so focused on preparing for interviews that I didn't know what to say when I got hired.

"How much do you pay?"

"$10,000 a year."

"$10,000! That's half the starting salary for a..."

"And room and board. Do you live in Marin County?"

"No."

"Do you know what rent goes for around here?"

I stood silently. The steady clicks from the grandfather clock were the only sound.

Darryl only let a few of them tick before he demanded, "You want the job, or don't you?"

*** BREAK ***

It didn't take me long to pack up the things I brought to the Bay Area. I brought just enough clothes to last a few weeks of interviews. I could have Mom ship up my Commodore 64 and anything else I needed. But I needed her advice more than anything from the house.

"The first job out of college never pays well." Her soothing voice comforted me through that long-distance line. "You'll be getting experience you can use to get a better paying job later on."

I exhaled. "That's what I thought too, but still..."

"Is it true what that guy said about rent in Marin?"

"Tina says she pays $650 for her place."

"Wow. That's twice what I pay on our mortgage. Of course, your dad and I bought our house in '65, before he went to Vietnam. It wasn't easy for people like us to buy a house in Reseda back then."

I was one of the few Hispanics at my elementary school. When they started the school integration program, many of my classmates assumed I was bussed in from East LA.

Mom brought things back to the present. "So, if they actually include your room and board, you'd be saving..."

"I've already done the math. It's $7,800 per year plus utilities. That comes out roughly to about $8,250, which means I'm actually getting $18,250. Still, that's not even close to..."

"It's a start, Laura. And a chance to prove yourself is the most valuable thing you can get."

*** BREAK ***

I wasn't sure what to wear. I was going to work, but I was also moving into a house. I chose black dress slacks and a plain blue polyester blouse that could pass as a dressy t-shirt. I brought a gray college t-shirt with CSUN in red letters with black trim, and my white Reseda High School gym shorts with navy blue stripes down the sides and along the bottom. I assumed they would stay in my suitcase because I'd never wear them around people I had to work with.

I opened the hatchback and took out my two suitcases. I didn't want to leave my things in my car, especially with Grandma's pearls were packed in one of the suitcases. I also figured I'd save myself a trip. I locked the car and carried the suitcases along the stepping stones and up the well-worn steps. I set down the suitcases and rang the doorbell. Again, the loud buzz came from inside.

I expected Darryl to open the door, but it was a woman. She wore cutoffs and a white spaghetti strap tank top. Her nipples and areolae were visible through the thin fabric. Her blond hair was sculpted into a layered wedge with a few stray strands dangling over her forehead. When she opened the screen door, I saw that she was barefoot. She was definitely nothing like a professional businesswoman.

"You're new."

I could tell from the yellowed teeth, thick stench, and the rasp in her voice that she was a smoker. Definitely something I didn't want to deal with. Still, I had to be professional.

"I'm Laura Rodriguez."

I smiled and held out my hand. She just stared at it.

"Don't ask me to carry your damn bags."

She turned and headed towards the stairs. She expected me to follow her with my damn bags. I had to manage picking up my suitcases while using a free finger to open the screen door. I maneuvered through the opening with two bulky suitcases before the screen door slapped shut behind me.

"Close the door behind you. Mrs. Posner doesn't want any bugs getting in the house."

"Mrs. Posner?"

The woman didn't turn around. "It's her house."

I used the side of my foot to nudge the front door closed. The woman continued up the stairs. I had to bring in my arms so both bags fit in the narrow space between the wall and rail.

"Is Darryl her son?" My voice strained from the effort to climb and the compression on my chest from carrying the bags in an awkward way.

The woman glanced back at me. "You really are a programmer. Figure things out quickly, don't you?"

I made a turn at the landing. The top half of the stairway seemed narrower than the bottom. I swung out my arms, so one bag was in front of me, and the other was behind. The one that was behind kept banging against my legs. I was grateful to reach the top. I set both my suitcases at the landing, but the woman continued. I exhaled and picked up my bags again. The woman stood by a door.

"Your room."

I set down the suitcases and opened the door. Spartan didn't begin to describe it. A bed with a pine headboard. On top of the bed were a single pillow and a white quilt with faded embroidery. A dresser was pressed against the corner. It had a lace doily on the top. One of the drawers didn't have a handle. Next to the dresser was a pine desk that had the finish worn off the top. A plain wooden chair with no cushions had been pushed into the desk. The room had no telephone. No computer. Nothing that indicated that any work has or can be done there.

I turned to the woman. "Where is the office?"

"That's Peter's room."

"Peter?"

"Peter Posner."

"Darryl's brother?"

She planted her hands on her hips. "Anything you don't know?"

"Your name."

She stared at me. "Kathlynne."

"Kathleen?"

"Kath*lynne*." She pronounced the second syllable with a short, clipped *I* sound. I couldn't imagine how it would be spelled.

"Posner?"

She folded her arms. "Working on it."

"So, is, um, well…"

"I've been with Darryl for three years. We have the bedroom next to yours. We tend to get loud, so get used to it. I usually start my period on the eleventh. Women sync when they live together, you know. Smoke?"

"No."

"Good. Mrs. Posner doesn't allow smoking in the house. I go in the backyard. Unless it rains, then I go on the front porch." She unfolded her arms and let them relax by her sides. "We have two phones. One in the kitchen, and one in Peter's room. Local calls are fine, but you pay for your own long distance. You can't use the phone between nine p.m. and midnight. That's when Peter needs it for his computer. God knows what he uses it for."

"Do you know anything about this business?"

"That's Peter's thing. I have no idea."

"When can I meet him?"

She folded her arms again. "When he wants to."

I blinked in confusion. Kathlynne stared at me for a moment. Then, she looked me up and down.

"This place doesn't have air conditioning. You should change into something cooler."

She turned and left the room.

*** BREAK ***

I brought in the suitcases and set them on the bed. They sunk in slightly. I pressed my palms against the mattress. It gave way. It felt old and worn. I wasn't going to sleep well in this house.

Kathlynne left the door opened, so I walked over and closed it. It got dark in the room. A small light hung from the ceiling with a single bulb in a frosted glass shade. But where was the light switch? I found a pair of buttons by the door. One was pressed in, and the other was popped out. I pressed the popped out button. The light came on. What kind of wiring did they have in this house? Was it some sort of retrofit from gas lamps? How could this antiquated electrical system handle the demands of a modern office?

And what type of office was it? There was a computer, but it was in Peter's room. What am I supposed to program with? Peter must know enough to ask for someone who can program in 68000 assembler, but why? What was he trying to create? And what computer was he creating it with? What type of business is this? How was it going to make enough money to pay me $10,000?

I looked at the suitcases on the bed. It wasn't too late to pick up those suitcases and head out the door. I didn't sign any contracts. I didn't even shake anyone's hand. I could leave the Bay Area and be back in Reseda before bedtime. At least I would have to hear Kathlynne and Darryl get, as she put it, loud.

She was right. It was getting hot and stuffy. I walked over to the window. The metal latch was stuck. I pulled on it hard until it finally unlatched. I slid open the window. That's when I noticed the freeway was just past the backyard. The steady whoosh of traffic filled the room. That was probably why the window had been kept latched for so long.

A trickle of sweat ran down my stomach. I didn't want my blouse to get sweat-stained, so I pulled it off. I felt a little cooler standing in my bra. I could change into my gym shorts and t-shirt, but what if Peter needed to meet me?

The door creaked open. I clutched my arms around me and looked over my shoulder. Kathlynne stood behind me.

"Do you knock?" I growled.

"Peter said to give you this."

I turned around. Kathlynne held a thick white binder towards me. I had to unblock my torso to take it.

Kathlynne looked me over. "You clearly never ditched gym class. And I'm sure you can get a good boyfriend with tits like those."

My jaw tightened. Kathlynne looked directly at me.

"Mrs. Posner invited you to lunch. Put your top back on."

She turned around and closed the door behind her. I exhaled hard. My irritation was overcome by my curiosity about the binder Kathlynne gave me. I carried it to the desk and opened it. I stared at the title page for a while. I straightened my glasses and started thumbing through the pages. I realized that whatever Peter was working on was something new, something special. Something that was worthwhile. Something that might make the embarrassment, discomfort, low wages, and heat more bearable. I flipped back to the title page and stared at it.

Amiga Programmer's Reference Manual.

CHAPTER FOUR
October 2016

Scraping and a click from downstairs. My eyes flung open.

"Hear that?" I whispered anxiously.

"Hear what?"

"Didn't you hear that? From downstairs?"

I pulled back the covers and climbed out of bed. I was in my sleep shorts and tank top.

"What are you doing?" Kevin mumbled as he rolled over on his side.

"Checking it out."

I put on my glasses. I didn't have enough time to put in my contacts. I headed to the closet and slid open the door.

"You're not getting the bat, are you?"

I was reaching for Henry's old Little League bat, which we kept propped against the closet wall for moments like this.

Kevin sat up. "It's probably Stacy."

"She wouldn't be awake." I went back to my nightstand and picked up my phone. "It's 4:28 a.m."

"What if she went out?"

"She wouldn't be out."

"When you were her age, didn't you try sneaking back home at four in the morning?"

I exhaled. "OK, but I'll take the bat. Just in case."

*** BREAK ***

I stepped slowly, quietly down the stairs. The lights were on. Clanking came from the kitchen. Could it really be Stacy? She'd still be asleep from chemo and possibly finishing the rest of Dr. 420 Healthyherb's magic cookie. Who could it be? I kept the bat down as I snuck to the foot of the stairs. I crept past the small side table next to the staircase and dashed to a wall by the opening to the kitchen. I pressed my back against the wall and peered around the corner. A shadow grew along the white tile floor. I raised the bat over my head. The tip of a tennis shoe crossed the threshold from the kitchen onto the hallway carpet. I leaped around the corner.

"Agggghhhh!"

"Ahhhhhhh!"

"Mom!"

I lowered the bat to my side.

"Henry?"

*** BREAK ***

Kevin and I sat on the sofa across from Henry, who sat on the love seat. His bat leaned against the sofa next to me.

"That's my favorite DeMarini," he cried. "That's from the year I made All-Stars! You remember?"

"I remember." I crossed my arms. "I don't remember you telling us that you were coming."

"Didn't I tell you I'm moving back?"

Kevin and I blurted together, "What!"

"I told you, I'm moving back. Didn't you get my email?"

I shot back. "What email? I didn't get an email from you in weeks."

"I didn't either," Kevin grumbled.

"Maybe it's in your spam folder..."

Kevin waved his hands at Henry. "Never mind all that. I want to know why you're here instead of Mountain View."

"I hate Mountain View! Everything is so expensive. And they've got those alt-right people there. They say the most fucked-up shit..." He turned to me with an embarrassed look. "Sorry, Mom."

"Sorry?" I felt my anger boil, but I kept my voice calm. "You got a job with Google. They started you at $105,000, plus stock options and bonuses. They even paid to relocate you. What happened to that?"

"I quit."

"What!" Kevin and I shouted in unison.

"I—I wasn't really doing anything important. I was just fixing bugs and writing APIs…"

Kevin slapped his hand on his forehead. "For crying out loud, Henry! You weren't stocking shelves at Walmart or serving sandwiches at Panera. You were working at Google!"

"But it isn't me. It isn't what I really want to do."

"But this was the perfect opportunity for you," I argued. "Programmers dream about having the chance you had. And you just walk away from it? Don't you remember me telling you how much I made in my first job after college?"

"But that was you, Mom. This is me."

Henry spoke with a conviction that surprised me. He wasn't just whining that he didn't get a more comfortable desk chair. Still, things didn't add up. Something else must have gone wrong.

"What about Lisa?"

Henry stiffened and looked away with me. "There's no more Lisa."

"You've been seeing her for a little over a year. Did you have a fight?"

"We—I just don't want to talk about it! OK, Mom!"

"So, you really did come home, didn't you?"

We turned our heads and stared at Stacy, who stood in the hallway in her nightshirt and open robe. Stacy glanced at Kevin and me and shrugged her shoulders.

"I thought he already told you."

*** BREAK ***

Stacy went back to bed, but Kevin and I couldn't. We watched Henry make trip after trip to his car. He walked in with a box tucked under one arm, and a duffle bag slung over his shoulder.

"I can't believe we're letting him do this," Kevin grumbled softly.

"He's our son. What are we supposed to do? Let him sleep out in the street?"

"He's 24 years old! He should solve his own problems!"

"What if he did?"

Kevin stared at me.

"Something terrible must have happened to him," I continued.

"Like what?"

"You know." I moved closer to Kevin. "It's not easy for people like us, especially now."

His voice softened. "Never was. Things haven't changed. We just refused to stay silent about it. That's what's really making those people angry."

I looked at the brownness of Kevin's face. We never thought much about race, even though he's African American, I'm Hispanic, and Henry and Stacy are both. We celebrate Kwanzaa and gave Stacy a quinceañera, but we paid more attention to the color to the carpet than we did the color of our skin. And whenever I was forced to think about it, it made me angry. Or as angry as a Hispanic woman was allowed to get.

"I brought everything in."

We turned to Henry. He lowered his head.

"You must be disappointed in me."

I put my hand on his shoulder. "No, Henry, it's just—If something was wrong, you should have talked to us. You know Dad, and I are always here for you. You can talk to us about anything."

"Not about this." He pulled away from me and headed towards his bedroom.

Kevin and I just stared at each other.

*** BREAK ***

Now, both of our children had problems we had to deal with. Stacy has leukemia. Henry left his job and came home for God knows what reason. And I had to shut those out so I could get into my Honda CR-V and drive to work.

The radio didn't make things even easier.

"I can't believe that someone could make those type of statements and even consider running for President of the United States. He completely disrespects women, not to mention all the horrible things he's said about minorities, military families..."

The last thing I wanted to listen to was the world going to hell. I tapped the button on the steering wheel to switch to satellite radio.

"Here's a classic for your morning commute. Mr. Mister and 'Kyrie' on the 80s Hits Channel."

I tapped up the volume. That song demanded to played loud. Something about it lifted my spirits and reminded me of...something, but I couldn't recall what. Still, that song raised my spirits. I leaned back and let the wailing synthesizers and Richard Page's powerful lead vocals reassure me. Nothing was going to ruin my day.

*** BREAK ***

"Hey, Laura. Got a minute?"

It was our engineering director Deanna Iverson. She rarely spoke to me. When she did, it was usually bad news.

*** BREAK ***

Deanna led me to the conference room. Chris, Bob, and Warren were already there along with a young woman with straight blond hair, plump cheeks, and black cat-eye glasses that looked like something I wore in elementary school in the sixties.

It was definitely bad news.

Deanna took the seat closest to the door. I had to go around the conference table where the only seat was next to the young woman. I didn't dare look at her because I didn't know what my working relationship with her would be. She did take a long look at me.

Deanna straightened her back. She spoke in the flat, measured voice of someone who had to rehearse a speech in front of senior management before giving it to us.

"As you know from Gerald's email yesterday, we've been focusing on integrating the resources we've acquired from Guacphix so we could leverage our expanded capabilities..."

It was typical corporate speak. We've been hearing it for decades. Chris, Bob, and Warren sat patiently, listening to words that attempted to cover up and justify something dreadful. But what about this young woman? I gave her a quick glance. She sat as silently and emotionlessly like us old-timers. She looked professional enough with a black blazer and a white and black houndstooth dress. Was that part of that hipster vibe that many of Henry and Stacy's friends tried to emulate? Or did she want to appear older than she was?

I noticed her eyes were sliding towards me. I turned my focus back to Deanna.

"Although it made sense for us to combine our graphics processing teams, it led to redundancies in our management structure. Vince Ulrich has been a valued member of the MHR Imaging team for the past eight years, but we were not able to find a position for him in the new organization. We wish him the best in his future endeavors..."

I had mixed feelings about the news. Vince was the Peter principle personified. Someone who was a good-enough programmer but horrible as a manager. That's why I never sought the management career track, even in jobs where it was the only path to getting raises. Fortunately, MHR Imaging had a dual-career track where I could get raises and "Senior" and "Principal" tacked on my title without having to deal with the politics and babysitting that went with management.

Vince was a terrible manager. He was a poor communicator. He never gave us information about product changes that affected our code until the last minute. He cut budgets on upgrades and training we needed. "We have to tighten our belts," he'd say. Meanwhile, other programming teams were two versions ahead of us in their tools and recently upgraded all their computers. Vince always came into work late, left early, and was never available when we needed help. In a way, I wasn't sorry to see him go. But as the saying goes, "He's a son of a bitch, but he's our son of a bitch." Vince came up through the ranks here. He was around our age, and he had the same experience and company knowledge as us. He was our son of a bitch.

But this young woman was an outsider. An unknown. And as Deanna explained, our new boss.

"Tammy Oberon has agreed to be located here in our Warner Center office. She has a Master's Degree in Computer Science from Cal State Fullerton. She has worked at Guacphix's Irvine office for three years, and she has been highly regarded for her technical insight and business acumen. We are confident that her perspective and energy, when combined with your experience and technical know-how, will move the Graphics Engineering department forward and enable MHR Imaging to achieve greater success." She then glanced at the young woman sitting next to me. "Tammy, do you have anything you would like to add?"

"Only that I'm excited about the opportunity to come here and work with such a talented and experienced team."

Her voice seemed a little soft to be a manager. Did we intimidate her?

Deanna smiled. "Then, I'll give Tammy the chance to get settled in and all of you the chance to get to know each other."

We all stood up. Tammy's dress only went to mid-thigh. She was indeed a millennial.

*** BREAK ***

Tammy went off with Deanna, and my coworkers instantly clustered around my cubicle.

Warren spoke low. "So, what do you think about this—what's her name again?"

"Tammy Oberon." Her name was already etched into my mind.

"Why would she want to move here from Orange County?" Chris puzzled. "It's ten degrees cooler there and closer to the beach."

"The Valley's becoming hipster now," Bob complained. "Craft microbreweries. Popup diners with artisanal, locally-sourced crap. Coffee shops with big-bearded baristas who draw leaves in your cappuccino foam. Even Reseda's becoming artsy-fartsy."

"Here's what I don't get," Warren said. "How did she get to be a manager? Three years into my first job out of college, I was still an associate. A senior programmer had to review my code before I checked it in."

Bob sneered, "Maybe she got it because of her looks..."

Warren, Chris, and I all groaned him into silence.

"Don't talk that way," Warren growled.

"Do you want to get hauled into HR?" Chris complained.

"C'mon," Bob protested. "The man who may be the next President of the United States talks that way."

"It doesn't make it right," Chris countered.

"Look," I interjected. "She's our boss now. We at least need to give her a chance. C'mon, we've all been there. We all know what it was like when we first started out."

Bob turned to me, "What was it like when you first started out?"

CHAPTER FIVE
July 1985

The Regulator clock on the dining room wall clicked louder than the grandfather's clock in the living room. Or perhaps it was my heart beating as I sat across the table from Mrs. Posner. Darryl may have hired me, and Peter may be the head of the business, but it was clear who really ran things in the house. And I knew I had to make a good impression.

The dining room followed the same museum motif as the living room. Ornate oak furniture and chairs with velvet cushions. The drapes were drawn shut, and a chandelier over the table had the lights dimly lit. A china cabinet was filled with gilt-edged plates, cups, and bowls with pastel paintings of roses.

Mrs. Posner dipped a tea bag into one of those fine china teacups. She used silver tongs to deposit a sugar cube into the cup. She daintily pulled out the tea bag by its string and set it on a separate saucer. She sunk a silver spoon into the cup and slowly stirred. She set the spoon on the saucer next to the used tea bag. After she took a long sip and set her cup down, she finally spoke to me.

"You seem to be an intelligent young woman. How important is computer programming to you?"

"Very important, Mrs. Posner." If she had a first name, I didn't know it. Or would be allowed to call her that if I did.

"When did you decide it was important to you?" She took another sip of tea. I waited until she set her cup back down before answering.

"When I was eight. We had a field trip to the computer lab at UCLA. They told us how they used computers to help the Apollo missions get to the moon. I decided right then and there I wanted to be a computer programmer. I wanted to use computers to help people do great things."

She leaned forward slightly. Her face became more visible in the faint light. I couldn't tell how old she was. Her hair was blond with a hint of white, and it was impeccably styled. Whatever wrinkles she had were covered by what was probably high-quality makeup. But her clothes were as old fashioned as her house's furnishings. Her floral cotton blouse and multiple strands of pearls would have been more fashionable in the 1930s than the 1980s.

She looked me over with her green and golden eyes. "What about marriage? When you are married and have children, what do you plan to do?"

"I—I haven't thought about marriage yet."

She leaned back and took another sip of tea.

"I have no objections to working girls. My mother was one. She worked in the War Department. You know, people were called computers long before machines were. She worked on trajectory tables for munitions during the war. She excelled at mathematics at school. Of course, when Father returned from Europe, she was expected to go back to home and hearth. That was how things were back then. Ah."

A plate was set in front of me with a sandwich on wheat bread with the crusts cut off. A small salad with thin slices of cucumber and curls of carrot. The lettuce appeared damp. Probably oil and vinegar. I looked up. The woman who put the plate in front of me looked about my age. She had dark brown eyes like mine and brown hair like mine, except hers was bound into a bun. She wore a conservative ash-gray dress and a white apron as if it were some sort of uniform.

"That will do nicely, Maria."

Mrs. Posner unfurled her napkin and set it on her lap. "It seems like such a pity. A woman as intelligent and ambitious as Mother relegated to ironing shirts and baking pies."

I glanced up and watched Maria disappear into the kitchen. I then turned to Mrs. Posner, who smiled at me.

"Bon appétit."

*** BREAK ***

I wasn't sure what to make of Mrs. Posner or any of the household after lunch.

The meal was pleasant enough. She told me about the history of the house. Work had started in 1929, but the landowner went bankrupt during the Depression. The Posners bought the land and finished the house in 1931. She was vague about how her husband's family got rich, except that they wound up owning large tracts of land throughout Northern California by the end of Prohibition. She quickly changed the subject by listing all of the cultural landmarks I had to see in the Bay Area.

Mrs. Posner struck me as one of those grand patricians, a dowager empress, a Californian Brahmin. I could see her giving lavishly to worthy causes, possibly to cover up some misdeeds in their past. Even though I felt a bit suspicious and unsure of her intentions, I felt a little better about my job. If she were bankrolling Peter's business, I could be assured of getting paid. She was able to pay Maria a salary to cook and clean for them.

But if I'm supposed to write programs for them, when was I going to get a computer? I should read the manual Peter gave me, but the best way to learn is to do.

I made my way upstairs. When I got to the top, I saw a door that wasn't open before. I found myself walking towards it. I stopped. I shouldn't be peaking in other people's rooms, but Kathlynne had no problems walking in on me half-dressed. So, I continued.

I stepped to the doorway and peered around. It was a bedroom, but it was unlike any of the rooms I had seen so far. One wall was taken up with a large metal computer bench. Lined up on it were several computers. A Commodore 64, a Commodore 128, and another one I couldn't identify. Each one had a monitor. Peripherals, manuals, and disks filled the spaces between the computers. Several 1541 floppy drives. An Epson RX-80 dot-matrix printer that was probably used to print the flyer I found at the Golden Dragon. A Supra modem, which probably tied up the phone line at night. Several bookcases against the wall were filled with computer books and magazines. In the center of the room was a black, high-back leather office chair.

At last, a room that wasn't a museum piece! But it also wasn't an office. It had an unmade bed with clothes strewn on the floor around it and the faint odor of male sweat.

I started feeling uneasy. Was I supposed to work in a bedroom with some guy? What was I really expected to do in this place?

Still, my curiosity got the best of me. I peered around the room and then peered around the hallway. When I was sure I was alone, I stepped in.

My attention was focused on the computer at the end of the bench, the one I couldn't identify. He must have just gotten it. It smelled of fresh plastic. A few white dots of styrofoam from the packing material clung to the top and sides of the monitor. I glanced down at the faceplate below the screen. Next to a rainbow-hued double checkmark logo, it said, "Amiga."

I ran my fingers along the textured plastic on the side of the monitor. I whispered, "I don't believe this." I broke into a smile. "This is it. This is the Amiga. A whole new computer!"

My fingers continued down the side until they reached the bottom of the monitor. They continued down the side of the CPU until I felt a toggle switch. I nestled my index finger on it. The computer was off. All I had to do was press that switch to bring it to life.

I looked over my shoulder. The hallway was still clear. Dare I start it?

A click. A whirring fan. A red light came on. But nothing appeared on the screen.

I glanced at the front of the monitor. On the right side was a button and an indicator light that was dark. I pressed the button. The indicator light came on, and the cathode-ray tube brightened.

I stepped back in puzzlement. The screen showed a picture of a hand holding what appeared to be some sort of floppy disk. It looked like one of those new plastic three-and-a-half-inch disks like the ones for the Apple Macintosh. In upside-down text, the disk said "Amiga Kickstart." It meant that I had to insert a Kickstart disk to enable the computer to continue booting. I looked at the mass of blue plastic floppy disks surrounding the computer. One of them must be that Kickstart disk.

"Don't."

I gasped and turned to the doorway. Darryl was standing there.

"Don't disturb his room. He will see you when he's ready, not one moment before."

"I'm sorry." I exhaled softly. I then glanced at the Amiga. "Should I turn this off?"

He stared at me for a moment and shook his head. "Whatever you did, don't do it again."

I lowered my head and walked towards the door. Darryl stepped aside as I walked through. He kept his eyes focused on me until I retreated to my room.

CHAPTER SIX
October 2016

"Hey."

I turned around in my chair. Tammy stood in my cubicle opening.

"You're Laura, right?"

"Yes," I stood up and offered her a handshake. Her grasp was a little too soft. Still, I smiled. "It's a pleasure to meet you."

"Likewise." She gave a small smile back. "I'd like to take the team out to lunch to get to know everyone better. Where do you usually like to go?"

"Islands at Westfield Topanga. It's close by, and they have things everyone likes."

"Sounds great. 11:30?"

"Sound good to me too. Thank you."

"Thanks to you too."

She quickly turned around. I assumed that she was going to ask the others. When I looked down, I noticed a tattoo on her right ankle. It was the outline of a heart with an interwoven infinity symbol, both in teal. I had an idea of what that could mean, but I wasn't sure. I was sure it wasn't polite to ask.

It felt strange to have a boss who was young enough to be my daughter. I wonder how it felt for Tammy to supervise someone who is old enough to be her mother.

*** BREAK ***

We had unspoken rules about what we can and cannot talk about at company lunches.

Politics. Definitely out, especially with this presidential election.

Religion. Also a big fat no. We had a programmer named Jane Michelson, who was an evangelical Christian. I've worked with other born-again Christians who studied their Bible at lunch and left us alone in the office. But for Jane, saving souls was more important than writing code. This didn't go over well with us. Warren is Jewish, Bob is an atheist, Chris is Mormon, and I only went to church for Easter, weddings, funerals, and when we took Kevin's mom to bingo night. Bob spoke his mind, but he also knew when not to. But Jane was in full proselytizing mode all the time. About six months after she started, she announced that she had a calling from God to bring her ministry to a Christian website headquartered in Colorado Springs. We think she really had a calling from Vince and HR about preaching when she should be working.

Some topics could be discussed. We could talk about our kids, but only the positive stuff. Even when I told my coworkers about Stacy's diagnosis, I just shared the optimistic parts. I tried to make her cancer sound like a nasty extended flu. I don't know what I'd say if, God forbid, the prognosis got worse.

We could talk about our spouses in the most flattering terms. We could talk about vacations and hobbies, but no bragging about what we do in the bedroom. Since Warren, Chris, and I have been married to our spouses for a long time, and Bob has been married more than once, there really wasn't anything new for us to discuss in that department.

I suppose we should tell Tammy all about the Valley. Where to go and where not to go. What the best places are to dine and shop. The only times I'd been to Orange County were the occasional family trip to Disneyland, so I didn't know how different it is from the Valley.

I assumed that Tammy, even with three years experience in the workplace, would know the unspoken rules.

*** BREAK ***

"So, what do you think about this presidential election? Crazy, huh?"

I had just stuck a fork in my salad. Chris hovered his burger in front of his face. Warren was in mid-sip of his Diet Coke. We all stared at Bob, silently begging him to keep Sean Hannity far away from the Broca's area of his brain. But Bob stayed quiet. He knew the unspoken rules.

Tammy clearly didn't.

"Do you watch John Oliver? He did this one bit about how the Trump family name was originally Drumpf. He's selling this cap that says 'Make Donald Drumpf Again.' Isn't that funny?"

No. Not at that place and time. I had to change the subject.

"So, how do you like the Valley?"

"It's surprising." She dug into her salad.

"How so?"

She finished chewing and then answered, "I thought people said things like 'gag me with a spoon' and 'grody to the max,' and nobody around here talks like that."

We all looked at each other. Then, Chris, Warren, and Bob stared at me. They appointed me to be the one to straighten her out.

I spoke softly, "That's just a song from the eighties. We never talked like that."

Chris suggested firmly, "There's a place called the Valley Relics Museum. You might also want to visit the Museum of the San Fernando Valley. I think you would be very interested to learn about San Fernando Valley culture and history."

Warren added, "There's also the Valley Performing Arts Center at Cal State Northridge."

Tammy smiled. So did I. It seemed like she was getting it.

But then she said, "Do you have anything like the Irvine Spectrum?"

"I'm not familiar with that," I replied.

Her voice brightened with excitement. "It's really great. They have all these wonderful stores, like Active Ride Shop, Adidas, and an Apple Store. They have all these great restaurants, and they have a Ferris wheel and carousel. My boyfriend and I have an apartment right across the street. Our bedroom overlooks the pool area, and they have a Starbucks in the complex. So, in the morning after we..."

She looked around the table at each of us. Her cheeks reddened. She spoke in a low, sheepish tone, "TMI?"

I nodded. Chris and Warren followed. Bob, who probably didn't know what "TMI" meant, nodded too.

Her hand shook a little as she dug her fork into her salad. "They have delicious food here, don't they?"

We nodded our agreement and finished the rest of our meal in silence.

*** BREAK ***

"Great lunch, guys." Either Tammy was being sarcastic, or she was oblivious to the awkwardness that hovered over the rest of the meal and the drive back to the office. "We'll touch base this afternoon to discuss projects, and I can get up to speed, OK?"

"OK." We each answered asynchronously. Our voices made a jumble of Os and Ks.

Tammy smiled and turned towards her office at the end of the hallway. We then turned to each other.

"What a piece of work," Chris grumbled. "If she loves Irvine so much, why doesn't she move back?"

Bob snorted. "I'd give her three weeks."

Warren added, "More like two."

I just stared at Tammy's door. I felt bad for her in a way. Sure, someone in her position should know the unspoken rules. But how did I learn those rules when I was in my twenties? How can you follow rules you've never been taught?

CHAPTER SEVEN
July 1985

"Uhh! Uhh! You fucking asshole! Uhhh! Ahhhh!"

My eyes popped open. Kathlynne was even louder with Darryl than she warned. But it sounded less like sex than a really heated argument.

I had to pee. The top floor had two bathrooms. The one next to Peter's room was a half-bath with a sink and toilet. The one closest to my room also had a shower/bath. But I had to get to it before...

"Uggghhh! Uggghhh! Agggggrrrhh!"

The way Darryl bellowed, it sounded like he ejaculated a bowling ball.

The other bathroom would have to do. I usually slept in just my panties, but I had to get dressed before venturing into the hallway. I put on my gym shorts and t-shirt.

The bathroom looked like a museum piece too. The floor had white hexagonal tiles. The toilet tank was high overhead with a chain that dangled down. I assumed I had to pull on it to flush. The sink also looked like a relic from the thirties. The steel handles had porcelain caps with "Hot" and "Cold" in ornate script. I looked down at the toilet. The light oak seat was up. Clearly, a man was here before.

I lowered the seat and checked the door. Fortunately, there was a lock in the handle. If there was one place I needed my privacy, it was there.

Although the fixtures were antique, the toilet paper was, mercifully, a modern quilted two-ply. I washed my hands, unlocked the door, and stepped outside.

I gasped.

Standing in front of me was a man I hadn't seen before in that house. His light blond hair was mixed up in a wild case of bedhead. His white t-shirt and gray sweat pants sagged loosely on him. He had a rounded face with a small mouth and a barely visible chin. He straightened his aviator glasses.

"Laura?"

"Yes?"

He glanced at my legs. "You have lovely kneecaps."

"Um...thanks?"

"Will you help me with a problem?" He extended his arm towards his room.

I glanced at his room and saw the side of his bed.

I gestured to my room. "Actually, I was going to go..."

"It's a problem with the Amiga. I think you can help me."

I froze. I stood there wearing shorts and a t-shirt. A man I didn't know, who had just commented on my bare legs, asked me to come into his bedroom. But this man was obviously Peter, the person who wanted me to program for him. And he was giving me my first opportunity to work with a new computer. What do I do? What should I say?

"Sure."

But I could feel my heart pound as I took each step to his bedroom.

*** BREAK ***

He rushed to the high-back leather office chair in front of the computer. He had his own large white binder with smudged and dogeared pages open next to the Amiga's keyboard.

"You see, I was following the tutorial in the *Amiga Programmer's Reference Manual,* and I just can't seem to..."

He looked up at me. He must have noticed that I stood just inside of his bedroom door, my hands clasped in front of me. The only place I could sit was on his bed, and there was no way I was going to sit there. He must have understood that. He got up and brought a metal folding chair from the side of his desk. He placed it next to his chair and patted the seat to encourage me to sit next to him. I did. But I kept as far away from him as I could. The cold metal chilled the back of my thighs.

He pointed to the Amiga's screen. "I entered the program exactly as it appears in the tutorial, but I when I try to run it..."

He reached for the mouse. I had seen those on a Macintosh, but the Amiga's had two buttons instead of one. As he moved the mouse, a red pointer moved on the screen. He moved the pointer over something that looked like a balloon with lines inside of it. Below the balloon, in block serif letters, it said "Program Tutorial." He tapped the left mouse button twice. The whole screen went black. A rectangle with a blinking red border appeared at the top that said, "Software Failure. Press left mouse button to continue. Guru meditation," which was followed by a long number.

I leaned forward to take a closer look at the screen while maintaining a distance from Peter.

"What's that?"

"A Guru Meditation error."

"What does it mean?"

He looked at me. "I thought you could tell me."

"Can you hand me your..."

"Sure." He lifted the binder and handed it to me.

I flipped back to the index to look for a page reference to a list of error codes. I figured that long number after "Guru meditation" meant something. I then flipped over to the page with the codes, but those codes didn't really tell me what was wrong.

"What happens when you press that mouse button?"

Peter did. I was sorry I asked. The black screen with the blinking red box went away. The floppy drive made a brief grinding noise. Then, that hand holding the Amiga Kickstart disk appeared. I assumed that he had to reboot the whole system. He pressed a button that ejected the disk that was in the drive, and he inserted another one with "Amiga Kickstart" handwritten on the label. He knew enough to remember to make a backup. After a few grunts of the floppy drive, another hand appeared holding a different floppy disk. This one said, "Amiga Workbench."

"You have to go through this every time you boot this computer?"

Peter nodded as he ejected the Kickstart disk and inserted another one with "Amiga Workbench" written on the label. The screen turned blue. Something that looked like a command window displayed a series of messages. Then a white bar appeared across the top that said "Workbench release. 383096 free memory." The floppy drive kept grunting. Each grunt made more windows and icons appear on the screen. The floppy drive finally fell silent. The screen was filled with windows and icons.

I wasn't sure what to think about this method of starting a computer. I worked with terminals and PCs that displayed a bunch of green text when I turned it on until a blinking cursor appeared. I used a Macintosh that only required one floppy disk to start up. But the Amiga's blue, white, and orange screen did look attractive.

"Let me see your code."

I didn't notice what icon Peter tapped on, but it opened a blue window with a white frame and white text. It was 68000 assembly. And something looked wrong.

I put my finger on the screen, being careful not to touch Peter as I reached. "Shouldn't that d0 be a d1?"

He looked at the manual. "It says d0 in the book."

"It may be a typo. Try changing it."

He backspaced the 0 and typed a 1. He then pressed Esc to open the command prompt and typed A. The messages indicated that the code was assembled correctly. The balloon icon with the lines and "Program Tutorial" label appeared.

"Do you think it will work?"

I shrugged. "Only one way to find out."

He moved the pointer over the balloon icon and tapped the left mouse button twice. This time a small window appeared with black, orange, and white lines swirling and bouncing off the sides.

He smiled. I smiled with him. He then stared into my eyes.

"How did you know?"

I could tell him how the previous line loaded the window's right edge into the d1 parameter, so the routine for the line collision had to read the value from there. But I thought about what Louise said, "Men like girls who are smart, but not too smart, and certainly not as smart as they are."

So I said, "The previous line loaded the window's right edge into the d1 parameter, so the routine for the line collision had to read the value from there."

He looked at me for a moment. Then his smile grew wider. "I'm really impressed. I'm so grateful to find a programmer like you."

"Thanks." I didn't want to blush, but I couldn't stop the warmth burning from my cheeks.

"There are some more things I really want to show you."

"I really should..." I turned my face towards the door.

"Sorry." His voice softened. "I know it's late."

He nodded. I stood up.

"We'll work on this more in the morning." I gave him a reassuring smile.

"Sounds great."

He nodded and turned back to the computer. I saw that as my cue to leave. I turned around and stepped out of his door.

"And thank you."

I turned around. His head turned toward me.

I nodded. "You're welcome."

*** BREAK ***

I was tired, but I couldn't get back to sleep. I laid on top of the covers, still in my t-shirt and shorts.

I saw a sliver of what the Amiga could do, but I was impressed with what I saw so far. A color screen, but one with graphics that could keep up. It seemed easy to use, even if it took two disks to boot.

And Peter, he seemed like a nice enough person. It felt awkward working in his bedroom, but he seemed to respect and understand me. If only I hadn't blushed. That seemed so unprofessional. So was coding in a t-shirt and shorts.

I still didn't know what to think about this job and this place. Noisy sex, antique toilets, and offices in bedrooms. But that Amiga. It would be worth sticking it out to see what the machine could do. And what I could do with it.

*** BREAK ***

"Laura! Laura!"

My eyes opened. I was surprised to see they could focus. I still had my glasses on. I put my hand over my chest. I felt the fabric of my t-shirt. I must have fallen asleep on top of the bed. I looked up. Kathlynne hovered over me. Her face turned cross.

"You better go downstairs. It's time for breakfast."

*** BREAK ***

After Kathlynne left, I changed into a floral blouse and navy blue slacks. I didn't have time to shower, but I couldn't go to breakfast in a t-shirt and shorts.

When I reached the bottom of the staircase, I glanced at the brass figurine on top of the marble pillar. I could tell it was the goddess Diana from her quiver of arrows and the deer she held by its antlers. It was a beautifully detailed figure, but it had a small dent on the side of her head. Still, it reinforced the image of the Posners as a family of refinement. I wouldn't feel out of place eating breakfast in business clothes.

But in the dining room, Kathlynne was dressed in a tank top and cutoffs. Darryl wore a white t-shirt, light blue boxers, and a robe. The household didn't seem to stand on formality for breakfast. Mrs. Posner was the exception. She wore a long pale pink and white lace dress with a cameo brooch.

She looked up at me as I entered the dining room. "Laura, so good you could make it."

"Thank you," I replied softly, so I didn't reveal my residual exhaustion.

Mrs. Posner turned her attention to a hard-boiled egg that had been shelled and set into a white and blue porcelain holder with a tall stem. She sprinkled some salt from a cut crystal salt shaker. Then, she picked up a spoon that seemed to be designed specifically for eating hard-boiled eggs.

She smiled and declared, "Ab ovo usque ad mala."

I didn't know if she intended this to be some sort of a toast that required some sort of response. But Kathlynne had already dug into her egg, and Darryl was almost finished.

I glanced at the egg in front of me. "Isn't Peter coming to breakfast?"

Mrs. Posner replied, "He comes when he pleases. Coffee?"

*** BREAK ***

After breakfast, I headed upstairs. I glanced at Peter's door. It was still closed. Who knows when he would be up, and I could work again?

I figured I better take a shower. The polyester in the floral blouse and navy blue slacks was starting to itch.

Like the other bathroom, this one was a museum piece. It also had white hexagonal tiles, a toilet with an overhead tank and a chain to flush, and an antique sink and metal handles and ceramic caps. It also had a large cast iron and porcelain coated bathtub. The handles were at the center, and a pipe extended up from the faucet and curved at the top with a large showerhead. A knob on top of the faucet diverted the water to the showerhead. A thick white shower curtain hung from the ceiling. The shower appeared to have been retrofitted.

I was about to pull off my blouse, but first I had to lock the door. I jiggled the handle once, twice just to make sure it was secure. I didn't want anyone walking in on me in the shower, especially Darryl.

*** BREAK ***

I felt much better after the shower. I couldn't wear my clothes from this morning since I already sweated in them. I looked at my gray CSUN t-shirt and white and navy blue Reseda High School gym shorts lying on the still unmade bed. It was going to get warm today, but I put on my light blue dress blouse instead. I thought about the skirt, but I grabbed a pair of gray slacks. Summer weather or not, I wasn't going to show any more of myself in this house than necessary.

When I stepped out of my room, Kathlynne was there in her tank top and cutoffs. She stared me up and down.

"Do you always dress like you're working in an office?"

"This house is my office."

"Well, I gotta take a cigarette break. Want to come outside?"

*** BREAK ***

"Some office, huh? Bet this wasn't what you expected."

She took a long drag from her cigarette and tapped the ashes on the ground. I didn't like cigarette smoke, but it wasn't too bad outside. The rising heat was something else. I wished I had something other than office clothes.

We stood behind a small storage shed with the same redwood siding and green trim as the house. The center of the yard was a square of unkempt grass with a bare dirt patch in the center. The garage sat at the other end. A long concrete driveway led from the street to the garage. A ten-year-old Cadillac was parked there, one of those long ones with the protruding chrome bumpers. Perhaps that was Darryl's since he always drove to work. I suppose I could park my Civic in the driveway too, but I hadn't gotten around to ask Mrs. Posner. Her house still didn't feel enough like home.

The garage door was open. Two cars were inside. One was a pale yellow Mercedes-Benz that appeared to be a year or two old. The other car was a new red Pontiac Fiero. I wondered who could have owned that. Certainly not Mrs. Posner.

Kathlynne took another drag and flicked off some more of the ash. "Where you from?"

"Reseda."

"*The Karate Kid* Reseda?"

I smiled and nodded.

"So why'd you come here?"

"I was looking for a job in Silicon Valley."

She took another long drag. "This ain't Silicon Valley."

I nodded. "That's south of here, right? Cupertino, Mountain View, San Jose..."

"I'm from San Jose." She turned slightly to face me and leaned against the side of the shed. "Dad took us there after he was discharged from the Navy. Actually, we bounced around the Bay Area a bit. Richmond, Oakland, Novato. He then went to The Haight without Mom, my brother, and me. We never saw him again." She took a long look at my face. "Don't feel sorry for me. It's just something that happened."

"How did you wind up here?"

"Got a job at this bar on Tamalpais Avenue. Darryl came in a lot, and well, one thing led to another." She took another long drag.

"Do you still work there?"

She shook her head. "Darryl gets too jealous."

I felt my muscles tighten. The people in this house seem to have quirks and little respect for privacy, but this was the first time I felt uncomfortable.

Kathlynne crushed out her cigarette against the side of the shed and tossed the butt on the ground. I stared at it. She then looked at me.

"Maria cleans those up."

CHAPTER EIGHT
October 2016

"Come in."

I could tell that Tammy hadn't gotten settled in. Her office had several unpacked boxes. She was staring at her laptop. It was a MacBook Pro, not one of the Lenovo laptops supplied by the company.

"I can connect to your Wi-Fi, but I can't access your network."

"You need to put in an IT request to authorize your laptop for the network. Is that a company-supplied laptop?"

"Mine. I'm a card-carrying member of the Cult of Mac." She leaned back and smiled proudly. "This one is a few years old. I can't wait until they announce the new ones."

Her MacBook Pro had a sticker with the same teal heart and infinity symbol tattooed on her ankle. The sticker was positioned so that the Apple logo glowed through the center. I couldn't imagine IT authorizing that computer for the network or any other one Tim Cook might announce.

"Why don't you take a—Oops, sorry."

She rushed around her desk and removed the open box of books on the guest chair. I sat down.

"How long have you been programming, Laura?"

"A long time."

I smiled. I had to be careful not to tip off anything about my age. I didn't want her to draw any conclusions, especially since I've been programming longer than she's been alive. So, I thought I'd flip the questioning to encourage her to talk about herself. Besides, I needed to know as much about her as she needed to know about me.

"How did you get into programming?"

"Well," She leaned back in her chair. "There was this game my dad bought me for Christmas when I was seven. It was called Robot Factory for Windows 95. Ever hear of it?"

"Yes, I think I have."

Actually, I bought it for Henry when he was about her age. It was how he got into programming.

Her eyes widened, and her voice became more excited. "It was really neat. You'd make these robots by dragging pieces from an assembly line, then you can make them do all sort of tricks by moving around programming boxes. I made one called Tommy because I was really into *Rugrats*, and...I'm not boring you, am I?"

"Of course not."

She wasn't because I was remembering what Henry and Stacy were like when they were younger. I'm not sure this was how I wanted to relate to someone who was my boss.

"Then, I took my first programming class in sixth grade. We used an iMac. Remember those big Bondi Blue G3s with the round mouse? It was so exciting. Writing code and have a computer do something new. You must still remember when you first did that."

I smiled and nodded. How do I tell her it was on a mainframe with punch cards?

Her iPhone buzzed. She picked up it and stared at her screen. Her eyebrows raised. Her lips parted. I couldn't tell if what she saw pleased or upset her.

She looked up at me and forced a smile.

"Sorry. I have to take care of something."

"No problem." I stood up.

"Thank you, Laura. I really enjoyed our talk."

"I'm glad."

I thought this was just a nicety, but I noticed how intensely she was staring at me.

*** BREAK ***

Their eyes demanded answers.

Warren, Bob, and Chris stood by my cubicle. They didn't have to speak. I knew their questions. And I couldn't answer them all. Especially the most important ones, like what she intended to do with us.

"She's actually quite pleasant. She has a passion for programming. She's been doing it since childhood." I gave a small smile. "And she liked *Rugrats*."

"What's that?" Bob grumbled.

We didn't answer. We already knew that he wouldn't know. Besides, everyone kept their eyes focused on me, demanding more answers.

Warren spoke softly. "So, she didn't give any hints about any changes she's planning?"

I thought about her reaction to something on her iPhone, but I didn't know enough to talk about it.

I shook my head. "We didn't have much time to talk. Not now. I'm sure she will give us opportunities to learn more about us and for us to know more about her."

Bob chimed in with a smirk, "Will she tell us what that bluish-green tattoo is on her ankle?"

Warren and Chris turned their scowling faces towards Bob. He started shifting uncomfortably.

"C'mon! If she didn't want people to ask her, why'd she put it on her ankle for everyone to see?"

Our eyes gave him the answer: Because it's rude. Because there may be some personal story that she might not be ready to tell us. It must be something important because she also had that symbol on her laptop. But Bob had a point. Why would she make something visible that she didn't want others to know?

"I'm sure that she'll tell us when she wants to," I assured them.

Something made Warren, Chris, and Bob scatter towards their cubicles. I turned my head. Deanna was heading towards our aisle.

I stepped into my cubicle and sat down. I noticed a text on my phone. It was from Kevin.

> S's appt. was rescheduled to 4:30. I have a late customer call. Can you pick her up after? See you tonight. Love you.

I texted back.

Sure thing. Love you too.

I set the phone down, wiggled the mouse a little to wake up my computer, and logged in. I exhaled softly. I understood what Tammy was feeling about her tattoo. If I had something deeply personal, I might not want to talk about it, especially with people I just met. Even if it were out there for the world to see.

CHAPTER NINE
July 1985

"That's $20, $30, $35." I straightened the bills I laid on the counter and placed the receipt on top of them. I handed the cash and receipt to the young woman with the red hair and lavender headband on the other side of the counter. "Thank you for banking with us and have a pleasant day."

"You too." She put the bills and receipt in her wallet and stepped away from the counter.

I straightened some papers at my station. "Welcome to West Valley Savings and Loan. May I..."

All I could see was the barrel of a gun staring at my face. Behind it growled a deep disembodied male voice. "Empty your drawer into this bag."

I looked down at the counter as a large canvas bag was pushed towards me.

I spoke calmly and softly. "I have to unlock my drawer."

A button next to the drawer sounded an alarm for the police. I slowly reached for it.

A loud pop above me. I couldn't hear anything. Rough hands grabbed my blouse. The back of the counter blurred around me as I was flung face down on the floor. When my ears cleared, that male voice shouted above me, "You try anything, I'll blow your brains out! Got it?"

My hands were forced behind my back. A tearing, scraping sound, like something being peeled away. Duct tape? My heart pounded against the floor.

Someone grabbed my shoulders from behind. He shook me hard.

*** BREAK ***

"Laura?"

My eyes flung open. I found myself face-down on a bed in a darkened bedroom in San Rafael.

"Laura?"

I glanced over my shoulder and gasped. I grabbed the sheet and covered my chest as I rolled on my back. Between the dark and my nearsightedness, I could only make out the vague shape of a person hovering over my bed. I could only identify him by his voice.

"Peter! Don't you believe in knocking?"

"But I have something to show you! It's really exciting!"

I exhaled hard once, twice. "Can I get dressed first?"

*** BREAK ***

I waited until he left. I threw on my t-shirt and gym shorts. I slipped on my glasses and ran my hand through my hair just to get it out of my face. I exhaled hard one more time just to get my heart to stop pounding. Then I walked slowly, stiffly towards Peter's room. Part of it was from still being half-asleep, but it also reminded me of how I felt after my boss untied me.

The robbery happened 6 years ago when I was 18 and worked as a teller. I stopped having nightmares about it years ago. Why was I thinking about it now?

*** BREAK ***

PBUM. PBUM-PBUM-PBUM. PBUM. PBUM-PBUM.

I heard the sound before I even stepped into Peter's room.

PBUM. PBUM. PBUM-PBUM. PBUM. PBUM-PBUM.

I stepped towards the Amiga. Peter's smile grew as I moved closer.

PBUM. PBUM-PBUM. PBUM. PBUM-PBUM-PBUM. PBUM-PBUM.

He slid in his chair away from the desk. I stepped into the space he vacated. I leaned over and stared at the Amiga screen.

PBUM-PBUM-PBUM. PBUM-PBUM-PBUM. PBUM. PBUM-PBUM.

A 3-D white-and-red checkered ball bounced against a gray background with a purple grid. With each bounce, the ball spun and cast its shadow against the background. It gave a realistic hollow and echoing PBUM like a real rubber ball against a wall.

I couldn't stop watching that ball.

PBUM. PBUM-PBUM. PBUM. PBUM. PBUM-PBUM-PBUM.

"You wrote this?"

"No," he replied. "It came on a demo disk."

PBUM-PBUM. PBUM. PBUM-PBUM.

I considered all of the processing power, local memory use, object-collision tracking, 3-D modeling, and audio synchronization needed for this computer to produce this effect. But I couldn't stop watching that ball. It was hypnotic, engrossing. It didn't feel like I was looking at a computer anymore.

PBUM. PBUM-PBUM. PBUM. PBUM-PBUM-PBUM. PBUM.

I whispered, "How did they make this?"

*** BREAK ***

The source code didn't tell me much. I tried to track the hexadecimal codes passed in and out of the registers, the instructions, the conditional processing, but they seem to go somewhere that wasn't familiar to me. I tapped on the screen.

"That's not 68000 code."

"It's running off the Denise chip."

I turned to him. "The what?"

"The Denise chip."

I turned back to the source code. "Denise? That's a strange name for a chip."

Peter continued. "The Denise chip is the graphics processor. It communicates with the CPU through the Agnus chip, which also processes memory and copies bits in parallel."

"Parallel? It must be fast."

"The whole system is optimized for video display."

"And what about the audio?"

"It comes from the Paula chip."

"Is it anything like the C64 SID chip?"

"It's more powerful than that. Four DMA-driven 8-bit PCM sound sample channels that produce stereo sound."

"Stereo?"

He nodded.

"So what's the 68000 doing?"

"The Amiga chipset offloads processing to specialized chips. This frees the 68000 for additional tasks."

"So, this computer can…" I couldn't believe what I was about to say. "Multitask?"

Peter nodded. "Preemptive multitasking. It's handled by the operating system. Watch."

He moved the mouse pointer to the white bar with "Workbench release," which was at the bottom of the screen instead of the top. He held down the mouse button as he moved the mouse up. It pulled up the window until the blue Workbench screen with its white and orange windows and icons emerged again. This was something the Macintosh couldn't do.

He double-clicked the balloon icon for the bouncing lines tutorial I helped him with. It ran in its own small window on the Workbench.

"Now, watch this."

He moved the mouse pointer to the white "Workbench release" bar and pulled it down. The red-and-white checkered ball was still bouncing with its PBUM, PBUM, PBUM. He then moved the bar until the bouncing ball took up half of the screen. In the bottom half of the screen, the lines were still bouncing in the Workbench window.

I shook my head. "How is this even possible?"

Peter just grinned.

"A computer like this should fill up an entire room, not sit under a monitor."

"This is the future, Laura. The things the Amiga can do, the things we can do with it, they can open up all sorts of possibilities."

I turned to Peter. "So, what are *we* going to do with it?"

"I'll show you."

He stood up rapidly and took my hand. I found myself pulled out of his room and down the stairs.

*** BREAK ***

He took me to the kitchen, where he finally let go of my hand. It was still dark, but he didn't turn on the light. I heard a drawer slide open and jingling and clanging as he was rooting around for something by touch.

I didn't know what to make of him. Part of me understood what he was doing. He was going to show me what he wanted us to create with that incredible computer. And with all the things the Amiga could do, who knows what he had in mind?

What if it was something underhanded?

He's a man. I'm a woman standing in my shorts and t-shirt with cold tile against the bottoms of my feet and the coolness pricking my bare skin. He wakes me up in the middle of the night and expects me to work in his bedroom. What really were his intentions? Does he expect me to write computer programs? Or did he have something else in mind?

Was that why I had that nightmare of getting robbed and tied up at the bank?

"Come on," he whispered.

A door creaked open, and a blast of cold air came from outside. I stepped into that coldness. I clutched my arms around me as I shivered. My bare feet stepped on icy concrete, uneven and wet tufts of grass, and scratchy dirt. The steady whoosh of traffic from the freeway floated from overhead. Then something stabbed at my right sole. I lifted my foot. I must have stepped on a pebble.

Soft clinking and a click came from the shed I stood next to earlier. A door creaked open.

"Come in."

I was grateful to get out of the cold, but my heart pounded as I stepped into complete blackness. The door creaked and closed behind me. Whatever was in this room couldn't have anything to do with computers.

My voice trembled. "Peter, what are you going to..."

A click and the room filled with a faint red light. Benches lined all of the sides. Empty plastic bins, bottles of chemicals, and a brown cardboard box with the label, "Photography paper. Do not expose to light." A string with clothespins hung across one wall.

"A darkroom?"

"Yes."

Peter's face was red and deepened by shadows, but somehow, I felt less afraid.

"Photography was my father's hobby." He stepped to one of the walls. "He was a lawyer and a judge, but I think he'd rather have been a photographer."

I didn't recall seeing a Mr., I mean, a Judge Posner at the house. Mrs. Posner hadn't mentioned anything about him. If something happened to Judge Posner, I figured this wasn't the right time to ask about it. I let him continue.

"I think a lot of people would like to be photographers. Capturing special moments, special people, preserving memories. It's just so hard to do. You snap pictures, and you wind up with a roll of film. You're not sure whether those pictures turned out right or if they turned out at all. You have to pay someone to develop the pictures for you."

"What about Polaroids?"

"They're limited in what you can do. You can't change lenses, focus, or exposure. Pictures are only one size, and there are no negatives for making copies."

"What does this have to do with the Amiga?"

"What if we can take everything that can be done in a photoshop like this and have a computer do it? Adjusting exposure, cropping, correcting contrast, retouching, special effects. You can do it the moment you take the picture, so you know it's the way you want it. And these images would be digital. You can make as many copies as you want and share them with all your family and friends."

"But how would you get the pictures from the camera to the computer?"

"I've been doing some research. There are some products available, including video cameras that transfer images directly to the computer. Perhaps someday, it will all be in one device. You can take computerized pictures as easily as taking them with a regular camera."

Getting a computer to work like a camera seemed impossible. But it also seemed impossible for an ordinary computer to run two resource-demanding programs at the same time. I looked at Peter, and the red lights glinting in his glasses. He saw something in the future I didn't see. A camera that didn't need film and produced images people can develop instantly and share with others. He was on the threshold of something revolutionary. If I followed him, I could be a part of a revolution.

Yet, I still didn't completely feel comfortable with him. He seemed to sense it.

His voice softened. "I can't do this alone. You are a talented programmer, I can see that. You can help me create something wonderful. Will you help me, Laura?"

I stared at him for a moment. His body, tight t-shirt, and baggy sweats cloaked in red and shadows. I then stared at the redness glowing on my skin and the shadows in the folds of my t-shirt and gym shorts. It was like we were both baptized in red light. I looked into the shadows on his face.

"When do we start?"

*** BREAK ***

I stood on a tuft of grass as I watched Peter click the padlock closed. The sky started to lighten, and the whoosh from the freeway increased. I estimated that it was four or five in the morning. I couldn't go back to sleep, and I didn't want to. I wanted to start programming.

But as Peter stepped from the door, he froze.

"What did I tell you?"

I turned around. Mrs. Posner stood in the backyard. She was cloaked in a quilted pink robe. Her arms were folded, and she had a sour expression on her face.

Peter and I glanced at each other. He then stepped towards Mrs. Posner.

"But Mother, I had to show Laura..."

"Your father's shed is off-limits. You know that."

"But Mother..."

"Peter!"

He fell silent and lowered his head.

Mrs. Posner looked past him and glanced at me. She then stepped to Peter's side. She spoke softly as if she didn't intend for me to hear. I did anyway.

"And you should know better than to have a young woman alone in a room with you. You will move your computer into the living room."

"But I have it all set up..."

"Peter!" She took another step closer to him. "May I remind you who's funding..."

"I know. I'm sorry."

He trudged into the house. I remained fixed on the grass. Mrs. Posner walked towards me. Fortunately, she was wearing slippers. She spoke calmly to me.

"Breakfast will be served in a couple of hours. I suggest you get some sleep."

I nodded. I was too afraid to speak. I followed Mrs. Posner into the house. Before I stepped in, I took a quick glance at the shed.

CHAPTER TEN
October 2016

The game had long ended, and cleanup crews were busy sweeping between the seats in the Matadome. But Stacy and her teammates were still huddled on the gymnasium floor. Gaby raised Stacy's Samsung Galaxy high above their heads. She shifted it left and right until they were all in the frame.

"Smile!" Gaby tapped the button on the screen. The phone made a shutter sound. Gaby handed the phone back to Stacy. Her teammates closed the huddle around it, oohing and laughing.

"One more! One more!" Stacy cried.

They moved back, and Gaby raised the phone again.

Kevin, Henry, and I kept a fair distance from the huddle. I felt a soft touch on my shoulder. I turned and saw Stacy's coach, Sheridan Thornburg standing behind me. She was a woman about my age with short and graying blond hair.

"If they keep taking selfies, we're going to get kicked out of the arena."

She smiled. I smiled back. She clasped my hand.

"I am so glad that Stacy was able to come. Everyone misses her so much. I sure could have used her at net tonight."

I patted the top of her hand. "She can't wait to get back. I'm sure she will as soon as she's able."

The huddle broke up. Allison had her arm around Stacy's shoulders. They let Stacy wear her uniform. The gray long-sleeve jersey and black shorts that were once skin-tight now hung loosely on her.

Coach Thornburg squeezed my hand and gazed at us. "If you need anything, anything at all."

I patted her hand again, "Thank you, Coach Thornburg."

*** BREAK ***

Kevin finished brushing his teeth in the bathroom. I was in bed checking email on my phone.

"Henry asked me if Stacy's going to die. I think he wants her room."

I didn't look up from my phone.

"Just joking," he blurted apologetically.

"That's not funny."

"I know." He pulled the covers back. "But everything's going to hell. What else can we do but try to laugh about it?"

I put the phone on the nightstand. I didn't answer him.

He covered himself up. "How's it going with your new boss?"

"I don't know. She's just a kid. She's young enough to be dating Henry. If she weren't already banging her boyfriend in Irvine."

"Now, you're trying to make a joke."

"No, she pretty much told us that."

"At work? That's unprofessional. Even when you and I started dating..."

"They're not like us, Kevin."

"Who?"

"Millennials."

"Honey, our kids are millennials."

"And they're not like us. How could Henry just walk away from that job at Google? And why won't he tell us what happened?"

"It's not because he's a millennial, honey. It's because he's still young. He's still trying to figure it all out."

"I thought he did."

"Things change." Kevin looked directly at me. "They change for all of us."

I nodded slowly.

He took my hand. "We should go to sleep."

"I better take out my contacts."

*** BREAK ***

I put the lenses in the case and tightened the lids. My world was again in its natural blur. I leaned closer to the mirror so I could see myself. Standing so close amplified every wrinkle and pore. The gray hairs in my eyebrows and roots. Even the color of my skin seemed to have faded.

I complained about millennials, but the truth was that I didn't understand myself. What gazed back at me in the mirror wasn't the person I thought I was. I was the young girl in Reseda swimming in our backyard pool. The newlyweds who passed up the luau at the Polynesian Cultural Center so we could make wild, screaming love on our honeymoon. The young mother holding my babies for the first time. I was not the middle-aged woman in the mirror.

Tammy was old enough to be my daughter. And my own daughter, Stacy, she could be...

I covered that wrinkled, pore-filled, and faded face with my hands and exhaled hard.

CHAPTER ELEVEN
July 1985

Maria set the plate in front of me. An egg sunny-side up, two pieces of crispy bacon, and a slice of wheat toast.

I looked up. Mrs. Posner was the only other person at the breakfast table. Maria set the plate in front of her.

"Very good, Maria. Thank you."

Maria said nothing and quickly disappeared. I found myself alone with Mrs. Posner.

She unfurled her napkin and set it on her lap. "Lovely weather we're having."

"It is." Yes, the weather is a lovely thing to talk about when there is something you didn't want to talk about. Especially when it happened a couple hours ago.

"We will get warmer weather as the summer goes on. The Bay Area may seem cool, especially in the evening, but this part of San Rafael can heat up."

I took her hint, but all I had were interview clothes. I wore a seafoam green blouse and black slacks that I used at a couple interviews. I could ask Mom to ship me some clothes. I had some lightweight blouses and cotton slacks. I even had t-shirts and shorts at home, but I still didn't feel comfortable wearing them for work. I suppose I could wear them to bed. People in the Posner house feel that they can come into my room whenever they please, so I had to stay dressed.

Mrs. Posner turned to her plate, neatly bisecting the yoke and letting its innards spill over the whites. I dug into my food too. The only sounds were our clinking utensils and the steady clicking from the Regulator clock.

Until the banging from the staircase.

"Ow! Ow!" It sounded like Darryl.

"Sorry," That was definitely Peter.

Mrs. Posner got up from her chair and set the napkin on her seat. I got up and followed her.

"Watch the turn!" Kathlynne snapped.

"I am watching it!" Darryl snarled.

Peter's metal computer bench stood on its end at the landing in the middle of the staircase. Peter stood on a step on the bottom part of the stairs. Darryl was behind the bench. Kathlynne's arm hung over the railing. I stood next to a tense Mrs. Posner near the foot of the stairs. She probably dreaded that bench tearing up the stairway carpet or smacking holes into the walls. I knew that was bound to happen. To get that bench down the rest of the stairs, Peter and Darryl would have to lift it straight up so that Peter could pull out the bottom end and walk it down to the bottom.

That was what they were trying to do. Peter was straining. I couldn't tell what Darryl was doing, but the top of the bench started to wave.

"Oh, dear!" Mrs. Posner gasped. She grabbed the Diana figurine and clutched it close to her, afraid that it might get damaged.

"Pull out your end, Peter!" Darryl yelled.

"I'm trying! I'm trying!" He panted.

"C'mon, Peter! It's your fucking bench!"

Mrs. Posner protested loudly, "Language! Language!"

I rushed up the stairs and knelt next to Peter at the bottom of the bench. I shouted up the stairs. "We're going to lift the bench straight up. Darryl, hold your end steady and be ready to grab the back end."

I then spoke softly to Peter. "I grab this corner. You grab the other."

He shifted to the opposite end of the bench.

"We're lifting it on three. Ready?"

Peter nodded. Darryl grumbled something inaudible.

"One, two, three!"

The bench rose. Peter's end started to wobble, so I slid my hand towards the center to steady it. We lifted the bench high enough so the legs could clear the end.

I shouted. "We're going to start walking our end down. Darryl, keep the sides steady and watch out for the legs. Here we go!"

The bench really wasn't that heavy with Peter, Darryl, and me working together to carry it. It floated down the bottom of the stairs. We then had to get it into the living room.

"Keep going straight." I didn't have to shout to Darryl because the bench was no longer blocking us. "Peter, you and I will swing out this end. Darryl, you back it into the room."

I pulled on my end to swing the bench clockwise. Darryl figured out what we were doing. He swung his end, so the bench lined up with the entryway. Fortunately, the bench was able to fit through it without having to tilt it.

I would have asked Peter where he wanted the bench, but I could tell from his sweat-coated face, and the furious expression on Darryl's that they had enough with moving furniture for the moment.

"Let's set it down here for now."

We lowered the bench in the middle of the floor.

Mrs. Posner stepped into the living room, still clutching that Diana figurine. She stared at Peter with the same cross glare she gave us earlier that morning. She turned towards Darryl and gave him that same scowl.

"Such language! Did I raise you boys in a barn?"

She didn't include their father, Judge Posner.

"Clean up and come to breakfast." She stopped at the pillar and set the Diana figurine back on top of it. She then continued to the dining room.

I turned around to follow Mrs. Posner. Then, I heard Darryl's voice behind me.

"You had to get a girl to help you because you can't do a man's job."

I glanced over my shoulder. Peter hung down his head.

My muscles twitched. I kept walking. I could talk to Peter later. I had to get back to my breakfast before it got cold.

*** BREAK ***

After what happened with the shed and the bench, I needed some time away from the Posner's house. The shopping district on Fourth Street was just a fifteen-minute walk. And I needed more exercise.

I looked in the clothing stores. Maybe I'd buy some outfits instead of bothering Mom to ship things to me. It was all summer stuff. Shorts, miniskirts, swimwear, and whatever Madonna wore in her latest video. I came across a Macy's. It had summer-weight business clothes that looked pretty nice. Or did until I saw the price tag.

I had money saved from the summers I worked, and I paid off my credit card each month. But I spent a lot on gas and on meals when I lived with Tina. I didn't know when the Posners were going to pay me. Darryl said I'd get $10,000 per year, but when would I get paid? Weekly? Monthly? When they felt like it? When I complained loud enough? I still felt confident they would pay me. I wished I had pinned them down on specifics.

I also wished I had brought more clothes because I didn't feel comfortable about spending money on new ones.

I walked to a nearby payphone and reached into my wallet for my MCI card. That was another expense I'd have to deal with.

*** BREAK ***

"Are you sure you don't need your swimsuit?"

"They don't have a pool."

"Well, if you need me to send anything else..."

"I'll be fine, Mom."

"Are you sure, Laura?"

I watched as a couple burst out of the restaurant next door, arguing loudly.

"I'm sure, Mom."

"I'm proud of you, honey. I want you to know that."

My heart glowed. "Thank you, Mom."

"I better let you go. And oh..."

"What?"

"Greg sent you a postcard from West Germany. He said he'll be on leave next month. Should I send him your new address?"

"I'll send it to him. Thank you, Mom. I love you."

"I love you too, honey. Take care of yourself in San Rafael."

"Take good care of yourself too. Bye."

"Bye."

The phone clicked. I hung up the receiver. I clutched my hands to my heart. Greg!

*** BREAK ***

I knew where I had to stop next. I flipped through the postcards in a convenience store. Golden Gate Bridge. Golden Gate Bridge. Golden Gate Bridge. San Francisco. Fisherman's Wharf. Golden Gate Bridge. San Francisco. "Dig those crazy California earthquakes!" Golden Gate Bridge. Finally, I found one of San Rafael. It was a picture of the mission. Greg and I were both Catholics, but we weren't too into it. Still, it was a pretty picture.

I bought the postcard and a stamp. I looked for a counter and a pen I could borrow and tried to keep my hand from trembling as I wrote.

> Hey, Greg. I got a job in the Bay Area. Write me and let me know when you'll be on leave. I'm at 27643 Irwin St., San Rafael, CA 94901.

I should give him my phone number, but I was afraid of who might pick up the phone.

> Can't wait to see you. Love you, Laura.

On the right side, just below the stamp, I wrote "Sgt. Greg O'Bryan" and his APO address.

I stared at his name. Six months. Six months since I last saw him, felt him.

"Excuse me." A woman stood off my left shoulder. Her eyes were fixed on some necklaces dangling from a rack.

"Sorry."

She gave me a funny stare as I retreated from the counter. I didn't care. I nearly skipped to the mailbox in front of the store. I dropped the postcard in the slot and gave a small schoolgirl sigh.

*** BREAK ***

When I got back to the Posners, I figured I'd see what help they needed with the bench and setting up the computers. The bench was moved against the wall at the end. I stepped towards it. Underneath the bench, Peter's legs and butt stuck out. His jeans sagged, exposing the sliver of a crack and butt cheeks covered with fine blond hairs.

Peter quickly scooted out from under the bench. He remained kneeling on the floor by the bench.

"I put the phone line here. My room is overhead. I removed my jack and spliced 15 feet of telephone wire to the existing cable. Then, I dropped the line into this room and put in a new jack. We can now connect the modem in here."

I nodded. "Let's see Darryl do that."

"There are still plenty of things he can do that I can't."

I fell silent, but I had questions. Questions about him and his brother. Questions about his father, a man I had never seen. But they were questions I knew I shouldn't ask.

He stood up and moved in front of me. "I really appreciate you helping me today."

"You're welcome."

He smiled. I smiled back.

He then said, "Do you think you can help me bring down the rest of the equipment..."

"Of course."

We started walking towards the staircase and his room.

*** BREAK ***

That night, we discovered a problem with moving the computer into the living room.

"I love it when a plan comes together..."

Peter didn't look up from the Amiga. "Can you please turn it down?"

Darryl protested. "We're watching our show!"

"We're trying to work."

"Mother!"

Mrs. Posner spoke calmly, "You heard your brother. He and Laura are trying to work."

"But, Mother! We want to watch our show!"

"For pity's sake," Mrs. Posner hissed. A click, and the TV went silent. "It's just four louts driving around in a van and causing explosions."

"It's my favorite show!"

"It's just a TV show, Darryl!"

"And I can't watch because of them!"

Darryl's shouts forced both Peter and me to turn around, just as Darryl thrust a quivering arm towards Peter.

"He's supposed to work in his room! But you made us drag down that...that..." He must have remembered his mother's injunction against swearing. "Now, we can't watch TV! Why did you do that to me?"

I froze. I was afraid Mrs. Posner was going to talk about what happened early that morning. And I would get blamed because, as a woman, I shouldn't be alone with Peter in his bedroom.

Instead, she spoke calmly and firmly. "It is my decision that..."

"Mother!"

"My decision stands. This is my house."

Darryl twisted his arms tightly in front of him. "You mean yours and Peter's. It sure as hell ain't mine."

Mrs. Posner's face tightened it. "Then if you don't want to..."

Kathlynne bolted from the sofa and rushed to Darryl's side. She leaned in close to his ear. "Babe, please don't..."

The room fell silent, except for the steady clicks of the grandfather clock.

Mrs. Posner's face relaxed. "We can move the TV into the dining room if you agree not to watch during meal times."

Darryl relaxed his arms and face to give his silent acceptance. Mrs. Posner nodded and headed out of the living room.

He then turned to Kathlynne. "Let's go to the bar. Maybe we can catch *Hunter*."

"They probably have the Giants game on..."

"Nobody cares about the Giants. They suck this year. Lou will change the channel if you ask him."

Kathlynne nodded and left the room, leaving us alone with Darryl. He glanced around the room, probably to make sure his mother was gone.

"This fucking computer thing of yours better make us rich, Peter." He then stared directly at me. "Especially when you made me hire a girl."

He swiftly turned and rushed out of the room.

Peter turned around and started typing on the Amiga again. But I was trembling too badly to even think about programming.

My voice shook, "Do you think, maybe, we can take a break?"

Peter looked at me. "We had to fight to keep our workspace. We have to keep going."

It took me two long, deep breaths, but I was able to turn my attention back to the computer screen.

He went back to typing a file saving routine. He typed fifteen lines of code. The steady clacking helped me forget what just happened. Halfway through writing a routine to call the Save dialog box, he stopped.

"Laura, do you have any older brothers and sisters?"

"No." The metal chair squeaked as my back stiffened. "I'm an only child."

"Consider yourself lucky." He went back to typing the routine.

CHAPTER TWELVE
October 2016

I tried not to pay attention to office gossip, but I couldn't ignore the Guacphix people clustered in small groups. I knew they were from Guacphix because they were all young. They also knew nothing about business attire. I saw my first man-bun. One woman wore Lululemon running shorts and an Atari ST t-shirt. She probably wasn't even born when the Atari ST came out. I just walked past them and headed to my cubicle.

I settled into my desk chair, wiggled the mouse to wake up the computer, and looked over my C# code.

Bob's grumble broke my concentration. "My God, he's coming."

I stood up and watched Ray Bifo saunter towards our cubicles. He broke out his typical salesperson smile. We knew whenever he came to us, he always brought some unreasonable request and impossible deadline.

He exceeded our worst fears.

"It would be so cool if we could use the 2X optical zoom camera on the iPhone 7 and extrapolate the pixels to..."

"You mean the iPhone 7 Plus."

"The iPhone 7 also has an optical zoom."

"No, Ray. Only the iPhone 7 Plus has the second telephoto camera lens. The iPhone 7 only has one lens, and it cannot perform optical zoom."

"But the lens is bigger, right?"

"Yes. It's an f/1.8 aperture."

"Then, it can do telephoto, right?"

Chris, Bob, and Warren gave me the "thank God you're dealing with this instead of us" look. I always found myself stuck with dealing with Ray. He came to MHR Imaging from a company that made frozen pizzas. When he was hired as marketing director, he knew nothing about imaging. Six years later, he still knew nothing.

"The iPhone 7 doesn't have a telephoto lens."

He pulled his iPhone out of his pocket and tapped the Camera app. He pinched in and out, in and out. "Why can I zoom like this?"

"That's a digital zoom, not an optical zoom. I told you the difference between the two, remember?"

"So, I can do this digital zoom as much as I want."

"The iPhone 7 only goes up to 5X. The 7 Plus only goes up to 10X with digital zoom."

"So, why can't our software zoom some more?"

Warren looked down. Bob pawed the carpet with the tip of his shoe. Chris looked ready to explode.

I softly exhaled. "We can only work with the image captured by the camera."

"But you can program it to make it zoom more, can't you?"

*** BREAK ***

For all his flaws, Vince had the ability to quash most of Ray's wild requests. He did this mostly by promising to do further research and then forgetting about it. Or he used his poor communication skills and propensity for BS to make Ray give up.

We didn't know what to expect when we took him into Tammy's office.

In our favor, Tammy was a programmer from a graphics company. She must know enough to see through Ray's ignorance. There was also no generational advantage. Ray was 39. We knew that because he kept telling us how much he dreaded turning 40. But working against us was Tammy's lack of experience. How would she work with some marketing guy with an oversized personality?

By saying, "You don't know what the fuck you're talking about."

Chris gasped. Warren's eyes flung wide open. Bob raised an eyebrow. I stood emotionless, but I had to admire her guts. Her unprofessional, career-limiting guts.

Ray boiled. "I'll tell Deanna!"

She leaned back in her chair. "Good. Do it. But first, go to Amazon and buy yourself a copy of *Imaging for Dummies*."

Chris, Warren, Bob, and I exchanged glances. Tammy said everything we've dreamed about saying to Ray. This seemed unreal to us. It certainly must have felt that way to Ray because he just stared blankly at her.

After his shock wore off, he raged, "You stupid little girl! By the time I'm finished with you, you'll be back making Frappuccinos at Starbucks!"

She smirked. Really.

"I never worked at Starbucks. I got my first paid programming gig when I was 16. What did you do when you were 16? Roll blunts?"

Ray stormed out of Tammy's office. He brushed against my arm as he charged.

Our eyes all turned to Tammy. She stared back at us.

"Dude was blowing smoke out his ass." She leaned forward in her chair. "But I'd think, with your experience, you'd know that."

Chris, Warren, Bob, and I looked at each other in stunned silence. Tammy gnawed a huge chunk out of our asses too.

*** BREAK ***

"We're taking you back to 1982 on the 80s Hits Channel. Here's Hall & Oates and 'Maneater'."

I gripped the steering wheel tighter. The bite Tammy took out of my ass still stung.

Still, I was impressed with how she put Ray in his place. How many times I wished I could have said the same things Tammy did. But I knew I couldn't. Even when I was in my twenties, I knew there were things I could and could not do. Certainly, cussing out a marketing manager was one of them.

So, why did Tammy do it? Was it a generational thing? Immaturity? A lack of professionalism?

Or was something else going on?

*** BREAK ***

I heard the noise before I opened the door. Was it music? It had a rhythm like music, but it didn't sound like anything I would call music. The noise got louder as I climbed up the stairs, and it exploded when I opened the door to Henry's room.

Somewhere in the sound was a muffled "Mom?" Then, Henry shut off the sound.

I looked around his room in amazement. I had no idea where this so-called music came from. It certainly didn't come from his Fender bass in the corner or the saxophone he played in marching band. Henry sat in front of a MacBook Pro and a bunch of equipment I didn't recognize.

"What's all this stuff? And when did you start using a Mac?"

"Mom, I was making my jam!"

"Jam?"

"My music! Do you like it?"

*** BREAK ***

"He quit Google to become a DJ!"

I stood in front of Kevin and Henry as they sat on the couch. I had to have Kevin there to hear my outrage.

"But Mom, I hated Google. I—I was doing the same thing every day. I was fixing bugs and adding comments to the source code for APIs."

"And I once spent three months refactoring code because we switched from Java to .NET."

Henry stood up. "Mom, when I'm on stage or mixing beats, I feel energized! I feel alive! I feel happy! Don't you want me to be happy?"

"Family makes you happy! When you get married and have kids, how are you going to support them?"

He looked at the ground. "I make money DJing!"

"How much?"

"Um...I made $500 at a bar mitzvah." He looked up at me and smiled proudly. "And I sell my beats on iTunes. I call myself HamilDown."

"And what's the most you made on iTunes?"

"Uh...There's this one...it's my favorite..."

"How much did you make?"

"Uh...$15?"

Kevin stayed planted on the sofa. "Son, only a handful of musicians ever made any money from their music. And most of them are dead."

I folded my arms. "And you walked away from a job with a six-figure salary."

"What good is making money if you feel dead inside? What good is having a nice car if you drive it to a job you hate? Didn't you tell me about what that one guy said to you? 'People have the right to change their mind.'"

"But you worked for Google! They give you free gourmet food!"

"Mom, it's not me! It's not me!" Henry's voice began to quiver. "Maybe you can spend the last 30 years moving bits around, but it's not me!"

He dashed out of the room. Kevin and I stared at each other.

*** BREAK ***

Kevin and I still didn't know what to say when we got into bed. He muttered, "I don't know what has gotten into him."

I scrolled through some emails on my phone. "Maybe it is a generational thing."

"Did something happen with your new boss? What's her name again?"

"Tammy." I put the phone in my lap and turned to Kevin. "She cursed out Ray."

"You mean that marketing guy that always causes you trouble?"

"Uh-huh."

"And what do you mean by cursing him out?"

"She used the F word."

"Really?"

"Really."

"Good. About time someone chewed out that motherfucker…"

"Kevin!"

"What can I say? It was unprofessional, but he deserved it."

"Maybe. But what if I did something like that? Or you? We'd be out on the street so fast, it would make our head spin."

"So, did your boss get called into Human Resources?"

"No. Not as far as I know."

"Maybe the rules have changed, Laura. Everything seems to be changing."

I put my phone on the nightstand and plugged in the charger. Then, I set my glasses by the alarm clock. I felt Kevin's warm palm against my shoulder.

His fingers started massaging my muscles. "But I know something we can do to make ourselves feel better."

I turned to him. "Sorry. I'm just too stressed right now. Rain check?"

"We have a lot of rain checks."

"I know. It's just with Stacy being sick, work, and now Henry…"

"It's OK." He glided his hand down my arm and squeezed my hand. "We'll get some sleep. Good night. I love you."

We leaned towards each other and kissed.

"I love you too, Kevin."

*** BREAK ***

"Up next on the 80s Hits Channel, we have 'You've Lost That Lovin' Feelin'" by Hall and Oates."

"I don't think so." I tapped the button on the steering wheel to change the channel.

"The fallout continues over the latest statements by Republican presidential candidate..."

"Dear God, no."

I reached over and turned off the stereo. One thing I liked about having a short commute is that I didn't have much time to listen to crap on the radio. Or to think. I'd wind up thinking about what was happening at home with Stacy and Henry. And with Kevin. I hated to refuse him again. He never complained about it. Should I be worried about that?

And should I be worried about work? Would Tammy get in trouble for what she said to Ray? Would we? In a way, it felt good watching her put him in his place. But what would be the fallout...

Fallout? Oh, this damn election! I can't wait for it to be over. Unfortunately, it would mean that one of those fools would get elected. I had enough going on in my life to have to decide whether Clinton or Trump would do the least amount of damage. Not to mention having to read through all those propositions.

MHR Imaging appeared on the right. At least, I would be able to deal with only one set of problems.

*** BREAK ***

I sat down at my desk and logged into my computer.

"Hey, Laura."

I turned around. Tammy stood behind me.

"I just wanted to touch base with you about our meeting yesterday."

"Sure. What's up?" It was hard to sound professional when my throat was tightening.

"That request from marketing yesterday, you don't need to worry about it. It won't be pursued, and you don't have to waste any more time with it."

"That's good." I nodded and tried to force a smile.

"Good."

She smiled and turned towards the entrance of my cubicle. I saw that as my cue to turn back to my computer and go back to work.

"Oh, and Ray Bifo is no longer with the company."

I swung back around, but Tammy had already started walking back to her office. I caught a glimpse of her teal ankle tattoo.

All I could do is stare blankly towards the hallway.

CHAPTER THIRTEEN
August 1985

After breakfast, Maria would go to the kitchen to do the dishes, Mrs. Posner would go upstairs to her bedroom to read, Darryl would go to work, and Kathlynne would go to the backyard to smoke and flip through tabloids. Peter wouldn't be up until noon. I had the living room—and the Amiga—to myself.

The whirring of the computer's fan drowned out the clicking of the grandfather clock. Seeing that Workbench screen take shape in vivid blue, white, and orange brightened my mood. Unlike other computers, working with the Amiga didn't seem like work.

My first task was to make backups of the disks we used for our code. I learned the importance of backups the first time I spent four days writing a program for class on my Commodore 64, only to have a flaky 1541 drive corrupt my disk. Then, I looked over the code Peter and I worked on the night before. I had to get on him about adding comments. He had gotten better at it, but I still had to look at the code to figure out exactly what we did and where we left off.

Weeks of programming enabled us to make a rudimentary drawing program. We could draw lines, circles, rectangles, and free-form polygons in any of the basic 32 colors. That was twice the colors of a Commodore 64 or an IBM with a CGA card, but not enough to be useful for photographs. The Amiga has a hold-and-modify mode capable of 4,096 simultaneous colors. My task that morning was to coax the Denise chip to let us use it.

I flipped to a page in the *Amiga Programmer's Reference Manual*. I found the register, but I also had to look at the DMA channels and the Copper. I studied the instructions and poured over the sample code.

KNOCK-KNOCK.

I straightened my back. It was a soft knock, but I heard it clearly. I had learned how to block Darryl and Kathlynne's screaming sex, but I could still be drawn to soft sounds. I figured I better answer it. I stood up and brushed flat the front of my magenta polo shirt and lime green Bermuda shorts and headed to the door. When I opened it, I gasped. The thick, wavy red hair. A face full of freckles. Broad shoulders.

"Greg?"

"Laura!"

He wore his Army jacket with a t-shirt and jeans. I swung open the screen door and rushed out. I pulled him to a spot between the windows and pressed him against the redwood siding. I kissed him long and hard. I thrust my tongue between his teeth. I reached inside his Army jacket and caressed those firm back muscles underneath his cotton shirt. My hips nestled onto his. We pulled away to catch our breath, but our chests continued to rise and fall together in sync. My heart pounded. Our eyes locked.

When I could catch my breath, I whispered, "Where are you staying?"

*** BREAK ***

I found myself naked on his motel bed. The sheets below me were rough and over-washed, but his skin felt so smooth and warm against mine. The Army built up his muscles until they were taut, bulged, and round. His pale skin made him look like a Greek sculpture, but with bright copper hair. I dipped my hands into those soft, loose curls and twirled them around my fingers.

My glasses were off. The world past Greg blurred, but I didn't care. My body was on fire. My hard nipples gave way to the roughness of his tongue. His white skin on top of my tan. Yin and yang.

He plunged into me. My whole body trembled. I closed my eyes, leaned back my head, and let out a loud moan that came deep from my gut. He pulled back and thrust again. I arched my back and let out another deep, involuntary moan. I wrapped my legs around his thighs. I needed to feel those thick veins as they rubbed inside of me. Our bodies ebbed and flowed together, undulating in a single motion. Each thrust shook my body loose. I was ready to explode, but I didn't want him to stop. I clasped the back of his head. My fingertips trembled against his scalp. My jaw fell slack as moans and cries burst uncontrollably from my open mouth.

He stopped and pressed hard against my pubic mound, driving himself deep inside of me. Underneath his condom, he throbbed and pumped as he let go.

My heart skipped. My body seized. Waves of heat burned from my chest. It faded after a moment. I drove the air out of my lungs with a hard exhale. I let go of his hair and let my body settle into the mattress. I unwrapped my legs and rested them by his sides. I opened my eyes. The world was even blurrier. Hormones sloshed inside my skin while my heart pounded.

He lowered himself on me, nestling his sweaty face between my breasts. He exhaled hard.

I caught enough of my breath to speak. "Six months is too long, isn't it?"

*** BREAK ***

After we cleaned up, I drove Greg into the City. I had gotten familiar enough with the Bay Area to know my way around and call the different areas by their proper names. And where to find the best sourdough bread bowls and clam chowder on Fisherman's Wharf.

The waiter brought us our wine. I unfurled my napkin and set it neatly on my lap. I guess Mrs. Ponser was having an influence on me.

Greg studied his glass. "Is this that white zinfandel you ordered?"

"Yes."

"It's pink."

"It's delicious." I raised my glass. "To the Bay Area."

"To us." He clinked my glass and took a long sip. He nodded in approval. "It's good. One of those Napa Valley wines?"

"Sutter Home." I took a sip and set down my glass. "I heard they have great wines in West Germany."

He nodded. "There's a place near where I'm stationed in Stuttgart. It's called Freiburg. It's at the base of the Black Forest."

"They don't have evil queens and witches who eat children, do they?"

He chuckled and shook his head. "They do have great wines. They even have a vineyard in one of their parks. Beautiful place."

I looked around the wharf and the bay in the distance. "It's lovely here too. I've come to like it."

Greg took another sip. "So, how is the job treating you? Do they pay you well?"

"They haven't paid me anything yet, but they do cover my room and board."

"So they own you."

I leaned forward. I could feel my face tighten. Greg let out an embarrassed smile.

"Hell, Uncle Sam owns me. Thank God the Soviets have that new guy Gorbachev. He seems reasonable. Perhaps President Reagan won't get us fried in a nuclear war after all."

My face relaxed, but I still shook my head. "You know I don't like discussing politics, Greg."

"I know, but in my line of work, politics is pretty important. What happens in Washington is a life-and-death matter for me."

"I never thought of it that way."

We scooted back as the waiter set the sourdough bowls in front of us. I never heard of these things before I came to the Bay Area. A large sourdough loaf was hollowed out and filled with steaming clam chowder. Greg started shoveling into his chowder. I found myself dipping the spoon in slowly, carefully scooping a small portion. Mrs. Posner really did have an effect on me.

"So, how much longer does Uncle Sam own you?"

"Six months, 8 days, 11 hours…" He glanced at his watch. "Twenty-three minutes and 19 seconds. Not that I'm counting."

"I can't wait either."

"Will you still be here when I'm discharged?"

I stared at my clam chowder for a moment before I looked up and answered him. "That's what I expect I'll be doing."

"But how is your company going to make money? Do they have a business plan? A marketing plan? Do you know who's the target customer for your program?"

I leaned forward and smiled. "You still remember Business 201."

"Professor Conroy. He was checking you out."

"He was checking out all the girls."

"But especially you. I don't blame him though."

Greg's hand caressed my knee underneath the table.

*** BREAK ***

I thought about taking Greg to all the cultural landmarks Mrs. Posner pointed out, but we really wanted to go to a baseball game. Greg and I grew up as Dodger fans, so Candlestick was out. Fortunately, the A's were in town playing the Royals. We crossed the bay to Oakland for the game.

The A's must have been having a bad season too because Oakland-Alameda County Coliseum was sparsely filled. The row in front of us was empty. My legs felt cramped, so I perched my feet on the seat back in front of me. The legs of my Bermuda shorts slipped towards my lap, baring more of my tanned thighs. Greg placed his white freckled hand on one and gently massaged my muscles between his thumb and index finger. I closed my eyes and tried to keep my moan inconspicuous.

"Keep touching me like that, we'll start doing it right here in the stands."

He chuckled. "It'd be more interesting than the game."

The crowd gave a collective groan. I opened my eyes. The Royals in their powder blue uniforms dashed off the field towards their dugout.

"The Royals pitcher is really good." Greg let go of my thigh and picked up his program. He thumbed through it until he found the bio for number 31 on the Royals roster. He squinted as he looked at the name. "Saber...Sayer..."

I glanced over at the page. "Saberhagen. Really, Greg. I'd think with all the years you've been stationed in West Germany you could handle names like that."

"It's not that easy. German has vowels that will break your lips. Where's that Saberhagen from anyway?"

I leaned closer to look at the program. "Wow."

"What?"

I tapped on the page. "Graduated Grover Cleveland HS, Reseda, CA, 1982."

He brought the page closer to him. "Our crosstown rival."

I nodded and smiled.

He smiled back. "Small world."

*** BREAK ***

The first of the orange Art Deco towers of the Golden Gate Bridge passed above us, the top shrouded by night. I had my driver's side window open. The cool air of the bay rushed in, tousling my hair, and stroking my face. Greg had his arm around my shoulders. The thick khaki of his Army jacket felt good against me. The second tower stood ahead. Sadness came over me. Beyond that tower was Marin, and San Rafael, and the motel parking lot where I'd have to say goodbye.

*** BREAK ***

And my heart sank when I pulled in.

"When do you leave?"

"In the morning. I'm going to Reseda to see my folks."

"Tell them I said hi."

"Of course."

I exhaled and shut off the motor. "I had a wonderful day."

"So did I."

We turned to each other. He put his hand on my knee. "Sleep with me?"

I lowered my head. "I have to go back."

"Sure?"

"We even work at this time of night."

His face remained solemn.

I smiled. "But it won't be too long before you're discharged. Then, we can be together for good."

"Six months, 8 days..." He glanced at his watch. "Oh, 7 days. And 23...um..."

I silenced him with a kiss. Long, passionate, full-mouthed, but one I knew I had to end. I pulled away and smiled.

"That day will be here before you know it."

*** BREAK ***

I stepped through the front door. The clacking of the Amiga keyboard came from the living room. I looked at the stairway. I could continue upstairs and go to bed. It had been a long day, and I was tired. But I should go into the living room to check on Peter. I turned and then stopped again. What if Peter was upset that I went out today? I hadn't had a day off since I moved into the Posner's house. I'm sure he'd be fine if I had one day to relax. But I never told him about Greg. Will he be jealous I have a boyfriend?

I set my purse on a table by the front door and walked into the living room. I took the metal chair next to Peter. He didn't look up.

"Take a look at this." He used the mouse to pull the Workbench screen over the programming window. He double-clicked the icon for our application. "I got hold-and-modify mode to work. Notice how the resolution and screen color changes, and look at this palette."

He pressed the Amiga and C keys. Usually, our color selector window had 32 tiny blocks for each color. Now, it was a solid block of changing colors. Shades of red blended into shades of green that blended into shades of blue. Peter moved the mouse pointer into the box and clicked on a color. The color selector window went away, leaving a white screen. He held down the mouse button and dragged the mouse over the canvas. A squiggly line appeared in his selected color.

"You can see the responsiveness of the Amiga screen, even in this special color mode."

"Impressive."

He pressed the keys and opened the color selector window again. "I think we can make it easier to select colors by choosing RGB values."

"What about hue, saturation, and brightness?"

He turned to me, his eyes opened with excitement. "What would be really useful is if you can go to your existing image and click on any pixel to select that color. That would be perfect for retouching."

"That would be perfect. How do we code it?"

"Let's see what's already in the API..."

Peter flipped to a page in the *Amiga Programmer's Reference Manual*. We went back to programming the Amiga as if nothing happened to me that day.

I felt both relieved and saddened.

CHAPTER FOURTEEN
October 2016

I was determined not to let what happened at work bother me at home. I had too much work to do at home, anyway. I had to make dinner. Or thought I did until I smelled that aroma coming from the kitchen.

"Clam chowder?"

Henry stood proudly by the stove. He stirred our large stockpot. "I found the recipe online. Here. Taste some."

He reached for a spoon and dipped it in. He kept one hand under the spoon as brought it to me. I blew on the steaming white cream before tasting it. I smacked my lips and smiled in approval. He smiled back.

"That's one thing I'm going to miss about the Bay Area, great seafood. I even got some sourdough bread to go with it." He set the spoon in the sink. "And guess what, I got a job!"

"That's great!" I beamed with excitement.

"A DJ job!"

"Oh." My excitement faded.

"On election night, I'll be in Lake Balboa performing at a Democratic victory party."

"Victory party?" I leaned against the counter. "They seem pretty confident they're going to win."

"Of course they will! Have you seen the polls?"

"I don't follow polls, Henry. That's because I studied statistics. Numbers are only as good as the data collected."

"But don't you want Hillary Clinton to be elected president?"

I walked over to him and put my hand on his shoulder. "I want some of that delicious clam chowder you worked so hard to make."

"Henry?"

We turned to the entryway into the kitchen. Kevin was waving his razor.

"Did you use this?"

"No, Dad."

"My razor's all jacked up."

"But I didn't use it. I have my own razors."

"Then, if you didn't use it..."

"How do I look?"

Stacy stepped into the kitchen with a huge smile and a completely bald head.

"I was going to lose it all anyway, and I was sick of having it come out in clumps." She stroked her bare head. "Besides, that's what's great about being a black girl with cancer. We can rock this look."

I stayed planted by the counter. I was afraid if I spoke, I'd burst out crying. But Kevin stayed calm. He set the razor on the counter and walked over to her.

"Stacy, you look beautiful."

He threw his arms around her and held her close.

"Thank you, Dad."

He rested his head on her shoulder. I watched a tear trace down his cheek.

*** BREAK ***

I finished washing the last of the dishes. Stacy sat at the kitchen island, tapping on her phone. As I passed by her, I snuck a glance at her screen, like nosy parents are supposed to do.

"Hey, Mom."

Caught. But Stacy smiled back at me.

"I got 92 likes on my new photo." She stroked her bald hair. "People love the look."

"Hopefully, it won't be your look for much longer."

"I also got a friend request from Ruben."

I grimaced. "I hope you declined it."

"You still don't like him?"

"You were 16."

"We used protection. We were responsible."

"And then he cheated on you with that…"

"It's over and done with. Besides, I'm not sorry I did it with him anymore."

"Why's that?"

She lowered her phone and stared right at me.

"I might not get another chance."

She got up and headed out of the kitchen.

*** BREAK ***

Kevin pressed his lips hard against mine, His hands grabbed at the waist of my sleep shorts. I put my palms on his chest and gently pushed him a few inches away.

"We don't have to rush."

He nodded and moved closer. He kissed me, but not as hard.

I reached into his pajama pants and stroked his butt. His muscles weren't as firm as when he was younger, but they still felt soothing to touch.

He slid his hands under my tank top, gliding them over my curved belly and reaching for my sagging breasts. He rubbed my nipples with my fingertips. The way his strong fingers gently traced around the edges, it made me moan like I was 24 again.

His hands slid down my sides to my hips. He clasped them and rolled me on my stomach.

"Kevin?"

I heard his pajama pants slide down.

"Kevin."

He pulled my shorts and panties down over my butt. One of his hands slid to my crotch. He parted my labia.

I pulled away from him and rolled on my back.

His face froze.

I held my hands up towards him. "You know I don't like it that way."

He backed away from me. "I'm—I'm sorry."

"C'mon, Kevin. You know how I feel about that."

"I know, honey…"

"Then why? What were you thinking!"

"It has been too long. I just wanted to try something new."

"This isn't like picking a Korean barbecue." I exhaled hard. "Kevin, you should know why I don't like it. What it reminds me of…"

"Honey, that was almost 40 years ago. Don't you think it's time…"

"He stuck a gun in my face! He tied me up! He could have killed me! You don't forget something like that!"

He turned his face away from me. "But you can forget how to be a wife."

"Excuse me!"

He bolted off the bed and stood up in front of me. "Laura, I love you. I want to love you the way a husband should love his wife. But there's always an excuse with you. 'I'm tired. I'm stressed. Stacy has an appointment with the oncologist in Pasadena in the morning. My HRT medicine isn't working right. Can you take a rain check?' Always some excuse!"

"You're upset you can't get your rocks off? Is that it?"

"No!" His shout shook with tears. "I'm scared of losing our daughter. I'm scared about what will happen to our son. I can't afford to lose you too."

I held out my arms to him. He climbed into bed and collapsed into them. I closed them around him and gently stroked his back. I leaned in and kissed his shoulder.

"Kevin, I'm sorry. So sorry."

I held him tight. I was afraid holding was all I could do for him.

*** BREAK ***

I felt just as useless walking into work the next morning.

The Guacphix people were chatting again. I slowed as I approach them, trying to pick up some of the conversation.

"For real?"

"That person's a genius…"

"But why come here?"

"What I heard was…"

The guy with the man bun raised his head. I picked up my pace before he noticed me.

But I stopped when I saw Warren in front of my cubicle. He waved me over and started walking towards Tammy's office. I followed him.

*** BREAK ***

My heart pounded as Warren and I stood in front of Tammy's still cluttered desk.

"I don't know what the problem is." She leaned back in her chair. "All I said was the MHR Imaging Graphics Library was put into maintenance."

Warren stiffened. "And the version 12 upgrade was canceled."

"We're still providing bug fixes through service packs."

I looked at both of them. We had never relegated a product before. This left us with dozens of products we had to support, some of which haven't had a new customer in years. But this was MHR Imaging Graphics Library. We spent evenings and weekends on the initial release and were rewarded with generous sales and laudatory industry reviews. That product was a labor of love to all of us, especially Warren as its chief engineer.

"You don't know what a big deal this product is," he begged. "We've been enhancing and improving it for 15 years."

"That's the problem." Tammy gestured to him. "That product is 15 years old."

"It's our flagship product."

"It's a cash cow. According to management, it's not producing as much milk as it used to."

"If we can only produce that upgrade..."

"An upgrade can't fix a rickety core architecture. Your product supports Windows XP. Not even Microsoft supports Windows XP anymore."

Warren lowered his head. "My schedule was booked for the next six months on that upgrade. Shoshana in Tech Comm is slated to update the user documentation, and Faisal has five engineers lined up in Mumbai for QA testing. What are they supposed to do?"

"They will be redeployed to other projects. So will you." She turned to me. "Do you have any concerns, Laura?"

I glanced at Warren and then turned to Tammy. "No."

Warren didn't look up. I'm sure he knew there was nothing I could say or do.

Tammy leaned forward. "Things are changing. Get used to it."

CHAPTER FIFTEEN
August 1985

"I think we should put together a business plan."

The faces around the dinner table didn't encourage me. Peter had a blank, puzzled gaze. Darryl glared. Kathlynne looked away. Mrs. Posner, who I thought would have enough business acumen to support this idea, seemed disinterested. Maria poked her head into the doorway and looked with curiosity, but she quickly ducked out.

The steady click of the Regulator clock was finally broken by Peter.

"Why do we need a business plan now? We don't even have a product."

"That makes it the perfect time to put together a business plan."

Peter gestured to me. "But if the product is good enough, won't people buy it?"

I dug into what I learned at lecherous Professor Conroy's class years ago.

"People won't buy it if they don't know it's there. Look, this isn't a hobby. We want to make money." I looked at Darryl. "*You* want to make money."

Darryl scrunched his face and shook his hands. "Who do you think you are? I hired you as a programmer! Who are you to tell us about business?"

"Like you're such a financial whiz," Kathlynne grumbled. "You lost $15,000 on that multilevel marketing scam you got us into. That's why we had to move back into this fucking..."

"Language!" Mrs. Posner snapped.

Kathlynne shrugged her shoulders and leaned back in her seat. "Sorry."

I spoke directly to Darryl. "I took business classes in college. I worked at a bank. I know something about money. And if you keep spending money with no plan on how to cover costs and make a profit, you'll eventually run

",

out." I looked at Mrs. Posner. "This is your money and your family's money. Certainly, you want to don't want to run out. Certainly, you want to do something to make more."

Mrs. Posner looked back at me. "I wonder if you're making things unnecessarily complicated, Laura. Our family became wealthy, and we didn't need some sort of plan."

"It doesn't have to be complicated, Mrs. Posner, but we have to decide on the basics. I mean, what is our company going to be called? What will be the name of our product? How do we document it, test it, market it, sell it? How do we convince people to buy it?"

Peter stood up. "Why does anybody buy anything? Because it makes them feel good. Because it makes them feel powerful. Because it lets them do something they couldn't do before. That's why I want to do this, Laura. You know this program makes me feel. It's a way I can honor my…"

He looked around the room. The bitter expressions on his mother's and brother's faces silenced him and forced him to slink back in the chair.

Kathlynne folded her arms and leaned back in her chair. "You know, Laura, you're just wasting your time."

"You know, Kathlynne? You're right."

I got up and left the dining room.

*** BREAK ***

I rushed up the stairs. When I got to the top floor, Maria was in the hallway with an armful of bath towels. She didn't notice me as I reached for the doorknob to my room.

"Laura."

It was the first time I heard her voice. It was heavily accented like I would expect from an immigrant, but strong and confident. She walked over to me and looked into my eyes.

"You are a smart woman. Rich people do not like smart women. They like to think they are the smart ones. Even when they are not."

Maria turned and walked towards the linen closet. I opened the door. I knew what I had to do.

*** BREAK ***

I opened the closet and took out the suitcases and the box Mom used to ship my extra clothes. I then took a hard and deep breath out. I thought about the Amiga. How that blue, white, and orange screen made me feel. The things we could do with it. Peter was right, we do buy things because of how they made us feel.

But I felt cheated. Like this was a lost cause. How I could I dedicate myself to this project if Peter and his family won't even do the rudimentary work of running a business? Even naming the damn program was too much work for them!

"Please don't go." Peter's voice was soft and plaintive. "I need you."

I didn't turn around. "What you need is someone to kick your ass and make you take this project seriously."

"What makes you think I'm not taking this seriously? Look at all the time we put in..."

"And it will all go to waste if we don't run this like a business."

"But that would take all the soul out of it."

I turned and stomped towards him.

"You know what takes the soul out of things for me? Getting screwed! I'm not going to see a penny of that $10,000, am I?"

"So, is it the money you care about?"

"I have a car loan, credit card bills, long-distance phone charges, and insurance. My first student loan payment is coming due. And I can't pay those with soul!"

"If you want, I can write you a check..."

"I want is to know I'm not wasting my time working with you. I want to know that when we finish this program—this program that means so much to you—that others will buy it and reward us for our hard work. This is your dream, Peter. *Your* dream! I want you to give a fuck about it!"

We both looked up and down the hallway. Mrs. Posner wasn't around to scold us about language.

Then Peter looked at me. "If I work with you on a business plan, will you stay?"

I folded my arms. "Why do you want me to stay so badly?"

"Because you're my amiga."

"Excuse me!" My whole body shuddered.

Peter reeled back. "I didn't mean to offend..."

"Then what are you thinking, Peter? You think because I'm Hispanic..."

"That's not it! It's like when I think about the Amiga, the computer..."

"You're comparing me to a machine? A thing?"

"Amiga means friend!" He had never spoken so loudly and firmly to me. "You're the first person who has ever been a friend to me."

I fell silent. He put his hand on my arm. It was the first time he ever made physical contact with me.

"I need a friend. Especially now. Especially to do this. Please don't go, Laura. Please."

I looked at him. Through my glasses. Through his.

*** BREAK ***

This time, Darryl and Kathlynne sat quietly on one side of the dining room table. I handed them a dot-matrix printed, stapled document containing our business plan. Mrs. Posner stood in the furthest corner of the room, next to the Regulator clock. She kept her arms tightly folded. When I attempted to hand her a copy of the document, she shook her head.

I returned to the dining room table and sat next to Peter and across from Darryl and Kathlynne.

Peter straightened the document in front of him. "Our product will be called PhotoLab. Our goal is to demonstrate it at the Consumer Electronics Show this coming January in Las Vegas. That's less than five months from..."

Darryl interrupted. "Is that where we make money on this thing?"

Peter continued. "To make this product a success, we need to cultivate resources we don't possess. We're looking for corporate backing, someone who will make the investments we need or a large company that can buy our product outright. Barring that, we can sell the product ourselves. At least, we need to find leads for customers. But if we're going to establish a positive impression at CES, we have much work to do, and we need your assistance."

He glanced at me as my cue to speak.

"Darryl, we'd like you to do our marketing for us."

His eyes opened wide. His surprise surprised me. I continued.

"The first thing you need to do is to get us set up at the show. We need passes to get in and a booth to do our demonstrations. I will get you the forms, and you will get the check from your mom. We also need you to reserve hotel rooms for us. Once we get to CES, we need you to make contacts with partners, distributors, resellers, and the press."

He grumbled, "Why do you want me to do this?"

"Because you have marketing and sales experience."

"Right," Kathlynne grumbled. "He sells lemons at a used car lot."

"Hey, all of our vehicles have a 24-point quality inspection!"

"That's a good point, Darryl."

Darryl blinked several times. He stared at Kathlynne in confusion.

"We have to make sure our product is the best possible quality before we demonstrate it." I turned to Kathlynne. "We want you to be our QA tester."

She turned her face to me. "A what?"

"You'll test the software. Peter and I will tell you what to look for. If something doesn't work, you write down some notes so Peter and I can fix it."

Her eyebrows raised. She seemed interested.

"But how am I supposed to get this done?" Darryl complained. "I have work."

"You can make calls at lunch, in the evening, and on your days off," I replied.

Peter jumped in. "We all will be putting in extra effort to make this work. Laura and I especially since we have to write the software. But if we work together, we can get this done. What do you say?"

"All right," Kathlynne nodded.

"I guess," Darryl said.

Mrs. Posner remained silent.

"Well," Peter gave a well-deserved smile, "Let's get to work."

Darryl and Kathlynne got up from the table, business plans in hand. I turned to Peter and patted him on the shoulder.

"I'm proud of you. You handled it so well…"

"Don't be too overjoyed."

We turned around. Mrs. Posner, with her folded arms, looked sourly at us. She spoke to Peter.

"I will continue to fund your project, but don't use it to honor your father."

Peter lowered his head.

"And Laura." I turned around. "You got a telephone call."

*** BREAK ***

"Yes, this is Louise Stansfield."

"This is Laura Rodriguez. I understand that you called me."

"Yes, Miss Rodriguez. My, you are difficult to reach. I had to get your phone number from your mother."

I made a mental note to talk to Mom about this. I didn't want her to give out the number to the Posners, precisely for this reason.

"How can I help you, Ms. Stansfield?"

"I'm prepared to give you an offer…"

"An offer?"

I pulled the handset away and glanced at it for a moment, just to make sure that this was really happening. Then her voice came faintly from the receiver. I pressed it against my ear again.

"...The position of Associate Programmer. This is an entry-level position, but it has plenty of room for advancement."

"I thought you weren't interested in me."

"The managers are. So much so that they are offering you a starting salary of $27,500."

I looked around the living room. I was alone, but I worried that Peter or someone else could walk in.

"We can also offer you a comprehensive benefits package with health and life insurance and educational reimbursement. We are also prepared to offer you 500 shares of stock options. We can also arrange a relocation package to our area."

I glanced around the living room again to make sure I was alone.

What she was offering was the reason I came to the Bay Area. A normal programming job in Silicon Valley with a normal salary and normal benefits. Even though Peter agreed to a business plan and handled himself well in presenting it, who knows if he and his family would follow through? And what was the deal between him, his mom, his dad, and his brother anyway? I didn't have to be part of all that drama and uncertainty. I could leave this house, leave San Rafael, and get a normal, stable job.

Louise Stansfield's voice came on the phone again. "Miss Rodriguez, will you accept our offer?"

Her nasal, condescending tone brought me back to that interview. The stares. "Are you an American citizen?" "Wear a skirt." Did I really impress them as a programmer? If so, why did they wait so long to extend me an offer? Did they really want me on their team? Or did they have to hire me to check off some boxes in an EEOC audit? Would I be respected at that company? Or would I get paid $27,500 per year to have men stare at my breasts and legs while I made coffee and carried boxes of floppy disks from the storeroom?

I looked at the Amiga again with our business plan in a text editor window. Blue plastic floppy disks with code Peter and I had written.

"Miss Rodriguez?"

"Thank you for getting back to me, Ms. Stansfield." I swallowed hard. "But I already found a position."

"Then, I congratulate you and wish you the best of luck."

"Laura?" Peter had entered the living room.

"Thank you, and have a pleasant day." I hung up the phone quickly.

"Who was that?"

"Um...uh, a telemarketer."

"I hate those." He sat down in front of the Amiga. "Always asking us if we want to change our long-distance service."

"Yeah."

He closed the window for the text editor and double-clicked the icon to open our source code. "I have some ideas for the user interface."

I forced a smile. "Let's get started."

CHAPTER SIXTEEN
October 2016

Saturdays were my day to help Mom.

She lived by herself in the house I grew up in on Vanalden Avenue. At 78, she still took care of a lot of the household tasks herself. She needed my help with cleaning, maintaining the pool, and shopping. I didn't mind because I was always happy to spend time with her. And it gave me a respite from all of the craziness going on in my life.

When I stepped into her living room, something seemed different.

"Do you like it?"

I walked to the triangular shadow box on the mantlepiece.

"Dad's flag?"

"I found the case at Michael's. I never knew they had such things, and his flag had been put away for so long. Now, I have a place I can remember him."

I sighed and stared proudly at Dad's flag.

"And when I die, you can have it."

"Mom!"

She patted me on the shoulder. "We have to talk about these things, Laura. And when I found your dad's flag, I found some other things too."

*** BREAK ***

"I can't believe I ever wore this." I unfolded the lime green Bermuda shorts that I had taken out of the box.

"That used to be your favorite," Mom replied.

"I probably can't fit into it anymore." I set the shorts on the bed.

Mom kept my old room the way it was when I moved out. Everything was still in its place. My yearbooks. Manuals for computers and programming languages I hadn't used in decades. Certificates and plaques. Even my *Blade Runner, Tron,* and *Koyaanisqatsi* posters. Stepping into this room was like stepping into a time machine. Mom kept everything clean and dusted. Even the cardboard box in the center of the floor seemed in good repair.

I sifted through that box, which contained clothing older than my children. "I can't believe you saved all this."

"You didn't throw it away."

Something caught my attention. I grabbed something white with faded navy blue stripes. It was my old Reseda High School gym shorts.

"I should have thrown *this* away." I stared at the brown streaks of dried blood on the front.

Mom rubbed my shoulder. "Some things can't be thrown away."

I exhaled and lowered my head.

"That reminds me." Mom let go and walked to my closet. "I found something else of yours."

She slid open the door. The old and worn wheels rumbled on the track.

"I don't really have the room for it here. Perhaps you'd like to take it home with you."

The closet door revealed boxes with a monitor, external floppy drive, my cables, and other equipment, and my Amiga.

*** BREAK ***

I drove home in my 2015 Honda CR-V with a 1985 computer in the back. My climate control system probably had more computing power than that 31-year-old computer. My backup camera certainly had better video. I wanted to help Mom out by taking that bulky computer off her hands, but what was I going to do with it? It can't connect to our Wi-Fi or the Internet. My old floppy disks may have degraded to the point I can't run them. I didn't know if it even boots after sitting for years.

And to think, there was a time when that computer...

I shook my head. I had no time to think about the past when I had too many other things to deal with.

Maybe I can sell it on eBay. Or donate it to Goodwill. Or maybe I should take it and my old clothes and throw them all away.

But Mom was right. Some things can't be thrown away.

*** BREAK ***

I had to figure out what to do with this Amiga when I got it into the house. I could put it in the garage or in the attic. But I wanted to see if it still worked.

Our home office had a wall unit that was designed for a large monitor and tower computer. That space was occupied by a five-year-old Windows 7 desktop computer Kevin and I were no longer using but kept for the kids. But Stacy mostly used her phone, and Henry got a—heaven help us—MacBook Pro. So, the desktop collected dust.

I disconnected and took out the old desktop and monitor and set it next to the sofa. I unboxed the Amiga's monitor first. I had to see if that old CRT would even fit in the space used by an LCD flatscreen monitor. It fit with plenty of room to spare.

Next, the CPU. I opened the flaps. I found the letter and newspaper clipping on top of the first layer of foam. I set them and the foam aside and unboxed the CPU, keyboard, and mouse. I could set the CPU on its side, but there was enough room to put it under the monitor, the way it was designed. I then had to plug in the cables, unpack the disks, and put the foam, letter, and newspaper clipping back in the box to get them out of the way. I didn't want to hook up the camera, but I wound up doing it anyway.

The computer looked the same as when I last laid eyes on it. No yellowing, no smudges, no missing keys. I suppose I could get top dollar on this if I were to sell it on eBay. Some nostalgic middle-ager or a hipster would want to buy it. Maybe that woman in the Lululemon shorts and vintage computer t-shirts might want it.

But in a strange way, the Amiga seemed to fit in that wall unit as if it belonged there. My Lenovo laptop looked puny next to it, even though it had many times more power than its distant predecessor.

But was the Amiga more than just a room decoration? I had to find out.

"What's that?" Henry stood in the doorway with his Beats headphones wrapped around his neck. Kevin and Stacy stood behind him.

"My old computer. Grandma had it in storage."

"Is it from the nineties?"

"1985."

Stacy squinted. "They didn't have computers like that in the eighties!"

Kevin gave her a sour look.

Henry urged, "Does it work?"

"Let's find out." I turned on the monitor and the CPU. The fan whirred. The screen showed a picture of a hand holding the "Amiga Kickstart" floppy disk. I was relieved to see the computer got that far.

But Henry muttered, "Is it broken?"

I gazed back at him. He shrugged.

"Then why doesn't it boot?"

"I have to insert a disk."

I fished through the ancient blue floppy disks until I found the one with "Amiga Kickstart." The floppy disk drive whirred and grunted. Henry and Stacy, who had never seen a computer that didn't boot instantly from a hard drive, looked at it in puzzlement. Especially when the hand with the floppy disk prompted for the Amiga Workbench disk. I ejected the Kickstart disk and inserted the Workbench one.

Henry turned to Kevin. "Did your first computer work this way?"

"Mine used cassette tape."

Stacy looked at him. "What's cassette tape?"

The screen turned blue, the AmigaDOS window appeared and displayed the startup messages, and each grunt of the floppy drive made windows and icons appear. The Amiga Workbench emerged in its blue, white, and orange glory as if all those years hadn't passed by.

Henry gasped in amazement. "Wow! That's so eight-bit!"

I turned to him and smiled. "Actually, it's a 16-bit with a 32-bit processor."

Stacy leaned forward. "What does it do?"

I turned back to the Amiga. "Wonderful things."

*** BREAK ***

I spent the rest of the day going through my old disks. Programs I wrote and programs I bought. Things I had forgotten about, and things I was better off forgetting. The Amiga was still running by the time we were ready for bed.

"Why did you set it up?"

I turned around. Kevin leaned against the doorway.

"I was curious to see if it still works."

"Is that the only reason?"

I looked at him for a moment. "If you want me to put it away..."

He shook his head. "I understand. When things are stressful, people want to go back to a simpler time..."

"The eighties weren't a simpler time for me. Well, they weren't until I met you."

I got up and walked over to him. I wrapped my arms around him. I couldn't reach as far around him as we were younger, but his skin felt just as warm and soft. We exchanged smiles.

"Do you want to go to bed?" His voice softened.

I glanced back at the Amiga. "I should it shut down first. Remember phosphor burn-in?"

He chuckled. "It caused me to replace more than a few monitors. I'll see you when you get in."

We kissed. I let go. He flashed a smile as he left.

It turned out I had to do a few other things besides shutting down the Amiga. I forgot to charge my phone. When I plugged it in, I saw a notification on my lock screen. It was a Facebook friend request. I had to look at that screen for a moment.

*** BREAK ***

BOOCHEE-BOOCHEE-BOOCHEE-BOOCHEE...

I grabbed my glasses and kicked the covers off me. Kevin was still sound asleep. I couldn't imagine how.

I headed towards Henry's room. When I opened his door, I was hit with a blast of rhythmic noise. Henry shut it off immediately.

He pleaded apologetically. "I have to practice for my gig."

"And people have to sleep, especially on a Sunday morning."

"But my gig is a week from Tuesday. And I just made this really cool jam. Listen!"

I supposed I had to.

It was a sample of Hillary Clinton from her Democratic National Convention acceptance speech. She repeated, "I believe in science!" over an incessantly pounding beat.

BOOCHEE-BOOCHEE-BOOCHEE-BOOTCHEE

"I believe in science!"

BOOCHEE

"I believe in science!"

BOOCHEE

"I believe in science...science...science..."

He played each "science" at a different pitch ranging from Neil deGrasse Tyson to Alvin and the Chipmunks.

He stopped the music, but the beat didn't stop pounding in my ears.

He smiled proudly. "What do you think?"

"It sounds..."

He looked at me anxiously.

"...Great. It sounds great, Henry."

My approval seemed to fill him with joy. That was until I said, "What will you play if she loses?"

"She's not going to lose."

"Henry, she's not the only one running. What if Trump wins?"

"He won't win. The American people aren't that stupid."

"No, they're not. But they are frustrated and angry, and scared. And let's face it, there are more than a few who have gotten tired of biting their tongues for the last eight years."

The pride on Henry's face was quickly replaced with terror. "But if Trump wins, what will happen to us?"

Henry looked a lot like his dad. That was why I got afraid whenever he went into certain neighborhoods. I worried what would happen if he got pulled over for a faulty taillight or was mistaken for someone suspicious. All I could do was to reach out and hold his hands.

"I don't know what will happen if Trump wins. I don't know what will happen if Clinton wins. Just know that I'm here."

It wasn't enough to convince him. He pulled his hands away.

"Hillary is going to win," he said defiantly. "And I'm going to bump my jam all night long."

CHAPTER SEVENTEEN
August 1985

I got a postcard from Greg. He must have sent it to me as soon as he got back to West Germany. It had a picture of some lovely medieval church, one in dark brown brick with a tall bell tower with a clock in the front. On the back was something lovelier, Greg's handwriting.

> Hi, Laura. We've been marching in the heat the past few days. It gets hot in this part of West Germany. I bet it must be cool where you are in Marin. I hope to be on leave around Christmas. I'd love to see you then. Thinking of you. Love, Greg.

I sighed. Something about his postcards made me feel like I was crushing on him again in ninth grade.

Greg made a wrong guess about the weather here. It was unbearably hot too.

I was in my t-shirt and Reseda High School gym shorts. My business blouses, slacks, and that conservative navy blue skirt all hung unworn in the closet. My makeup sat unused in the drawer. In fact, the only things I wore were the t-shirt and gym shorts. I slept in them too, even though I wore them all day. I couldn't sleep in just my panties anymore because a Posner can wake me up at any time. It got hot in the house, so hot that even my nice Bermuda shorts were too uncomfortable to wear. It also didn't make sense to wear proper work attire in the living room office during the day and then change into shorts and a t-shirt at night. I gave up my professionalism and privacy to work at the Posners.

Fortunately, I didn't have to give up getting paid. I convinced Peter and Mrs. Posner to give me regular paychecks so I could cover my bills. My salary didn't leave me much money for anything else. It didn't matter because they provided me with everything, and I didn't have any time off to go anywhere or do anything anyway.

I wished that I could at least do something to cool off. I opened the window. I hated the rushing sound from the freeway, but I needed to break the stuffiness of the bedroom. Opening the window didn't offer any cool air. There was, however, another sound. Something like rushing water. I looked down at the yard. Maria held a garden hose that looped over the lip of a large aluminum swimming pool.

"Mrs. Posner had us set up the pool today." Kathlynne was already in her bikini. "Do you have a suit?"

I shook my head.

"You can borrow one of mine."

*** BREAK ***

Kathlynne's bikini top was almost the right size. I had to let the straps out a little. I guessed my breasts were bigger than hers. Maybe that was why she said they would get me a good boyfriend. Greg did like them. But her bikini bottom. The crotch had some sort of creamy, whitish-yellow stain in the crotch. I decided to wear my gym shorts and panties in the water. They needed to be washed anyway.

In the yard, the Posners surrounded the pool but didn't go in. Kathlynne was busy slathering suntan lotion on her arms and legs. Darryl sat in a lounge chair, drinking a beer. His gut did stick out like he was six months pregnant, and it was covered with fine blond hair. His swim trunks were short, tight, and revealed why Kathlynne screamed so much during sex. Peter was in a t-shirt and jeans reading the *Amiga Programmer's Reference Manual.* Even by the pool, he kept working. He certainly wasn't dressed to swim. Neither was Mrs. Posner, who sat poolside in a long cotton dress and pearls. Her hair so immaculately sculpted, even the heat couldn't break it down.

I was going in. The water wasn't going to cool me if I just sat around it. I took off my glasses, set them on the lounge chair, and walked towards the pool.

Growing up, we had one of the few real in-ground pools in our neighborhood. A previous owner had it built. Mom was a swimmer in high school and college. She taught me how to swim in that pool. When I got older, she taught me how to maintain the pool, check the water, and add chemicals. I aced my chemistry tests by learning how to maintain a pool.

The Posner's pool had a rickety ladder on the side. I was going to climb it anyway to get into that water. It was cool. A little too cool since it came straight from the tap. But it felt invigorating and refreshing. Diving into it took me into another world. The blue blurriness was soothing and liberating. Here, there were no assembly language subroutines, no API calls, no bills, and no drama. There was also no air, so I let myself breach the surface. I pulled the hair from my face. The water beading on my skin felt wonderful against the heated air.

I climbed out of the pool. Vague figures surrounded me. I couldn't clearly see their faces, but it seemed that Darryl was staring at me.

Back at the lounge chair, I slipped on my glasses and wrapped myself with a towel.

"The water must have felt good."

I couldn't tell from Mrs. Posner's voice if she was expressing disapproval. Then, I heard another splash. I looked around. Kathlynne was missing. Maybe she decided to go into the water too.

I also noticed that Darryl was still staring at me.

Maria had quietly stepped next to Mrs. Posner's lounge chair. Mrs. Posner told her, "I think we'll take our luncheon outside."

*** BREAK ***

A patio table had been set up behind the shed in the spot where Kathlynne usually smoked. Like the above-ground pool and lounge chairs, the table, umbrella, and iron lattice chairs with cushions seemed to materialize from nowhere. Where did they store all this? Probably the garage, but Peter's dad's old photo lab seemed a more logical choice. Why did it sit empty? And for how long?

Those thoughts didn't stop me from gravitating towards that table. Darryl was still staring at me. And Kathlynne was walking right next to him. I felt uncomfortable enough with Darryl gawking at me like I was Miss August, but he was doing it in front of his girlfriend! I felt as bad for Kathlynne as I felt unnerved for myself.

I exhaled as I lowered myself onto the cushion. I had dried off enough that I didn't worry about soaking the fabric.

Mrs. Posner took her seat. She unfurled her napkin and set it on her lap. She directed her glance towards me. "You swam beautifully."

"Thank you," I answered softly. I didn't like being the center of attention, especially when Darryl was searching for my nipples in his girlfriend's bikini top. I had to do something to shift the attention. "Kathlynne, you swam really well too."

"Please. I got kicked off the swim team." She set her pack of Marlboros on the table. "Does anyone mind if I..."

Mrs. Posner's frown answered her question.

"Ah." Mrs. Posner stared at the tray with tall glasses of ice tea that Maria placed in front of her. She took a glass. "Thank you so kindly."

Maria made her rounds, offering each person a glass of tea. Maria came to me last.

"Thank you..."

I looked at Maria's face. She seemed unusually uncomfortable being there. I smiled to assure her, but her expression didn't change. She handed me my glass of ice tea and quickly left with the serving tray.

"So, Laura."

I quickly turned to Mrs. Posner.

"You must have been on your school's swim team." She took a sip of ice tea.

"I was busy with academics. I swim for fun." I took a long sip of ice tea, hoping no one would ask me a question while I was drinking.

Mrs. Posner persisted. "You must do something special to stay in shape."

Her son Darryl was staring at my bare abdomen. I took the napkin off the table and unfurled it on my lap. I then positioned the napkin to cover as much of my skin as possible.

"Nothing special. I just watch what I eat."

I looked around the table. Everyone's eyes were still on me, except for Peter's. He looked away as if he were uncomfortable too. But he couldn't possibly feel as uncomfortable as me.

"Ah." Mrs. Posner moved back in her chair as Maria set a plate with a sandwich and green salad in front of her. "Lovely, Maria."

Maria's face stayed expressionless as she nodded. But her face tightened as she stepped away and handed the next plate. Did she know what was happening? Did something like this happen to her? And why were the Posners so interested me all of the sudden? They had seen me half-dressed for weeks. They knew almost everything about me. Was it because I wore a bikini top? Or was it because they didn't have anything else to talk about?

Fortunately, everyone fell silent as they ate their lunch. I picked up my fork and started eating my salad. I had a reprieve from answering any more questions.

"I've always wondered," Peter said between bites. "Why do you sleep on your stomach with your hands behind your back?"

I continued with my bite of sandwich. I then noticed that everyone had gotten quiet around the table. I looked around. Peter had asked me that question.

Mrs. Posner dabbed her lips with her napkin. "Don't you think that is a rather personal question?"

Peter hung down his head. His cheek reddened as if sunburned.

I waved his question away. "I was just having a bad dream, that's all."

I took another bite of my sandwich. The faces around the table were still staring at me. They wouldn't accept my answer.

I exhaled softly. "The summer after I graduated high school, I worked at a bank. We were robbed at gunpoint, and I was tied up. I just had a bad dream about it. That's all."

Mrs. Posner gasped.

Peter hung his head even lower.

Kathlynne cried, "That's horrible! I'm so sorry that happened to you!"

Darryl said, "What were you wearing?"

Everyone's eyes turned toward Darryl. The only sounds were the whooshing cars from the freeway.

I placed my napkin on the table.

"Lunch was delicious, but I'm quite full."

I stood up.

"I've got some coding to do this afternoon, and I have to shower. Excuse me."

I walked at a brisk pace.

*** BREAK ***

I made sure the bathroom door was locked when I showered and used an extra towel to wrap myself. I put my gym shorts, panties, and Kathlynne's bikini top in the laundry hamper and got dressed in my t-shirt and lime green Bermuda shorts. It was still too hot for business clothes, but I still wanted to show as little of my body as possible.

I headed downstairs, past the figurine of Diana, and into the living room. I booted the Amiga and kept my eyes focused on the screen.

"I'm sorry I brought that up." Peter's voice was soft and sincere, but I didn't turn around.

"Let's not talk about it." I kept typing.

"We should talk about the user interface. I have some design ideas." He reached across the computer bench for a file folder. He opened it to reveal a piece of paper with a sketch of a window with icons across the bottom. "I think we can keep the paint program paradigm with a large workspace for the image and icons with various tools in a toolbox on the right and options for the selected tool on the bottom. For PhotoLab, the icons would be specific for photography."

I nodded. I still felt unnerved and violated, and it didn't seem right to talk about computer programming as if nothing had happened at the pool. But it was a good way to take my mind off of it. I could go back to being a computer programmer instead of Darryl's walking centerfold and bondage fantasy.

I tapped on the paper. "How big are these icons?"

"How big should they be?"

"It depends. How many tools do you want to display?"

"Um...all of them?"

"Well, for HAM, the screen resolution is 320 x 200. There's a maximum of 360 x 400, but we should assume the minimum. We should allocate most of the screen to the image, but we have to allow room for the window borders and scroll bars. We'd have to go small on the icons. Maybe 8 x 8?"

"Can we go smaller? We have a lot of tools."

"If we go too small, the tools won't be recognizable."

"Do they need to be? Wouldn't people just know what they are..."

We heard some footsteps behind us. We turned around. It was Maria picking up a dish from a side table. I guessed Peter must have left it earlier.

"I'm sorry to disturb you." She turned towards the door.

"No, that's all right," I said. "In fact, I'd like to get your opinion on something."

Peter whispered, "Laura!"

I whispered back, "When you design, you need feedback."

"But..."

I shushed him. I smiled to encourage her to come forward. But Maria stood still.

"It is all right. My opinion, it does not matter." She quickly left the room. My heart sank as she vanished into the entryway.

Peter tapped my shoulder. "So, about those icons..."

*** BREAK ***

It had cooled off at night, but it was still too hot in the room to sleep. I had to keep the window open, even with the rushing freeway outside. I slept on top of the covers, still in my t-shirt and Bermuda shorts. My gym shorts were still drying. I should have put my t-shirt in the wash too because it was sticky and itchy. I finally had to take it off and toss it on the floor. Screw it. If Darryl wanted to see my damn tits so much, he could walk into my room and look at them. I clearly didn't have any privacy.

SPLASH.

I sat up in bed and covered my chest with my arm. I grabbed my t-shirt and glasses and looked out the window.

I hurried downstairs, past the figurine of Diana, and out onto the yard. I stood by the edge of the pool. Then, a gasp. Maria stared at me over the edge of the pool. She looked frightened. She cast off from the side of the pool.

"Maria?"

She swam hard to the opposite end. I ran around and met her there. She still looked frightened.

I spoke calmly. "It's not safe to swim by yourself. Especially in the dark."

"It's...it's the only time..."

I could tell she wasn't stuttering out of nerves. It was getting cold outside, and the water was getting colder.

"Let's get you inside."

*** BREAK ***

Maria climbed out of the pool. She shivered in her one-piece swimsuit. It was the first time I had ever seen her in anything besides her ash gray and white uniform. I wrapped her up in several towels and brought her into the kitchen. I started the stove to boil some water for tea. Maria shifted nervously to protest, but I smiled to reassure her. She probably never had anyone serve her before.

She finally relaxed when I handed her a cup of tea. "Usted es muy amable."

"Gracias."

She leaned toward me. "¿Habla usted español?"

"Un poquito."

She nodded. "I thought you would know some."

I looked at the pigment of her skin and the shape of her eyes. I could feel a bond between us that transcended what work we did and our standing with the Posners. She smiled at me. I smiled back.

I leaned forward. "How did you wind up here?"

She took a long sip. "I was thirteen."

"Thirteen?"

"Yes." She took another sip. "We lived in Hermosillo. My father, he worked in a factory. There was an accident. He..."

Her jaw tightened and twitched. I reached across the table and held her hand.

"I'm sorry."

She exhaled hard and calmed herself.

"My mother, she told me to go to the United States."

"Alone?"

"I have three younger brothers and sisters. She could not afford to take care of me too. I was old enough to work."

My heart broke listening to Maria's story. And the calm, clear-eyed way she told it made it break more. I realized she was about as old as me. Or did what she went through age her?

"How long have you been here?"

She thought for a moment. "When did that movie come out? The one with the spaceships?"

"*Star Wars?*"

"No, the boring one with the bald woman."

"*Star Trek: The Motion Picture*, 1979. Do you like science fiction?"

"I like to know there is a future. I like to think it can be better than today."

"That's why I like working with computers. We can help build the future."

She nodded. I nodded back.

"If you like, Maria, I can teach you all about..."

Her smile faded.

"Is something wrong, Maria?"

"I do not know if I can."

"Of course you can! You can..." I leaned closer to her and spoke softly. "Is there something going on that I should know about?"

"It is better not to ask questions."

"Did something happen to you? What…"

She put a finger to her lips. I fell silent. She removed her finger and whispered, "The rich, they feel they can do anything. Because they are rich, there are no consequences."

She got up and put the teacups and saucers on the serving tray.

"Ten cuidado, amiga. And thank you for the tea."

*** BREAK ***

"What do you think?" Peter leaned back and smiled.

It took a few days, but Peter had turned his user interface drawing into a prototype. I got up close to the Amiga screen to examine his work. It looked OK on paper, but it didn't look right in pixels.

I pointed to an icon of a plus sign. "What does this do?"

"It increases the contrast."

"And the other?" I pointed to one that looked like a minus sign.

"Decreases it."

"What about these?" I pointed to some icons near the bottom of the toolbox. "You have plus and minus signs here too."

"Those are for brightness."

"Those are the same buttons as contrast. How can you tell the difference?"

Peter looked at me as if there was something obvious I was missing. "You just know."

I noticed Maria dusting in the corner. I turned to her. "Could you come over here, please?"

I was surprised when Maria set down her feather duster and joined us at the computer bench. I turned my chair towards her.

"Maria, if you are watching TV, and you wanted to make the picture brighter or darker, what would you do?"

She answered right away. "I would use a knob or some sort of switch, something that slides back and forth. If I slide or turn it one way, it would make it darker. If I went the other way, it would make it lighter."

"Thank you, Maria."

"Thank you." She walked back to her feather duster.

Peter quickly leaned towards me and whispered, "You would ask a maid about a..."

"Maids take pictures too, Peter."

"But she doesn't know anything about computers!"

"A lot of people don't know anything about computers, including the photographers we want to sell this to. If this program is going to be a success, it should be easy for anyone to understand. Including a maid."

Peter stared at the screen for a while. Then, he exhaled hard.

"Sliders would be the easiest to implement. I can have different ones for contrast and brightness."

"That sounds like a good idea."

I glanced back at Maria. I smiled at her. She smiled back.

CHAPTER EIGHTEEN
November 2016

"That was 'The Warrior' by Patty Smyth and Scandal on the 80s Hits Channel. At the top of the hour, your news headlines. Remember, Election Day is a week away, so remember to vote…"

I shut off the engine and the satellite radio along with it. I listened to that oldies station to get away from the news, but the news seeps into it too. I glanced at my phone on the passenger seat. The Facebook friend request was still on my lock screen. It's rude to let friend requests sit unanswered for even five minutes, let alone several days. I should delete it. But I was still curious.

I had no time to reply anyway. I put the phone in my purse and headed to the office.

*** BREAK ***

After reading my morning emails and bug reports, I went with Warren, Chris, and Bob to the lunchroom for our mid-morning beverages. Chris always had decaf coffee with non-dairy creamer and an excessive number of Splenda packets. Warren would gulp down his second can of Diet Coke for the day. Bob drank bottled water. I always have tea. When we got to the lunchroom, the counter was filled with half-empty bags of leftover candy.

Bob stared at it, "You can always tell it's the day after Halloween."

Warren peeked at the different bags. He pulled out one of those small boxes of raisins. "What kind of sick person gives these out for Halloween?"

Chris poured his cup of coffee. "In our neighborhood, one person always gives out religious tracts. I think he got egged once or twice."

Warren turned to me. "How many trick-or-treaters did you get, Laura?"

"We went through three bags. The kids were so cute this year. Almost all the boys and girls dressed like superheroes."

"Same with us." Chris stirred his non-dairy creamer and Splenda. "We also got a whole family dressed in *Star Wars* costumes. They dressed their dog like BB-8."

"One kid was dressed in a Trump costume." Warren went to the vending machine to get his Diet Coke. "And his family are big Clinton supporters."

"I just turn off all the lights and go out for the evening," Bob grumbled. "By the way, have you seen Tammy?"

Warren and I shook our heads.

Chris turned his wrist until the Mickey Mouse face appeared on his Apple Watch. "Did anyone talk to her about core hours?"

Bob leaned closer to us. "I think something is going on."

We all leaned in closer to him.

"You know Dean, the VP of Engineering? He's retiring."

"Retiring?" Warren stood up straight. "He's around our age."

Bob spoke lower. "You know what *retiring* really means."

I blinked. "He's being forced out?"

Bob nodded. "I heard they're bringing in this new person. Some industry hotshot."

Chris huffed. "Probably another millennial."

Bob grumbled. "Just what we need. Another kid who grew up watching *Rugrats.*"

"Hey, guys." Tammy had the exhausted voice and walk of someone hungover on fun-sized Snickers bars.

I gazed at her. "Are you all right?"

She held a coffee mug with a teal ribbon design. She put it under the coffee dispenser and pushed the regular button as hard as she could.

"Just drove back from Irvine. You won't believe how horrible traffic is in LA."

I blinked. "You drove all the way here from Irvine?"

"My boyfriend and I, we had a Halloween party at our apartment. He dressed as Pikachu, and I dressed as Nurse Joy. I slept over and..." She looked at all our faces and blushed. "TMI?"

I folded my arms. "Very."

*** BREAK ***

"It's obvious what they're doing." I turned back the covers and got out of bed.

"Ung, uhh." Kevin was still brushing his teeth.

I entered the bathroom. He had just spit out and started rinsing off his toothbrush.

"They're replacing our management with younger people."

"Isn't that age discrimination?"

"We know how companies are. They can always find some way to avoid getting caught."

"They wouldn't get rid of you. Would they?"

"Who knows? Maybe I should update my LinkedIn profile, just in case."

"They wouldn't let you go, Laura. You're too valuable to that company."

"Value doesn't matter anymore. Just cost."

I reached for my contact lens case and solution. I found a prescription bottle I hadn't seen before. I held it up to Kevin.

"When did you get this?"

"Today. When I was at the doctor's for my checkup, I asked for a prescription."

"You never needed medication like this before."

"The doctor explained that as men get older..." He exhaled hard and looked down. "I think it's me. I'm the reason you and I haven't been..."

I set down the bottle and wrapped my arms around him. "No, no, Kevin. It's just, things are really hard right now. Henry moving back and doing this crazy DJ thing. Stacy getting sick. My job. This stupid, stupid election."

"Honey, we've been through hard times before. Like when Henry broke his leg skateboarding."

"We were wrecks, and he was just upset he missed a season of baseball."

"And we lost our jobs after the S & L got shut down."

"It was so strange to see Harvey in handcuffs."

"You see, Laura. We made it through then. We'll make it through now."

"What if it's different this time? What if we can't make it through?"

"We'll find a way."

*** BREAK ***

When I got up the next morning, I checked my email and Facebook. I saw the notification on the Messenger icon.

I took a deep breath and clicked.

> Hi, Laura. Thank you for accepting my friend request. I'm so glad that we're able to reconnect. I'm looking forward to catching up and seeing how you're doing. Take care, Greg.

CHAPTER NINETEEN
October 1985

The mail was generous to me. First, it brought me another postcard from Greg.

Hello, Laura. Fall is beautiful around here, especially because it reminds me I'll be coming out to see you soon. I hope everything is going well at your job. Can't wait to see you. Love, Greg

The photo was of a thoroughfare in Freiburg called Kaiser-Joseph-Straße. I stuck it next to his other postcards from the Freiburger Münster, the Schwartzwald, and a water-filled channel in the middle of a street called a Bächle.

I wondered why all of Greg's postcards were from the same town. Was it because Freiburg happened to be the closest to his base in Stuttgart? Geography wasn't my best subject, but there had to have been some other places he could visit in that part of West Germany.

I shook my head. I shouldn't read too much into his postcards. He had more important things to do, like defending us from the Soviets.

The mail also brought me another care package from Mom. She shipped me warm clothing, including my favorite red CSUN sweatshirt. Her letter also offered warmth.

Dearest Laura,
I heard it can be cold in the Bay Area, so I sent your favorite

winter clothes. I was happy to hear about the progress you are making with the software. It sounds like you're working well with your housemates. Please keep me posted on how you're doing. I am proud of you, and I love you very much.
Love,
Mom

I was glad it had gotten cooler. I could wear my business blouses and slacks again. I hated having to wear shorts 24/7, but I still wore my t-shirt and gym shorts to bed. I had gotten used to sleeping in clothes and having to work at all hours.

Oddly enough, Kathlynne started dressing in business blouses and slacks. Did she wear those before she switched to sheer tank tops and cutoffs during the summer? Or was I having an influence on her?

I was feeling more at home with the Posners. I didn't mind the living situation and lack of privacy. I really felt like I was working better with them, even Darryl.

*** BREAK ***

But that afternoon, the Posners weren't getting along with each other. This was because of another package that came in the mail.

"I can't believe you let him spend all that money on that—that thing!" Darryl jutted his hands towards the computer bench.

"That thing" was something Peter and I had been searching for, the piece to make our product complete. We had searched for a way to bring photographs into the computer. There was a device called a flatbed scanner that converts already printed photos into a digital image. That was the most affordable and best quality solution. There were devices called still video cameras that worked like regular cameras and transferred images to special video disks. Canon tested some units at last year's Olympics in Los Angeles, but they were still in the prototype stage.

The closest thing we could find to a computer-based camera was a device called a MicronEye Camera. It looked like an ordinary camera with a lens affixed to the center of a box that was mounted on a tripod. The camera was tethered to the computer by an RS-232 serial cable. The product came with software, but none of it was for the Amiga. The only version we could run out of the box was on Peter's Commodore 64. We would have to write our own drivers and control software, but we had already planned to do that.

The hard part about the device was its price. That was what Darryl was arguing to Peter about in front of Mrs. Posner, Kathlynne, and me.

"$295!" Darryl shouted, "We can buy a new TV with that kind of money! But you! You spent $295 on a fu…"

Mrs. Posner's disapproving frown made him stop. But Darryl pleaded his case to her.

"Mother! I can't believe you gave Peter $295 for a stupid camera!"

"He needs it for his business."

"I need money too, Mother! I asked you for $150 for a real estate investment course…"

"Which was another one of your harebrained schemes."

"But you give Peter money for his harebrained schemes! You bought him that Amiga the day it was announced! And you pulled all those strings at Commodore to get it before everyone else!"

"And look what he's doing with it."

"We didn't know what he was going to do with it! *He* didn't know what it was going to do with it! If it weren't for Laura here…"

I took a few steps back. I didn't want to be a part of this fight.

Mrs. Posner didn't notice. She stayed focused on Darryl. "Peter has a goal…"

"So do I!"

"You have responsibilities, Darryl! How are you going to provide for Kathlynne if you two…"

Kathlynne waved her hands. "Mrs. Posner, please don't bring me into this."

Darryl exploded. "I'm not going to be able to do anything as long as I'm trapped in this house!"

Mrs. Posner maintained a calm voice. "You are not a prisoner here. You can leave."

"Fine! I will!" He rushed to Kathlynne and grabbed her arm. "Let's go, babe."

"Wait!" She then whispered to him. "Are you stupid? We're still deep in debt, and we have that eviction on our records! Where are we supposed to go…"

"We'll think of something." He tugged on her arm. "C'mon!"

Kathlynne glanced at me and then turned to Darryl. "What about that booth you're supposed to get for them? The one at that trade show?"

"Let them get their own fucking booth!" He then glared at Mrs. Posner. "That's right, Mother. I said fuck! Fuckity-fuckity, fuck, fuck, fuck!"

The room fell silent, except for the steadily clicking grandfather's clock.

I had to say something. "If Darryl doesn't want to be a part of the team, he doesn't have to."

Kathlynne pulled away from him and stepped towards me. "What about that Q...whatever that thing is you wanted me to do? Are you going to teach me how to do that?"

"If you wish to stay."

I continued walking to the Amiga. A number of voices whispered behind me, some of them angry. But I took my seat at the computer bench without saying a word. The manual for the MicronEye was still in its shrink-wrap. I tore off the cellophane and opened the manual.

"Fine!" Darryl burst from behind me. "We'll stay!"

Footsteps clomped up the stairs.

*** BREAK ***

Darryl would have been equally unhappy with the amount of money I had to spend. We needed three-and-a-half-inch floppy disks. A lot of them. A box of 50 cost $65. We needed books about the RS-232 serial interface and digital imaging so we can learn how to read the signals from the camera and convert them into a picture. I had to drive around town until I found them at a bookstore at UC Berkeley. The RS-232 book cost $24.95, and the digital imaging book cost $39.95. I had college textbooks that cost less than that. This was most I spent on a credit card for months. I hoped the Posners would pay me back.

I spent the following week reverse-engineering their libraries and rewriting them for the Amiga. Peter integrated the software with PhotoLab. But we ran into a problem.

*** BREAK ***

I plugged in the RS-232 serial cable into the Amiga and aimed the camera on our first subject, a teacup with a gold rim and pastel painted roses. It seemed like a simple subject, the first thing I drew in Miss Erickson's art class in eighth grade was a coffee mug, but getting the faint roses and gold rim with all the shadows would be a challenge for the device. We knew it would be because the *MicronEye Operator's Manual* had a whole appendix about optics selection and lighting.

Peter finished rebuilding the program. "Are we ready?"

"Ready as we'll ever be." I stepped away from the end of the bench, where I set up the camera and teacup. I stood behind Peter as he double-clicked the PhotoLab program icon. Every time he opened that icon, we worried that the program would crash. But there was no Guru Meditation error. The PhotoLab window opened with a blank white canvas for the photo and our toolbox.

"Now to activate the camera." Peter right-clicked the mouse to bring up the menus. He selected a bunch of commands, clicked on several windows, and then the camera came on. A black-and-white video image replaced the white canvas. It was a hand reaching for the teacup.

"Hey! Hey! Hey!" Peter bellowed at a volume I hadn't heard before. I held up my hand to stop him.

"Maria?"

She clutched the teacup close to her chest, afraid her trembling hands would drop it. "Mrs. Posner said she was missing one of her teacups. She told me to find it."

"You can tell her we're using it right now." I reached out my hand. Maria carefully set the teacup in my palm.

She turned her attention to the device. "Is that a camera?"

Peter fidgeted in his chair. I kept calm and smiled. "It is."

She stared at it from different angles. "How do you take the picture?"

Peter jumped in. "Well, the camera is operated from the libraries in our program, which sends initialization signals through the RS-232 port, and..."

"What he's saying," I interjected, "Is that you take the picture from our program on the computer."

Maria then looked at the computer screen. "So, how do you take the picture?"

"Well, you..." I then looked at the computer and the video of an empty edge of the table. "How do you take the picture, Peter?"

"It's easy. You first configure the RS-232 interface by pressing Amiga-R."

"R?" My eyes widened.

"R for RS-232."

Maria and I both looked at each other in puzzlement.

Peter continued undaunted. "You then use the Initialize command to open the channel to the device. Next, you have to set the configuration, such as setting the picture size and exposure control. Then, you activate the camera to allow the video stream to appear on the canvas."

Maria tensed. "But how do you take the picture?"

"I'm getting to that," Peter grumbled. "You then have to press Amiga-S to open the Save window. You select the destination of the file and enter the file name, including the .IFF extension, and then click Save. When you are ready to take the picture, you press Amiga-D."

"D?" I said.

"For download." Peter stared at me like he just told a joke I didn't laugh at. "You know, download the image to the disk?"

Maria stepped closer to the screen. "What if you just have a button?"

Peter turned to her. "What kind of button?"

"A shutter release button, just like a regular camera."

"But we can't just put a button on the screen."

"Why not?" I said.

"This is a computer!" He muttered, "You can't make a computer work like a camera."

"But that's what we're basically doing. Maria has a point. We should make taking pictures with a computer as easy as taking them with a regular camera."

"But what about the RS-232 port configuration? What about screen resolution and exposure control?"

Maria spoke calmly. "Regular cameras have settings too. They are on the control knobs and lens. You can set them when you need to. If you just want to take a picture, you press the button."

I turned to Maria and smiled. "You know a lot about photography."

She took a step back and clutched the collar of her dress. "Yes. I do."

I turned to Peter. He seemed stiff and uncomfortable too.

"It wouldn't be difficult to do, Peter. We can establish some default settings for the RS-232 port, exposure, and resolution. If the user clicks the shutter release button without changing the settings, it takes the picture using the defaults. If the user changes those settings, they will be used the next time the user clicks the button. We can give the user the option to save and load those settings to use later. In fact, we can save the current settings when the program closes so they can be used the next time the user runs the program. Does that sound doable?"

He gave a small stiff nod. "I think it can be done."

I glanced at both Maria and Peter. The tension between them didn't make sense to me. Maria gave us good user interface advice before. Was it because she's a maid? Or was it...No. Peter depended on me as a Hispanic woman to work with him on his program. Even when he called me his "amiga," I no longer sensed disrespect. But why didn't he respect Maria as much? Or was something else going on?

All I could do is sigh and smile.

"Well, we'll go ahead and make the changes. Thank you, Maria."

She squirmed out a smile and stepped away from us.

"Oh, and here's the teacup." I held it out towards Maria. "We'll be ready for it later."

"Thank you." She took it from my hand and bowed slightly. She quickly fled from the room. Peter stared tensely at me.

*** BREAK ***

It took another week to incorporate Maria's suggestions. It took as long to make the product easy to use as it did to make it work. Most of the time was spent haggling with Peter about what we should put on the screen. We finally agreed on two fields, one on one side to set the resolution, and one on the other side to set exposure. Between them was a large white button to snap the picture. And we were finally ready to test it.

While Peter finished rebuilding the program, I stood up from the metal chair.

"Where are you going?"

"To get a teacup."

"I have a better idea." He pivoted his chair towards me and leaned forward. "Let's take *your* picture."

"I thought we're taking a test picture first."

He gave a small smile. "No one will be interested in a picture of a teacup. We take pictures of people. Of...faces. Yes, faces are what we want to capture. That is the real test of this camera, this concept. How well can it take a picture of a person?"

I nodded. He was right.

"Then, we better set up." I moved away from Peter.

"Where are you going?"

"I'm repositioning the chair." I picked up the metal chair. It squeaked and slapped shut. "I have to position it far enough from the camera to get the right optics. We have to position lights..."

"Are you going to get dressed?"

I unfolded the chair and looked down at my forest green button-down blouse and black slacks. "I am dressed."

"I mean, dressed up. Makeup, a nice outfit. This is a special occasion, our first photo. We can also use it for demos."

"You realize this will be a 128-by-256-pixel monochrome photo. We'll be lucky if we can fit in my whole face."

He looked down in disappointment.

"Peter, I'd rather take the picture than worry about I'll look like. We don't even know if the picture will turn out." I gave him a small smile. "I can play model later."

"OK."

*** BREAK ***

It took us another fifteen minutes to position the lamps, the chair, and camera. I'd sit down for a moment, and we would have to reposition everything. I'd sit down again, and we had to reposition everything a little more. Finally, Peter said, "We're ready."

"Are you sure?"

He nudged the tripod a little bit. "Just to be sure."

"Peter, let's just take the picture. It doesn't have to be perfect. We just need to know that it works."

"OK," he said with a hard exhale. I could tell he was a frustrated photographer just like his father.

I took a seat and stared at the camera lens. I would have rather looked at the computer screen to make sure the program was going to work. I had to leave that part of the task to Peter. If only we could invent some way for people to take pictures of themselves.

He sat down in front of the Amiga. I could only watch his hand as it moved the mouse around, and he tapped the mouse buttons.

"Ready, Laura?"

"Ready."

"Smile."

I haven't had to pose for the camera since my senior class photo, but I smiled anyway. Then—nothing. No sound. No flash. Not even a little light that blinked. Nothing to indicate that something happened. I just noticed Peter was moving the mouse around again.

"Did you take the picture?"

"Yes."

I got up from the chair and rushed around behind him. I looked at the computer screen. The canvas was empty.

"What happened to it?"

He didn't look up from the computer. "I closed it. I wanted to see if it saved successfully by closing and reopening it."

He pressed the right mouse button to display the menu and then selected File and Open. I worked with Maria to create a custom window to open files because the one that came with Workbench wasn't very useful. He selected the external drive. I was relieved to see the file. He selected it and clicked Open.

The floppy disk drive grunted and spun, but nothing seemed to be happening on the screen.

"What's wrong?" My voice tightened.

"It's a big file. Just give it a moment."

The floppy disk drive continued to grunt and spin. I wondered if something really was wrong. I could picture the screen going black and displaying that dreaded Guru Meditation error.

Something stranger happened.

The blank white canvas disappeared from the screen. It was soon replaced by my picture. My face was rendered in 32,768 black-and-white pixels. The image looked boxy and grainy, but it was me.

I stepped back and stared at my digitized face. "I guess it worked."

He whispered, "You're beautiful."

I turned to Peter. He turned to me. His face flushed.

"I mean, *it's* beautiful. It turned out beautifully."

I nodded, accepting his backtracked answer.

CHAPTER TWENTY
November 2016

"Next up on the 80s Hits Channel..."

I tapped the button to change the channel.

"As we go into the bottom of the bottom of the third, the Cubs have a 1-0 lead..."

I tapped the button again.

"We will be able to immediately repeal and replace Obamacare..."

I reached over and turned off the radio.

I didn't know what was bothering me. I was just having dinner with an old friend, someone I hadn't seen a long time. So, why was I feeling so uncomfortable? Why did I feel like I wasn't being loyal to Kevin?

*** BREAK ***

As the maitre d' escorted me to the table, my heart pounded harder. What did he look like? How would I look to him?

"Laura?"

His wavy red hair had thinned and grayed. His face had wrinkled, and his freckles faded. He had put on a little weight, but he still had firm, broad shoulders. I had never seen him in a suit since our high school graduation, but it seemed to fit him well. He stood up and hugged me. I hugged back. No kisses, though. Not even on the cheek. We took our seats across from each other.

"You look great." He still had that broad grin and dimples.

"Thanks. So do you."

Our waiter came to our table. "Would you like something to drink?"

Greg grinned. "Do you have Sutter Home white zinfandel?"

I blinked.

The waiter replied, "Of course. Coming right up."

I smiled. "You remember."

"Fisherman's Wharf. Of course, I also remember when we used to sneak into my dad's liquor cabinet for Ripple. You threw up the first time you had it."

I chuckled. "No, *you* did. Remember? You thought your parents were going to kill you."

He chuckled too. "That's right. I remember now. They took away my car keys for two weeks."

"That was when you had that Ford Maverick. The brown one with the black vinyl roof."

"And you had that little yellow Honda Civic."

"That got me through the oil crisis. Remember Odd/Even days?"

"I'm amazed by how much you remember, Laura."

"There's a lot I'd like to forget."

Our smiles faded, but then the glasses with pink wine were set in front of us. We thanked the waiter. When she left, I raised my glass.

"Well, here's to old friends."

Greg raised his and smiled. "And finding them again."

We clinked and sipped. When we set down our glasses, we flipped open our menus.

"Have you been here before?" Greg asked.

"I went once with my husband." I had to make sure Greg knew about him. "He's not a seafood fan."

"I recommend the cioppino. Their clam chowder is good here too, but not as good as San Francisco."

I didn't look up from my menu. "A lot of things here aren't like San Francisco."

*** BREAK ***

The cioppino was reduced to empty clamshells and a small pool of broth at the bottom of the bowl. Only a few crumbs remained of the sourdough bread.

The waiter stopped by our table. "Would you care for dessert or coffee?"

I gave my head a slight shake. "I'm fine, thank you."

Greg smiled. "Just the check, please."

"Very well, sir and madam." He stepped aside as the server removed the plates and wine glasses.

After they left, I leaned forward. "The cioppino was a good recommendation."

Greg leaned forward as well. "It was so nice to see you again."

"Same here."

"It was great to catch up." His face turned grave. "And I'm sorry about your daughter."

I nodded. "We're staying optimistic."

"That's the best way to be."

I found myself leaning back in my chair. "You know, I've told you all about my family. I realize you haven't told me anything about yours."

His face contorted a little.

"You'll have to excuse me for a moment." He squirmed a small smile. "Little boys' room."

"That's OK, and..." He pulled out a cane that I hadn't noticed before. He got up slowly and with difficulty. His left leg trailed behind as he stepped away from the table.

"Do you need any help?"

He smiled at me. "I'm fine. Just a little gift from Saddam Hussein from the first Gulf War. I can't believe we had to go back and get that bastard."

"What happened?"

"Let's just say a battlefield isn't a safe place to be. A piece of an Iraqi shell found its way into my leg."

"I'm sorry..."

"Nothing to be sorry about. Price of freedom and all that. You know."

"I know." I thought about Dad.

"I'll be back."

I watched him move from the table. His leg kept dragging behind him. He had changed since the last time I saw him, but it was more than just a combat injury. He didn't seem the same person I knew when I was young. I wish he would have told me what else had changed.

*** BREAK ***

I could tell which car was Greg's. It had the handicapped placard hanging from the rear-view mirror and a California Purple Heart license plate. He had a 10-year-old Ford Taurus with a dent in the rear passenger side panel.

I didn't believe in judging people by their cars, but something about that car showed me that things hadn't gone well for him.

He turned to me. "I had a wonderful time."

"So did I."

"We should do this again."

I glanced away. "My schedule gets pretty busy."

"We'll find the time."

He embraced me. I embraced him back. I felt a warm peck on my cheek. I gave him a quick kiss on his cheek in return. We let go. His hand traced along my arm as we separated.

"Let's stay in touch."

"We will. Good night, Greg."

"Good night, Laura."

*** BREAK ***

When I walked in the house, I was surprised to see Kevin on the living room sofa watching TV.

"I thought you were taking Stacy to her team's game tonight."

He tapped the Mute button on the remote. "She wasn't feeling well."

I sat down next to him. "Should we have her see the oncologist again?"

"I already set up an appointment."

I nodded. I then glanced at the TV. "What's the score?"

"I'm not rooting for either team. Especially the Cubs. They beat the Dodgers."

"But if the Cubs win tonight, it will be their first World Series title in 108 years."

"Let's hope the Dodgers don't have to wait 108 years for their next World Series title. I'd like to be alive to see it."

I smiled. Kevin put his arm around me.

"So, how did it go?"

"Fine. We just talked about old memories. He definitely looked older. He got wounded in Desert Storm."

"Is it serious?"

"His leg got hurt. He walks with a limp."

"That's too bad. Where did you go to eat?"

"North Beach. It's that seafood place at Tampa and Nordhoff, near the mall."

"Well, I know how much you love seafood."

"It wasn't that special. It's OK. Not as good as San Francisco."

"At least you had a good...oh, look!"

Kevin hit the Mute button again.

"The Cubs did it! The Cubs win their first World Series since 1908! The final, 8–7 in 10!"

Kevin withdrew his arm and leaned back against the sofa cushion. "How about that?"

I exhaled softly. "Yeah."

*** BREAK ***

I slipped out of bed and went to the bathroom. When I was done, I returned to bed but didn't feel tired. Kevin was still in a deep sleep and snoring softly. I picked up my phone and brought it close enough to my face to read the time. Two twenty-three. I set down the phone and put on my glasses. I headed to the home office.

I don't know what bothered me more, my dinner with Greg or Kevin's nonchalant attitude towards it. Kevin and I knew about each other's exes, including his one girlfriend who won a gold and silver in Los Angeles. We haven't talked about them for years. And my dinner with Greg was the first time either of us saw one of our exes since we started dating.

So many things bothered me about Greg too. Why didn't he tell me about his life since we last saw each other? Did he get married? I didn't recall him wearing a wedding band. If he were married, he might not be now. Does he have any children? If so, why didn't he tell me about them? And why would he get back in touch with me after all these years? I guess it's understandable. I was able to find a lot of old friends through Facebook. Even Jenny Carruth, who went back to her original name.

I thought about contacting people from my time in San Rafael, but I had no desire to do so.

I stared at the Amiga. Why was it even here? Why did I set it up? Why hadn't I taken it down and put it away? I had forgotten much about that time. The things I did remember, I wanted to forget, like those blood stains on my gym shorts. And nothing that happened then has any relevance to what I was going through now. What if Stacy was getting worse? What if her cancer has spread? And Henry? Why did he quit Google and leave Mountain View? I didn't see how he could possibly make a living as a DJ. Perhaps if he met someone at that Democratic Party event...

And this damn election. I hadn't thought much about who to vote for. Clinton? I didn't care about that email stuff and Benghazi. All politicians cut corners and make terrible mistakes. Electing her would mean four more years of Obama, but not everything about Obama was great. This year, my medical premiums went up and coverage went down. Would we be able to afford Stacy's chemo if Obamacare continued this way? But Trump? My God! How could I vote for someone who acts the way he does? I knew too many people who would. I suppose I could vote for Gary Johnson or Jill Stein if I didn't want my vote to matter.

But this election was just another decision I had to make. I had to make tougher ones.

I decided to go back to bed, but I would first check Facebook and email. Then, I wouldn't have to deal with it in the morning.

There was a message from Greg.

> Hello, Laura. I really enjoyed dinner tonight. I want to see you again soon. Can we set something up, like this weekend? Talk to you later.

CHAPTER TWENTY-ONE
December 1985

Greg was pumping me hard that morning.

I should have enjoyed it. I had been craving him since we last saw each other four months ago, and I probably wouldn't see him again until his discharge in February. But I kept wishing he would get it over with. I kept thinking of all the things I should be doing. We had less than a month until CES. I had to fix the bugs Kathlynne found. I had to make sure we secured the booth, passes, hotel, and transportation. I had to get on Darryl and Peter to put together the demo. I still had all of my Christmas shopping, and I had to finish it quickly so I could get it in the mail.

Then, I started feeling guilty because I should be enjoying this time with Greg. This would be the last time I'd see him, be with him, before his discharge.

Then he discharged. He throbbed under his condom, but it didn't feel the same. He let loose. I didn't. And he just pulled out of me. Usually, he'd collapse on my body, physically spent and satisfied.

"Won't it be great when we can do this all the time?"

"Yeah." I watched him as he pulled off his condom.

"It's just 2 months, 7 days..."

"You're dripping."

"Sorry." He cupped his hand over his glans. "I'll wash off."

He stepped into the bathroom, leaving me sprawled on my back and naked on the bed. The overwashed sheets felt even rougher than the last time I was in this motel. I wanted to get out of bed, but I didn't want to move. My hand reached for my inner thigh…No, I didn't want to do that. I had my chance with Greg, and I blew it. And then I felt guilty for blowing it. And then I felt guilty for feeling guilty, especially when I already felt guilty for having sex when I had so many other things to do.

In the shower, Greg was whistling. I didn't know which song, because he drifted between two or three melodies. Clearly, he had no idea how I was feeling. That made me feel both relieved and angry. And I felt guilty about that because I really should be enjoying this time with him.

He was right. It will be great when we can make love all the time. And make a home. It will be great when he wasn't halfway around the world and would be in harm's way if the Kremlin, the Libyans, or the PLO decided to get nasty. I wanted a future with him. If only the present didn't get in the way.

The water shut off. He emerged from the shower with a towel wrapped around him. His pale, sculpted torso glittered from the beaded water. "Have you done your Christmas shopping?"

*** BREAK ***

We decided to go to the Northgate Mall, which was a short drive north on the 101. It was a typical mall with department stores, small shops, and a food court. Most of the stores were familiar. Some were not, like The Emporium. Greg and I didn't do a whole lot of shopping. We just loved wandering around together, taking in the glittering Christmas decorations, the aromas of roasted nuts and fresh-baked cookies, and the familiar strains of holiday music.

One song made Greg's face strain.

"God, I hate that song."

I listened closely. It was Wham! and "Last Christmas."

"What's wrong with it?"

"Just listen to it. It's about a guy who gets dumped by his girl. Why would the song be so cheerful, and bouncy, and grating? And what's with that singer? What's his name? Michael something?"

"George Michael."

Greg leaned in towards my ear and whispered, "I think he's a homo."

"Greg!"

"C'mon, Laura. Have you seen the guy? High, breathy voice. Wispy, girly hair. He might wind up with that AIDS stuff."

I stopped and folded my arms. "I can't believe you'd say something like that!"

"I'm just joking. What's wrong with that?"

"You think it's funny making fun of people because of who they are? People made fun of *you* because of who you are! You remember the things they said."

"Like mick, redhead, magically delicious?"

"And it upset you, didn't it?"

He exhaled hard and lowered his head. "I get your point."

I put my arms around him. "And who was on your side when the ridicule got too much?"

"I'm sorry."

I nodded and gave Greg a small smile and a small squeeze. "Let's get back into the Christmas spirit."

He smiled and nodded. We continued arm and arm.

*** BREAK ***

I was able to get my Christmas shopping done. I just got small presents for Mom, my grandparents, Greg, Tina, and my friends in the Valley. I couldn't afford big presents, and I certainly couldn't afford the postage to mail them. After an early dinner, we went to the Marin Headlands. The sun was setting on the Bay, casting its glow on the rippling waves and the Golden Gate Bridge with its orange Art Deco towers. It had gotten chilly. Even my CSUN sweatshirt wasn't warm enough to hold back the steady breeze off the water. But Greg held me close as we walked along the trail.

"So, what are we going to do when you leave the Army?"

"Depends. How committed are you to this Amiga program you've been working on?"

"Very. We have to get it ready for CES next month."

"Then what?"

"If it goes as well as I think, we'll make it a sellable product. Then, we have maintenance and upgrades..."

"But what if it doesn't go well?"

"What are you getting at?"

"Do you really want to stay cooped up in that house on Irwin Street?"

"Of course not. When you're out, we can get our own place around here..."

"I'm thinking bigger than that."

"Like what?"

"Like, let's leave California!"

"Leave California? This is the state everybody wants to move to."

"But there's a whole big world outside of here! The Army really opened my eyes. So many other places. Some many different cultures. There are parts of the US that are much different than California. Think of all the experiences we're missing out on by staying here! We can explore the world!"

"And how are we going to pay for it?"

"We can get jobs anywhere. There are computer programming jobs all over the world. I learned skills in the Army I can apply in any job." He clasped my hands and stared into my eyes. "Our lives can be such an adventure, Laura!"

"Or they will be in two months, se..."

His warm, soft lips silenced me.

*** BREAK ***

I don't know what time I got home after being with Greg. I just changed into my t-shirt and gym shorts and went right to bed. I didn't even brush my teeth. I slept soundly.

That was until I felt a hand on my shoulder, shaking me.

"Laura? Laura!"

My eyelids flung open. Everything looked clear. I forgot to take off my glasses again. It was light in the room, so it must have been morning. Peter stood over me.

I sat up and straightened my glasses. "What are you doing in my bedroom?"

"We have a problem."

*** BREAK ***

"I was busy! I have a real job! I don't have time for this!"

Darryl slouched on the living room sofa. All of us stood in front of him—Peter, Mrs. Posner, Kathlynne, and even Maria. We stood like interrogators giving him the third degree. And I stood in the center as Grand Inquisitor.

"So you didn't get us a booth? Or passes?"

Darryl blustered out a nervous laugh. "C'mon, do you really need those things? Can't you just show up..."

An angry glare from Mrs. Posner silenced him.

I folded my arms. "What about the hotel? Did you at least get us rooms?"

"C'mon, we're talking about Vegas. How hard is it to get a hotel room in Vegas?"

"Very, when it comes to CES! Hotels are booked up for months!" I found myself pacing around. "So, we have no booth, no passes, no hotel room. Transportation?"

Mrs. Posner spoke softly, "I can't afford airfare for all of you. I'm sorry, but we've already spent too much."

"No need to apologize, Mrs. Posner." I exhaled in frustration. "We won't be able to do anything if we get there."

"What do you mean?" Darryl stood up. "We can still cut deals. We can still show your program."

"Not if we can't get in the show!"

Everyone's eyes turned towards me. I didn't want to criticize Darryl in front of his family and girlfriend, but I had no choice.

"You had months to do this! I got the brochures and forms for you! All you had to do is fill out the forms, have your mom write a check, and drop it in the mail. And how many phone calls would you have to make to find a hotel? They're all toll-free. The hotels connected with CES have discount rates. You could have done this during your lunch breaks!"

Darryl stood up. "Gee, I'm sorry. Is there any way I could make it up to you?"

I just glared at him. He sat down on the sofa.

"Bust my balls, will ya..." He then turned to his scowling mother. "I know! Language! Sorry!"

Everyone was scowling at Darryl, except for Peter, who hung down his head.

"I guess we're not showing PhotoLab at CES. I guess it's all over." He looked at me. "Is it?"

"That's up to you. If you want to quit, quit. We can shut it all down if you want. I can go find a job with a company that actually wants to sell products."

Kathlynne and Maria looked at each other with nervous expressions.

I stepped to Peter. "But if you want even a chance of showing PhotoLab at CES, you have to work. You have to contact CES and see if there is some way—any way—we can get into the show."

"Why don't you do it?" Darryl grumbled. "You're the one who knows everything."

"Because this isn't my company! I didn't start it! I'm not funding it! If I have to do everything myself, I'd rather go out and start my own business and make my own products. And I'd do my job because I'd actually care whether it succeeded or not!"

Kathlynne stepped to my side. "And I'd join you." She then snarled at Darryl. "And you can go pound sand."

Darryl didn't reply. In fact, everyone fell silent and just stared at each other. They then turned towards me as if I was supposed to tell them what to do. As if they would actually listen and follow through. I stepped back from the group.

"I'm done doing the thinking for you. It's your money, your vision. You figure out what you want to do. If you get your act together, I'll help you. If you don't, I'll leave tonight. You decide."

I turned and headed out of the living room and up the stairs.

*** BREAK ***

I sat down on the bed and took several deep breaths. It took me several minutes for my head to clear. When it did, I had to admit that I was partly to blame. I shouldn't have waited so long to follow up with Darryl. And if he wasn't going to do his job, I should have assigned it to someone else.

But why did I have to take care of the Posners? This was Darryl's responsibility, Mrs. Posner's money, and Peter's passion. Why did I have to be the one to make PhotoLab a reality for them? They certainly weren't paying me enough to do that for them. Why should I care if they didn't? What's the point of even staying, even if they did come up with a plan of action? They'd just screw up again anyway.

"I would go with you if I could."

Maria stood by the door. I patted the mattress next to me to invite her to sit by my side. She took a seat.

"What's holding you back, Maria? Is it because you're an indocumentada?"

"There is more to it than that."

I turned my head towards her.

"Laura, part of me wants you to stay. You have been kind to me, you have taught me so many things, and you respect me as a person. No one has been that way to me for a long time. But part of me, I believe it would be better for you to go. It is not good for you to be here..."

Kathlynne poked her head into my bedroom. "We have a solution. Will you please come downstairs?"

"I'll be right down."

Kathlynne left the doorway.

I gave Maria's hand a gentle squeeze. She looked into my eyes. "Ten cuidado, amiga."

*** BREAK ***

When I returned to the living room, Mrs. Posner, Peter, and Darryl stepped apart from each other, as if they finished some secret huddle. Mrs. Posner took a step towards me.

"Laura, you are absolutely right. This is my money, and I should have taken more responsibility for how it is used. I have connections, and I can pull some strings and see what I can do about getting you into this show." She glanced at each of her sons. "Darryl, Peter, you will help me. I can't afford for everyone to go. I think you should go along with Peter, Darryl, and Kathlynne. We will see about getting an appropriate number of rooms. As for transportation..."

Peter mumbled, "Mom, you know how I feel about driving..."

She turned sharply to him. "Would you rather walk to Las Vegas?"

"I can see about renting a car from the lot," Darryl said.

"Are you kidding?" Kathlynne grumbled. "We'd be lucky if one of those lemons got as far as Oakland."

I spoke up. "We can take my Honda. It can fit four of us, and it saves on gas. We will be pressed for space, so we'll have to travel light."

"We'll reimburse you for gas," Mrs. Posner said. "We are fortunate that we have you working with us."

I wanted to smile, but I couldn't.

*** BREAK ***

"I can't read her handwriting."

Peter handed me the spiral notebook I gave to Kathlynne to track bugs. Her handwriting looked clear enough to me. I read the bug aloud.

"Program crashes loading color image in HAM mode. Guru Meditation error." I skimmed over the long number and then tapped on the page. "She wrote the steps to replicate the error, just as I asked."

Peter's expression soured. "You know what she did before she came here."

"She worked at a bar."

"She barely finished high school."

"Does it matter? She has potential. So does Maria."

Peter stiffened.

"What?" I leaned towards him.

"The things they say about Dad aren't true." He looked away.

I moved closer. "What happened to your father?"

He didn't answer. I moved back.

"If you don't feel comfortable about answering..."

He spoke without looking at me. "They found his car in a ravine off Highway 128 in Mendocino County. The sheriff wasn't sure what caused the accident. It happened at night, so he may have dozed off. Or he tried to avoid a deer and lost control of his car."

"Is that why you don't like driving?"

He nodded.

I reached over and put my hand on his shoulder. "I'm sorry."

He turned his head and looked at my hand, my arm, and then my face.

"May I ask you a question?"

"Sure."

"What's his name?"

I blinked in confusion. "Whose name?"

"Your boyfriend."

My heart skipped. "I—I never talked about a boyfriend. How do you know?"

"You were home late last night."

I exhaled softly. "His name's Greg. He's in the Army. He's on leave for the holidays, so he came to see me."

"He's the one who sends you those postcards from West Germany."

A chill came over me. I knew I didn't have privacy living here, but I didn't realize how much my personal life was being scrutinized.

"Yes."

He turned to the Amiga. "We should work on that bug Kathlynne found..."

"Does it bother you? That I have a boyfriend?"

"Why should it bother me? We're colleagues, teammates. What goes on in your personal life is your own business. Besides, we're friends. You're my amiga."

He smiled. I smiled back—in relief. I couldn't sense any jealousy in him, which reassured me. We could focus on our work and not have any strange emotional vibes get in our way.

I pointed to the screen, "I think the problem may be in the RS232ImageTransfer library..."

CHAPTER TWENTY-TWO
November 2016

I wrote back on Facebook Messenger.

Why do you need to see me in person?

The animated dots of a response appeared instantly. I glanced at the clock. I didn't have time for this just before work. But I decided I better reply to Greg now instead of messaging him during lunch.

Finally, his reply appeared.

I enjoyed seeing you, and there is so much more we didn't catch up on.

Then, another message.

Are you free for lunch one day?

The answer was no. I promised Kevin I would take Stacy to the oncologist because he had a big source control migration project to do at work. I suppose I could see him after I helped Mom on Saturday. But did I really want to see him at all? With things the way they were, it would feel good to reconnect with an old friend. Maybe I could learn something from his experiences that would help me deal with my situation. But he didn't tell me anything about what happened to him, except his war injury. And there was something about him that made me uncomfortable. Like I felt unfaithful to Kevin by talking to him.

So, I gave Greg the great Californian non-committal answer.

Let me check my schedule and get back to you.

Fortunately, he accepted it.

Sounds good to me. I look forward to hearing from you soon.

My shoulders relaxed. I bought myself some time. At least enough to get to work.

*** BREAK ***

I took another stroll past Tammy's office. She still wasn't there. I guessed she was late because of another overnight romp with her boyfriend in Irvine, but I then saw her MacBook Pro on her desk through the office window.

"Still waiting for her?" Chris and Warren each held a cookie. Bob chomped on his.

I stared at the treats. "Where did you get those?"

"Trinh's cube. It's her last day."

"Really?" I leaned against the wall. "Where's she going?"

"Some CAD software company in Thousand Oaks," Chris said.

"Gabriel in Finance is leaving too," Warren added.

I narrowed my eyes. "What's going on?"

Bob swallowed his bite of cookie. "You know what's going on."

"They're not planning a layoff, are they?"

Bob ate another bite. I had to wait until he finished.

"What else would they be doing? They'll either replace us with their people or close this office entirely."

Warren stepped closer. "Why would they do that if they're bringing in that new VP?"

Bob swallowed the last bit of cookie and licked his fingers. "Do we know anything about him?"

I folded my arms. "How do you know it's a *him*?"

"Hey, guys."

When Tammy's cheerful voice rang out. My coworkers smiled, waved, backed away, and left me alone with Tammy.

"What's up?" She unlocked and opened her office door. I followed her in.

*** BREAK ***

"I'm following up to see if you got my PTO request."

I always had to follow up with Vince. He didn't get around to approving them until the day before. Since all of my vacation time lately was to take Stacy to appointments, his delays posed a problem.

Tammy walked around her desk and sat down. She started scrolling through her MacBook Pro. I was surprised that IT connected it to the network.

"You put in for tomorrow, the fourth."

"And I have to leave at two on Wednesday the ninth."

She tapped on her trackpad and looked up. "No problem. I have you booked for tomorrow, and I put you on the calendar as off at two on November 9."

"Thank you. I'll block out those times on my Outlook calendar too." I started walking to the door.

"Do you have any plans?"

I froze. Vince never asked me what I did on my time off. I never told him about Stacy. I wasn't sure how he would react to all the PTO requests and the claims our company's health insurance had to process. But I had a new boss. And with all the rumors going around, it would be better to let her know. I softly closed the door and took a seat in front of her desk.

"My daughter has cancer."

Tammy's face scrunched. She gasped. She covered her mouth. Her voice quivered. "My God! I'm so sorry!"

Hers was the reaction of someone who never experienced cancer. It was the reaction I had before we experienced it with Stacy. We cancer families have our language of diagnosis, prognosis, treatments, and where to get the best deals on medical supplies. It was our secret handshake. So when someone reacts to the news with a tearful outburst like Tammy, we're not sure what to make of it.

Especially with all the things she said after.

"I think it's so terrible when I see little kids in those commercials, with their bald heads, and they have to stay in the hospital all the time, and they can never get the joys of a normal life with friends and playing outside. I just want to..." She started to sniff and weep.

I took a deep breath and thought about what our counselor told us. I spoke calmly.

"I appreciate your concern. We had many of the same feelings when we first got the diagnosis. Fortunately, we have a great team of doctors helping our daughter. We still have our fears, and things could turn serious. We try to stay hopeful and take things one day at a time."

"But that's so heartbreaking! Your poor little girl! How old is she?"

"She's 21."

The moment those words left my lips, I knew I made a mistake. Tammy's face, which had been scrunched in grief, now slacked in shock.

"She's just six years younger than me." She studied my face. "You're old enough to be my..."

She caught herself before she could commit an EEOC violation, but the damage was done. I couldn't believe she didn't realize how old I was before then. Now she knew it, and it couldn't be ignored.

And the tenseness and formality in her voice showed how much it affected her.

"Please wish your daughter my best." She brushed off her cheek. "If you need to take any additional time off for her treatment, please let me know."

"Thank you, Tammy."

I may have opened myself to her, but I may have cost myself a job.

*** BREAK ***

It was still dark when I had to wake Stacy. "C'mon, Honey."

She stayed in her pajamas and didn't bother with makeup. Neither did I. When we went downstairs, Henry was waiting in the kitchen.

"Can I come too?"

*** BREAK ***

Traffic slogged on the 101 to Pasadena. I needed something to listen to, so I turned on the satellite radio. It was "Kyrie" again. I cranked it up.

"Seriously, Mom." Henry groaned. "Do you listen to anything from this century?"

"I like it!" Stacy started singing along with the chorus, arms waving along to the melody.

Halfway through, she clutched her chest and started coughing. The coughing became violent.

I glanced at Stacy, then darted my eyes across the lanes of traffic. I looked for an offramp sign.

Laurel Canyon Blvd
1/2 Mile

I looked around. Cars and red taillights everywhere. No space to turn. A semi edged up to my right. Nothing outside the passenger window but the corrugated brick red of its semi-trailer.

Stacy coughed more violently than before.

"Mom?" Henry cried from the backseat.

My own breathing deepened as I gripped the wheel tightly. "Kyrie" continued on the radio, singing about a road that I must travel. But I was trapped on this road. How could I get out? If we had to call 9-1-1, how could the paramedics get to us?

Then, deep breaths came from the seat next to me. I turned to Stacy. The coughing had stopped. I reached behind her and rubbed her back. She caught her breath and started breathing normally again. So did I.

I glanced in the rear-view mirror. Henry's head was still trembling.

Behind him, high beams flashed. I turned my head to the front. Space opened up on the freeway ahead of us.

*** BREAK ***

The tests would take a while. Long enough that we got over the scare from the drive.

Henry brought his MacBook Pro and headphones. I checked my work email on my phone. I knew I shouldn't work on personal time, but I hated to see my work pile up.

Bob had sent an email to us.

I found this article about the new Engineering VP. You got to check this out.

I tapped the link, which took me to a press release on a news site. The person's first name looked somewhat familiar, but it wasn't someone I recognized. I wished they included a picture. The article said she was the founder of a software company called Huntress UX Design that was sold last year.

She. Bob was wrong, and I was right. I let myself smile and read on.

> "The merger of MHR Imaging and Guacphix is a great step
> forward in the graphics market. I also look forward to working
> with an old colleague..."

Old? By the time Guacphix was done with us, there would be no one
over 30...

I froze. Was I becoming paranoid like Bob? And I wasn't alone. I looked
at Warren's reply to Bob's email.

> Shoshana said the new VP stopped by Tammy's office yesterday.
> What's up with that?

I couldn't take any more of this office gossip. I glanced up. Henry sat
across from me in the waiting room. He was the model of concentration. He
kept his eyes focused on the screen. His fingers traced quickly and precisely
across the trackpad. Some of the beat seeped faintly out the headphones. It
seemed steady and danceable. I wondered if I dismissed his desire to become
a DJ too quickly. But I also wondered why he'd walked away from a great
paying job and a home in Silicon Valley.

He looked up. I looked away. Then my phone vibrated.

> Hello, Laura. Did you find a time when we can meet? Thanks.

I swiped the message away. This was not the time to deal with it. What
did he want from me anyway?

I leaned against the worn foam and scuffed wood of another hospital
waiting room chair, wondering what would happen to my daughter. I
wanted to be anywhere but there.

*** BREAK ***

The ride back home was silent. Stacy dozed off, Henry focused on his beats
with his headphones clamped around his ears, and I kept my eyes fixed on
the freeway ahead of me. I didn't bother turning on the radio. I didn't want
to hear music from any decade, and I certainly didn't want to hear another
bit of news about the election.

When we got back to the house, Stacy's friends Michelle, Hailey, Allison, and Gaby stood waiting for her. Stacy woke up and smiled.

"Hey, guys!"

She flung open the car door. When she got out of the car, her friends rushed towards her. It wasn't until I got out of the car that I realized what happened. Stacy's friends had to steady her. She shuffled slowly—bald, frail, and hunched—held up by her tall, athletic, and healthy friends.

I glimpsed at Henry. His shoulders trembled as he lowered his head. I sniffled as I unlocked the front door.

Stacy's friends helped her into the house.

"You want to hang out?" Allison's voice cracked.

"I want to," Stacy rasped, "but I'm so tired."

Gaby turned to me. "We'll take her upstairs."

I nodded and continued into the house.

"Mom?"

I turned around. Henry had his headphones around his neck, and his head lowered.

"She's going to die, isn't she?"

I put my hands on his shoulders. "Let's not give up hope, Henry. Things may get harder, but it doesn't mean it's over."

*** BREAK ***

By late afternoon, silence fell throughout the house. Stacy fell asleep. Her friends, still shaken, left soon after. Henry retreated into his room. It would be a couple hours before Kevin came home.

I headed into the home office. When I sat down at the desk, I started heaving. My face turned flush. The room spun. I covered my face and exhaled hard into my palms. My head slumped forward. It bumped into something hard and plastic. I pulled my hands from my face and sat up.

It was the Amiga.

I took several deep breaths and started breathing normally again. My hand fumbled for the power switch. The fan hummed. My finger had become steadier as I pressed the monitor button. That hand appeared again, telling me to insert the Kickstart disk. I picked it up from the stack of ancient blue plastic floppies, but I wound up tossing it back on the pile.

Why did I take the Amiga home? Why did I set it up? Why didn't I put it away? I had enough problems in the present. I didn't have time to play with a machine from the past.

I brought my hand to the side of the CPU, ready to flip the switch to turn it off. But I stopped. Instead, I pulled my hand away and reached for the Kickstart disk. Then, the Workbench disk. Then, the blue, orange, and white screen appeared. I couldn't help but smile.

My laptop was far more powerful than that old Amiga. It could connect wirelessly to the Internet. It could play high-definition video. Its RAM and hard-drive space were measured in terms we hadn't even imagined in the eighties. But it didn't bring joy. It brought viruses, spyware, spam, and foaming-mouthed hateful comments on social media. We used computers to buy things, curate photos of lunches, and scroll past memes that demanded, "Like and share if you agree!" Computers had become tools. They inspired as much passion as a hammer or wrench. Tracy Kidder wrote about a soul of a new machine, but our new machines had no soul.

The Amiga was different. Every click was a new discovery. Opening a program was an adventure. The Amiga had moments that made me exclaim, "Wow, I didn't know a computer can do that!" We had no industry standards or rules. We defined them as we went along. We were pioneers in pristine, unexplored wilderness before we paved it over with an information superhighway. The Amiga made me feel like anything was possible because when I was 24, *anything* was possible. Like when I was with the Posners...

Posner. That was a name I hadn't thought of for a long time. A name that reminded me of something else.

I picked up my phone and opened Facebook Messenger.

> Hello, Greg. I'm visiting my mom on Saturday morning. Want to go to lunch afterwards?

CHAPTER TWENTY-THREE
January 1986

If I have children, I hope they're not as difficult on long car rides as Peter, Darryl, and Kathlynne. The drive between San Rafael and Las Vegas was 580 miles long and would take at least 9 hours. We were all crammed in my Honda Civic hatchback. Its rear suspension sagged from the Amiga, its equipment, show materials, and our suitcases.

We weren't even gone a half hour when Darryl groaned, "How much farther?" And he groaned it every half hour. This would trigger Kathlynne to need another smoke break and Peter to go to the bathroom.

So, I suggested we'd pass the time by practicing the demo. This made things worse.

Darryl bellowed, "Haven't we gone through this enough?"

Kathlynne snapped, "No, because you keep fucking up!"

The language definitely took a turn without Mrs. Posner.

"Fine!" Darryl snapped. He cleared his throat, which sounded like him scrubbing his vocal cords with steel wool. I worried that he wouldn't have any voice left by the time we got to Las Vegas. He then went into our script. "PhotoLab is a new photography program for the Commodore Amiga. It enables users to take and edit images using analogues to common camera and darkroom techniques. Lighten and darken photos. Increase and decrease contrast. All with a click of a mouse. And...uh...um..."

Kathlynne prompted, "Photographs..."

"Yes, photographs can be taken and edited in Hold-and-Modify…" He broke from the professional tone and groaned, "Do I have to say all this techno mumbo-jumbo bullshit!"

"Yes." Peter kept his eyes focused on the endless farms passing by us.

"No one gives a fuck about that stuff!"

"Computer people do," he replied.

"We aren't supposed to sell to computer people! We're supposed to sell to photographers!"

I kept my eyes on the road. "Darryl's right. We should change the script."

Peter whined, "But I worked for hours on it!"

"And didn't I tell you it was a piece of shit!" Darryl mimicked in a snarky sing-song, "'PhotoLab is a new photography program for the Commodore Amiga. It enables users to edit images and blah, blah, blah.' Like, who gives a fuck! You got to excite customers! Make them want something they didn't even know they wanted! How about, 'PhotoLab is a revolutionary new product that will change photography forever!'"

Peter murmured, "What if it isn't?"

"Oh, for fuck's sake!"

Kathlynne grunted, "I need to stop for a smoke."

Darryl shot back, "You just had one!"

"Thanks to you, I need another one!"

I looked for the closest rest stop. I found one on the side of the freeway with a Texaco station and a Carl's Jr. When I pulled into the parking lot, I told them, "We won't be able to stop again until we hit Highway 99. If anyone needs to use the bathroom, use it now."

Peter and I got out of the front seats, and we then had to fold down the chair backs to let Kathlynne and Darryl out. I was glad we stopped to let Kathlynne smoke. My legs needed a stretch. I stepped towards the edge of the parking lot. Behind me, the cars on the 5 whooshed by like they did on the freeway behind the Posner's house. Around me, the faint smell of alfalfa. It seemed like an eternity since I first drove north on the 5 on my way to the Bay Area. The flat expanses of the San Joaquin Valley filled me with anticipation, knowing that my future awaited at the end of my drive. Now, I only felt a tightness in my neck, shoulders, and lower back, and a frustration that buzzed behind my eyes.

Behind me, a scuffling of gravel. Peter walked over to me. He had a nervous expression.

"What if we lie?"

I turned to him. "About what?"

"About PhotoLab. Darryl wants to say it's a great program..."

"It *is* a great program."

"But what if it isn't, Laura? What if we go to CES, and we find there are dozens of programs just like it? What if there are programs that are better than ours? What if we demo it, and it fails? What if no one is interested?"

"Peter, PhotoLab is great because you conceived of it. You worked hard on it. You invested money and months of work in it. Even if there are other programs at CES, they can't compete with yours because PhotoLab is *your* vision. You have to believe in it, Peter. If you don't believe in your program, no one else will. You have to sell it, or no one will buy it."

I turned to the Carl's Jr. I saw Darryl coming out of the side door. Kathlynne pointed to his zipper. I guess he forgot to close it.

I stepped away from the car. "I better go too. We have a lot of driving ahead."

*** BREAK ***

We were grateful when we finally arrived in Las Vegas. That was until we arrived at the place we were staying downtown, El Vaquero Hotel and Casino. It was the only place with vacancies we could find. It was easy to see why. It was far down on Fremont Street, away from the neon of the Strip or even the oldest downtown hotel-casinos. Its marquee was pocked by burned-out bulbs and broken neon strands.

Things got worse when we got to the front desk.

"There must be a mistake," I told the clerk with the greasy hair and overly oiled mustache.

"We only have one room reserved for you."

I looked behind me at Kathlynne, Darryl, and Peter. I then looked at the clerk, or tried to since one of his eyes had a droopy eyelid.

"We made a reservation for two rooms."

"But we only have one room available."

Darryl lunged forward. "Now listen here!..."

Kathlynne held him back. I had to express the urgency for all of us.

"We made a reservation for two rooms. There are four of us." I gestured to Peter, Kathlynne, and a raging Darryl behind me. "You can't expect four adults to share one room."

"I understand your situation, miss, but we are unable to fulfill your request for two rooms. We only have one room available for you."

"Surely, there must be some way you can accommodate us."

"We only have one room, miss."

"Then, can you find us a second room at another hotel?"

"We only have one room. There are no other rooms to be had anywhere in Vegas right now. If you wish to find a room on your own, good luck. Otherwise, here is your key and paperwork."

He slid a carbon-copy form and a tarnished brass key attached to a big plastic fob with chipped and faded white paint. I had no choice but to pick up the key and sign the form.

*** BREAK ***

And when I opened the door, my stomach knotted. One bed, not quite king-size, a threadbare carpet that probably had mites, and a bathroom with rust stains. The room had a faint chlorine smell as if someone tried to clean it by spraying bleach everywhere. The motel in San Rafael where I had sex with Greg was a lot nicer than this.

Peter picked up a brochure from the nightstand and read it aloud, "El Vaquero Hotel and Casino is a Las Vegas institution. One of the first hotels on Fremont Street, El Vaq, as the locals call it, opened its doors in 1940..."

"And they haven't maintained it since," Kathlynne snipped.

"Jesus Christ!" All our eyes turned to Darryl as he lifted the covers off the bed. "Foam blankets! How are we supposed to sleep on this?"

Kathlynne put her hand on her hip. "What do you mean, we?"

"We're sleeping together, right?"

"No, I'm sleeping with Laura on the bed, and you guys sleep on the floor."

"I'm supposed to be sleeping with you!"

"Darryl, we're not going to fuck in front of Laura and Peter!"

"Fuck? I thought we were making love!"

I thought I'd bite my tongue in half.

"Fine!" Darryl rumbled, "You and I can sleep on the floor, and Peter and Laura can share the bed."

"We can't." All eyes turned to Peter. "Laura has a boyfriend."

The room fell awkwardly silent. It wasn't just that Peter called me out for having a boyfriend, but he sounded disappointed about it. Like he was upset he couldn't sleep with me, especially the way his brother slept with Kathlynne. This upset me, especially because I thought there wouldn't be any emotional weirdness after I told him about Greg. I had to take a deep breath and shove that upset down.

"You and Darryl are giving the demo, so you both need your rest. So you share the bed, and Kathlynne and I sleep on the floor. Deal?"

*** BREAK ***

After figuring out the sleeping arrangements, we had to work out the bathroom arrangements. Kathlynne and I would have the shower in the morning, and Peter and Darryl had it in the evening. While the guys used the room, Kathlynne and I went downstairs to the bar.

I had never been to a Las Vegas casino before. Perhaps it was just this particular place, but the place was filled with dinginess, haze, and despair. The din of the room was tinged with anger. Someone groaned furiously at the blackjack table when the dealer turned up a card he didn't like. At the roulette wheel, an elderly woman with an oxygen tank seemed near tears as the croupier dragged away her stack of chips. Most of the patrons looked old. Morbidly obese men whose wide butts hung over the seats of their motorized scooters. Women who silently stuffed coins into slot machines and methodically pulled down the lever. They seemed like a part of the machine. They didn't even react when the machine dispensed their winnings with electronic bleeps and clattering coins. They just stuffed more coins in the machine and pulled the lever again.

I definitely needed a drink.

Kathlynne reached into her purse. "Do you mind if I..."

"Everyone else is."

We passed by a man who put his lit cigarette in the stoma on the front of his neck.

We entered the bar. The entryway had a plaster statue of some Greek god with its gold spray paint flaking off. The bar stools had torn and worn vinyl cushions. We took a seat anyway. The waitress who came to our table wore a short black dress with the skirt puffed out with numerous red and yellow petticoats. The top was low-cut and tight around her abdomen. Her forced smile showed how uncomfortable she was. Kathlynne's sympathetic smile helped the waitress relax.

"Can I help you, darlin'?" Her drawl showed she was a long way from home.

Kathlynne ordered with authority, "Scotch and soda."

"And you?"

"I'll have a glass of white zin..."

"Oh, no." Kathlynne held up her hand to stop me. "With what we're going to have to deal with the next few days, you need something stronger."

"You're right. Give me a shot of Cuervo, hold the lime and salt."

Kathlynne leaned back and opened her eyes wide.

"Comin' right up." The waitress left the table.

"Jeez, Laura. I didn't think you'd go for something that strong."

"With what we'll dealing with the next few days, I may need two."

Kathlynne took a long drag. "We're going to fuck it up, aren't we?"

I exhaled. "I don't know. The demos Peter and Darryl will give are important, but it also depends on where the booth is and how much foot traffic we get, and...who knows? Maybe things will turn out OK."

The waitress set down our napkins and drinks. Kathlynne and I thanked her and raised our glasses.

Kathlynne toasted first. "Well, here's to 'Maybe things will turn out OK.'"

I gave a small chuckle. "Cheers."

We clinked glasses. I knocked back the golden jolt and slammed the shot glass on the table. Kathlynne's eyes looked like saucers.

"Damn, Laura. I don't know anything about your boyfriend, but I bet you can drink him under the table."

I licked my lips. "I have."

Kathlynne raised her glass to me in salute and took a sip. She set down the glass. "So, what if things don't turn out OK? What are we going to do?"

I leaned back slightly. The tequila was starting to loosen me up.

"Instead, we better think about what we'll do if this demo succeeds. We have to turn this into a sellable product. We have to build a business around it."

"Do you think the boys can handle it?"

"If they can't, we can."

Kathlynne and I exchanged broad smiles.

The waitress returned. "Can I refresh your drinks?"

I looked at my empty shot glass and then at Kathlynne. "If I keep going, you might need to carry me back to the room."

Kathlynne smiled at the waitress, "I think we'll call it a night. We've got a busy day tomorrow."

"Thank you for comin' in," she said. "I'll get your bill."

After she left, Kathlynne leaned close to me. "Tip generously. These women are underpaid."

*** BREAK ***

The next morning, we went in search of our booth. It was at the Las Vegas Hilton, so I drove us there with the Amiga, our floppy disks, flyers, and press kits in the back, all ready to go. We also brought a handcart to wheel all of that stuff in.

We entered the main exhibit hall where the computer booths were located. All of the big companies were there: Commodore, Atari, and IBM, along with some I hadn't heard of before, like Nintendo. Huge and elaborate booths were being constructed with aluminum-colored pillars, large exhibition tables covered in color-coordinated fabrics, and enclosed rooms for private meetings. Above the booths, large logos hung from the ceiling.

If our booth was near one of those big booths, especially Commodore's, we would get the traffic, attention, and prestige we needed.

I led our group into the hall. "What's our booth number?"

Some papers rustled behind me. Peter called, "2917."

We passed by booths of different sizes, all busy with people setting up computers and hanging banners. Most booths had some type of giveaway. A number of them had baskets full of miniature candies. Pens, mouse pads, and floppy disk holders with the company logo. Some booths had drawings. "Drop in your business card for a chance to win a new Sony Walkman!" I was both impressed and uneasy. These were companies that had the experience and budget to make an impact, and we lacked both.

My uneasiness grew as we continued through the main exhibit hall.

Kathlynne must have noticed. "Something wrong, Laura?"

"If our booth is 2917, we should be in aisle 2900." I looked at the aisle signs hanging from the ceiling. "And I don't see aisle 2900."

"Maybe we're in the wrong hall."

"This is the computer hall."

Darryl spoke up, "Let's just keep looking until we find it."

"Don't be stupid," Kathlynne grumbled. "Just ask someone!"

I found a security guard. "Excuse me, do you know where booth 2917 is?"

"It's not here." He pulled out a map of the exhibit halls and tapped on a spot. "Booth 2917 is right here."

*** BREAK ***

When we finally found booth 2917, my heart sank. It wasn't anywhere near the computer exhibits. It wasn't near anything. It was in a hallway between exhibit halls.

Peter rolled the cart containing the Amiga into the booth. "Should we set up now?"

I slapped my arms to my sides. "What's the use? No one is going to stop at our booth!"

Darryl stepped towards me. "I thought you said that as long as we're at the show, we can make deals."

"No one can make deals with us unless they stop by and look."

Peter turned to me. "What makes you think they won't stop?"

"This is a hallway!" I spread out my arms to illustrate. "People are going from one place to another. They aren't here to stop and browse."

Kathlynne looked towards the end of the hallway. "What's on that side? If it's something people want to see, we might get people to at least pass by our booth."

*** BREAK ***

When I reached the end of the hallway, I gasped. The sign overhead said, "Adult Entertainment Pavilion."

From a distance, the booths were as elaborate and stylish as any in the computer hall. But what those booths displayed was far different. Shelves and shelves of videotapes. Every possible way a body part or other object could be inserted into an orifice. Every combination of men and women, including by themselves. One had a picture of a woman bound and gagged. I cringed and quickly moved away. I found myself in another booth stocked with dildos, all in anatomically impossible shapes, sizes, and colors.

I didn't see anything remotely computer related until I came across a company that made a game for the Commodore 64 called Pleasure Me 64. It showed what remotely looked like a naked woman. The player used the joystick to position a hand on different parts of her body. When the player pressed the fire button, it made sounds that were supposed to be her moaning, but it sounded like a car that couldn't start.

"Laura?"

I turned around and walked towards the woman in the booth across the way. She wore a shimmering red gown that used more fabric for ruffles than to cover her. Her hair was sculpted up in thick waves and curls. It took me a moment to look through her Nagel-style makeup to figure out who she was.

"Jenny? Jenny Carruth?"

She hushed me into silence. "Around here, you have to call me by my screen name. Call me Bambi."

"Bambi?"

"Bambi Swallows."

I stared at her iridescent blue eye shadow for a moment before I could speak. "Please don't tell me you picked that name out yourself. And you know Bambi is a buck, right?"

"Look, I have a pretty big name in the business..."

"You already had a pretty big name when we were in high school. Varsity cheerleader. Homecoming princess. Honor student. California Scholarship Federation..."

"I needed money for college."

"So you couldn't do something more respectable, like deal drugs?"

"C'mon, Laura. Look around you. Do you realize how much money this industry makes?"

"How much money do *you* make?"

"I get $500 per scene, plus an extra $100 for anal."

"You take it up the ass for an extra $100?"

"I made $50,000 last year."

I was scraping by on $10,000, and she made five times as much. If I accepted that other job, I'd still make barely more than half.

I stiffened myself. "So, you make a lot of money. What about your dignity?"

"What dignity? Laura, you know how it is. To make a living, we all get fucked up the ass. I'm literal about it and make much more money."

*** BREAK ***

All eyes fixed on me as I approached the booth. Kathlynne spoke up, "What did you find out?"

"We're screwed."

CHAPTER TWENTY-FOUR
November 2016

I carefully squeezed the reagent bottle, letting out five drops into the tube containing a sample of pool water. I put the cap on and swirled the water around. The water turned yellow, but not as yellow as it should. I opened the tub of granulated chlorine and scooped out some to dump in the pool. I had been doing this for so long, I could dispense the right amount without measuring.

"When was the last time you had the filter cleaned?"

Mom was reading the *Daily News* at a poolside table. "September. The pool cleaner was the nicest young man. He's planning to go to the Police Academy next year. Cute ass too."

"Mom!"

"A girl can look, can't she?"

I chuckled. "You're not a girl. Neither am I."

I sealed the tub and dumped out the water in the tube. I joined Mom at the table. Mom folded up the paper and set it on the table.

"We're still girls at heart, Laura. We mustn't let go of our youthful energy." She looked down at the newspaper. "Heaven knows we need it now."

I glanced at the front page with its pictures of Clinton and Trump.

"He's going to win," Mom declared with resignation.

"What makes you think that?"

"Give people a choice between safe and exciting, they'll choose exciting."

"Not when it comes to choosing a president!"

"They're like that when they choose a spouse. You could have done that."

I read her eyes for a moment. "Greg?"

Her silence meant, "Yes."

"I thought you liked him."

"I never liked him."

"Why's that?"

"You were 16."

"We used protection. We were responsible."

"You are. As for him, well..." She exhaled a disapproving groan, then relaxed. "Now, Kevin, he's a responsible man. Hard-working, dedicated, kind, even-tempered. A wonderful husband and father. I am so glad you're married to him."

"It's not all safety, Mom." I grinned. "He was exciting."

"Was?"

She and I stared at each other until I realized what I said.

"Mom, I didn't mean to say...We're happy. Really. It's just that with Stacy being sick..."

She reached across the table. "Please don't do something foolish..."

"What are you talking about?"

Once again, her stare answered my question.

"Greg? I'm just having lunch with him, that's all."

"That's all?"

"He's just an old friend..."

"You used to sleep with."

"Mom! My marriage with Kevin is important to me! I'd never do anything to jeopardize it!"

"Then why are you seeing him?"

"Why can't I be friends with someone from my past?"

"Have you forgotten?"

"I'm trying to forget."

Mom squeezed my hand. "Be careful, Laura."

*** BREAK ***

Mom's warning still rung in my ears as Greg and I sat across from each other in a Vietnamese restaurant in Reseda. I kept my spoon hovering over a steaming bowl of pho, but I hadn't taken a bite.

Greg leaned forward. "What's wrong?"

I set down my spoon. "I've told you everything about me, but you haven't told me about anything that happened with you since we...well..."

He gave a small smile. "What's there to tell?"

"You told me you went to the Gulf War, but that was 25 years ago. What happened to you since then?"

He stirred his spoon slowly in his pho. "I can tell you, 25 years is a lot of time to waste."

I leaned towards him. "What happened in the war, Greg?"

He looked down.

"You can talk to me, Greg. You know that I understand."

He set down his spoon.

"Can you understand having a dozen 18- and 19-year-old kids under your command, many of them haven't been in another state, let alone another country? Then, watching as those kids..." He winced. His body shuddered as he turned away.

I reached out and held his hand. I just sat silently with him. I knew that words were inadequate at times like this. Those men were Greg's responsibility, and he felt their loss deeply. Dad's CO felt the same way. Unfortunately, he never got past what happened in Vietnam. He died three years later from a heroin overdose. That was when I started worrying for Greg. War seemed to have broken him just as badly.

He then looked down at my hand on his, and then looked at my eyes. My hand reflexively retreated from his.

His voice became soft and apologetic. "I'm sorry to lay this on you. I mean, you have problems of your own with your daughter..."

"It's OK. We can help each other. We're friends."

"Friends." His gaze became uncomfortable again.

I cleared my throat. "One of my coworkers belongs to a support group for veterans and families who lost members in combat. I can put you in touch with him."

He nodded. "That's what I always appreciated about you, Laura. You're always kind and willing to help."

"Thank you."

"We don't appreciate the things we value until we lose them."

A chill came over me, but I calmed myself.

"But those losses can free spaces for something new."

He thought for a moment, then said softly, "I suppose you're right."

I gave a small smile. "We should have our pho before it gets cold."

*** BREAK ***

"That was Cyndi Lauper with 'Time After Time.' Coming up next on the 80s Hits Channel, we have Joe Cocker and Jennifer Warnes from 1982…"

I don't remember what song it was, but I knew I wasn't going to hear it. I had returned home.

I pressed the garage door opener. The garage door rolled up, revealing Kevin's Accord. I took a deep breath. I still felt unbalanced after lunch with Greg. I just hoped it didn't show when I saw them. When the garage door was fully opened, I pulled in my CR-V and shut off the engine.

I heard the thumping bass before I opened the door. When I stepped inside, I found Kevin and Henry in the living room. Henry turned off the music, but I could still hear it echo through the room. Kevin got up from the sofa and walked towards me.

"Henry was playing me some of his set list for his Tuesday night election party." He gave me a kiss. "He's really good."

I still wasn't ready to give my approval for him quitting Google to become a DJ, but I still gave him a smile. But Henry didn't smile back.

"So, how's Mom?" Kevin appreciated Mom as much she did him.

"She's great. I cleaned her pool and chatted."

"And lunch?" He spoke in a matter-of-fact way.

"Good. We went to that Vietnamese place on Sherman Way."

"Did you have the pho?"

"Of course. Best in the Valley."

"We should definitely go there sometime."

"Next time we go to see Mom together."

When I turned to put my purse and keys away, I caught a glimpse of Henry. He seemed tense and upset.

*** BREAK ***

I hadn't heard Stacy all afternoon. When I was upstairs, I peeked into her room. She was lying motionless on her side. My heartbeat quickened. Seeing her too still worried me. I slowly pushed the door open and stepped inside. I crept to her bed to get a closer look. Her chest and shoulders rose and fell at a steady rate. She was breathing. My heartbeat slowed.

I felt a hand softly touched my shoulder. Kevin whispered, "She's been sleeping all day."

We both left her room and quietly closed her door. Still, Kevin kept his voice low, "She needed one of those, you know, cookies. But she had a hard time even eating that."

We moved away from the door and headed to the bedroom. We sat down next to each other on his side of the bed.

"I'm worried, Kevin."

He wrapped his hand around mine. "So am I."

"I've never seen her so tired."

"She wanted to listen to Henry's set list, but she was just so sleepy. She slept through the whole thing."

"Is something wrong?"

"I'm worried about the outcome of her tests…"

"I am too, but I'm also worried about Henry. Is something wrong with him?"

"I didn't see anything wrong."

"When I came in earlier, he seemed like he was mad at me."

Kevin looked at the distance for a moment, thinking. "Well, perhaps he's upset that you don't accept his, well, career change."

"You don't either. You still think him quitting Google was a bad idea, right?"

"I don't know, Laura. I guess he has his reasons. You don't walk away from something important without them."

Kevin then looked directly at me. Was he accusing *me* of something? My paranoia grew with his next question.

"So, how's Greg?"

I shook my head. "The Gulf War really messed him up."

"War does that. The worst injuries are the ones you don't see."

"I wish I could do something to help him."

Kevin's voice turned firm, "I know Greg's an old friend who's suffering, but you can't make his problems your own. We have enough problems here."

"I know. I told him I'd get him in touch with a support program for veterans and families."

Kevin smiled. "That's good. That's the right thing to do."

We both stood up from the bed. Kevin put his hand on my shoulder.

"I think we should just try with Henry. He's having a hard time too with his sister being sick. Maybe this DJ phase will pass. Maybe he can turn it into a real career. But let's just support him."

I nodded. He smiled. We left the bedroom arm-in-arm.

But I still worried about Greg.

CHAPTER TWENTY-FIVE
January 1986

The response to our booth was as bad as I feared. People walked right past us on their way to the Circle Jerk Pavilion. Even worse, Darryl was nowhere to be found. Kathlynne had a good guess, and she was silently fuming. I thought she would explode when she saw him emerge from that hall. But then we saw the middle-aged man in a conservative charcoal gray business suit walking beside him.

"This is Arnold Hawthorne of Hawthorne Entertainment."

I didn't have to guess what type of entertainment he provided. But we all smiled, shook hands, and exchanged names with him. Even I did.

"Let me give you my business card." He reached into an inside pocket for a gold-tone business card case. Jenny was right. This industry did make a lot of money.

He presented me with a typical business card on thick ivory linen stock and embossed black Copperplate lettering. The address caught my attention.

"Chatsworth?"

"You're from the Valley?"

"Reseda."

"Lovely place.' Arnold smiled at me.

Darryl spoke up, "He's interested in our product."

Arnold looked to me. "He said that your program takes and retouches digitized photographs."

Peter piped in, "Yes, PhotoLab takes images captured from…"

Kathlynne tugged on his sleeve. "Let her explain."

I smiled. "I'll show you what it does."

"Thank you, um, Laura is it?"

"Yes."

He seemed so personable and professional, it made me forget he sold things for people to masturbate to.

I moved around the table and knelt in front of the Amiga. Arnold leaned forward to look.

"PhotoLab enables us to do everything we can do in a darkroom on a personal computer. You can see your photos the instant you take them. You can then lighten and darken the images, increase or decrease contrast, and do touchups. You can take photos on a video camera like this one." I put my hand on top of the MicronEye Camera.

"I've been looking at those," Arnold said, "But we haven't found an easy way to get good quality images."

A rush of excitement came over me. The pieces fit. We had a solution to somebody's problem! I calmed myself and continued the demo.

"With PhotoLab, we make taking pictures with a computer as easy as taking them with a camera." I positioned myself in front of the MicronEye Camera. My face appeared on the computer screen. "You can preview the picture right on the computer. You know how it looks before you take it. Then, all you have to do is click the shutter release button."

I moved the mouse pointer over the large white button Maria designed for us. Then clicked. I had added an effect that made the canvas turn white and bright for a fraction of a second, just like the flash of a camera. Then my picture appeared. Arnold leaned forward, brushing against my shoulder.

"Once you've taken the picture, you can use these tools to fine tune it. I circled the toolbox with the mouse pointer. "When you are finished, you can save the file." I right-clicked to display the menus, selected the File menu, and then the Save command. A Save window appeared. I typed in a file name and clicked Save. "We save files in Amiga IFF format so you can use them with other programs."

He then stood up straight. "That's amazing! And you make it look so easy!"

I stood up and turned around. I found that others had stopped in the hallway and were looking at us.

He then turned to me and smiled. "And you are very beautiful."

"Thanks." I felt both complimented and creeped out.

"Can you show me how you adjust the image?"

"Sure. I kneeled in front of the computer again and used the mouse to click one of the toolbox buttons. "This adjusts the contrast. Use the slider here to increase it and decrease it."

I moved the slider at the bottom to the left and right. My picture changed instantly from almost all black to almost all white.

"It's responsive and very easy to use. That's a brilliant design."

"I'll be sure to let Maria know. She came up with it."

Peter seemed to stiffen, but I ignored it. I stood up again. Arnold turned to face me.

"This can be an important product in our line of work. We've been watching the trends in computer graphics. The current generation of home computers have promise, but they are far too limited and difficult to use. But your program can really move things forward for us."

My shoulders shuddered. Had we devoted months on Peter's passion project just so it could be used for porn?

Arnold sensed my discomfort. "I know you're skeptical. Our industry doesn't have a great reputation. But we've been the ones to push technology forward. Look at VHS. The VHS tape player was a just a tool for classrooms and industrial training. It isn't even as good in terms of video and audio quality as Betamax. But our industry has pushed acceptance of VHS. Now, mainstream production companies are also producing videos on VHS. Twentieth Century Fox, Universal, Paramount, even Disney. Soon, there will be a VHS player in every home."

He gestured to our Amiga monitor.

"We can do the same thing for you, Laura. Today, a business like ours may be the only ones who can justify the cost for such equipment and software. But technology will improve, and prices will drop. Years from now, everyone will have a computerized camera like this. Someday, it may be small enough to fit in a pocket. They will need your software to take pictures and make them look great. You are on the ground floor of something exciting. And we can help you get to the top."

We all stood in silent amazement. So did growing crowd looking at our booth. I knew we had produced something special. We didn't realize how special it was.

Darryl stepped forward. "Let's talk business."

*** BREAK ***

I cheered when my Reseda High School and CSUN teams won in sports, and I was thrilled when the Dodgers finally beat the Yankees to win the World Series. But nothing compared to the burst of triumph and excitement that filled my body as we left the Las Vegas Hilton that night.

"We have to celebrate!" Kathlynne seemed unusually giddy.

Peter said, "I heard Circus Circus has a nice buffet."

"Fuck that!" Darryl burst out joyfully. "We're going to have the biggest steak dinner ever!"

"Let's go back to the hotel and change." I opened the car doors, and we all piled in. I was trembling so much from excitement, I could barely put the key in the ignition. Somehow, I got the Honda Civic started and backed out of the parking spot. Once we were out of the parking lot, I turned on the radio.

"Here's the latest from Mr. Mister, 'Kyrie,' on Vegas's hit music station..."

Kathlynne urged, "I love that song! Turn it up!"

I cranked the volume as high as my stock Honda radio would go. Instinctively, we rolled down the windows as if the music would burst them open. We started singing along. Peter pressed his fingers on the dashboard as though it were a synthesizer. We got some nasty looks when we stopped at red lights. We didn't care.

We had a sellable product. We had a customer. We had a sense of unity, purpose, and pure and unbridled joy. We had a feeling we thought would last forever.

CHAPTER TWENTY-SIX
January 1986

We also had a lot of work to do. We started polishing the product the moment we came back from CES. Kathlynne found more bugs to fix. Peter took care of those while I started writing a user's manual. It would've been better if we hired a dedicated technical writer, but we didn't have the budget. We needed that money for packaging and floppy disk labels.

Fortunately, I wrote enough policy and procedure documents at the bank and the CSUN computer lab that I could produce decent user documentation. I had set up Peter's Commodore 128 next to the Amiga so I could write while using the software. I used a program called PaperClip 128. I used the Commodore 64 version to write papers in college, so I was already familiar with it. I was glad that I could write in 80 columns without having to squint to figure out the characters.

I wrote in the mornings when I had the Amiga to myself. Darryl was at work. Mrs. Posner, Kathlynne, and Peter were watching TV after breakfast. The TV murmured in the background.

It was a typical Tuesday morning. We had a brief break from the rain, but it was near freezing at night. The Posner's house had a good heater, but the living room was a little drafty. I had to wear my CSUN sweatshirt.

I was writing the procedure on how to take the picture. Maria's changes made it much easier to describe how to do it, but I still had to figure out how to describe it to photographers who never used a computer and computer users who never took a photograph. I leaned close to the screen to look at a step I just wrote.

"AAAAAAAAAAAAAHHHH!"

The scream came from the dining room. It was Kathlynne! I shot out of the chair and dashed to the room.

*** BREAK ***

I found her standing in front of the TV. Her shoulders hunched. She clasped her hands over her face and sobbed hard into them. Mrs. Posner and Peter were still in their chairs. Her face looked grave. His dispassionate.

"What hap—" I mumbled before I looked at the TV.

The reporter's voice was both mournful and calm. "Let's take another look at the launch…"

The Space Shuttle was on the launch pad. The voices on the TV uttered dispassionately until the moment the engines ignited and sent the vehicle skyward.

"And liftoff! Liftoff of the 25th Space Shuttle mission, and it has cleared the tower."

I looked around me. Kathlynne was still sobbing hard. Mrs. Posner tensed. Peter sat passively. I knew I was about to see something horrible.

"Engines throttling up. Three engines now at 104%."

"*Challenger*, go with throttle up."

"Roger, go with throttle up."

The faded and flickering color screen, which probably showed Neil Armstrong walking on the moon, now showed the Space Shuttle crackle and burst into two white prongs of smoke. Death billowed in the Florida sky.

Only the clicks from the Regulator clock followed, occasionally broken with Kathlynne's sobs.

"Why are you crying?" Peter's soft voice showed irritation.

She peeled away her hands and turned to him. Her red-ringed eyes glared at him. "Why aren't you?"

Mrs. Posner glared at him too. Even I felt upset.

Peter spoke calmly. "Any complex technical system is prone to failure, including catastrophic failure. The Space Shuttle is one of the most complex systems ever built. A major malfunction like this was inevitable."

Kathlynne's voice rose. "But seven astronauts are dead!"

"Seven people who voluntarily accepted a job they knew was dangerous."

"But what about that teacher?"

"She was probably more at risk riding in a school bus on the way to a field trip."

Kathlynne stepped close to Peter. "Don't you care? Don't you have a heart?"

Peter's voice remained soft and flat.

"Every day, millions of innocent people are killed. Caught in the crossfire of war. Victims of terrorism and violence. Right now, throughout the Bay Area, thousands are in hospital beds and hospices dying of a disease for which no one has bothered to find a cure. They are sons and daughters, brothers and sisters, mothers and fathers. Every one of their deaths is a deep personal tragedy. Who mourns for them? Who cares when they're gone? If you want to cry for someone, Kathlynne, why don't you cry for them?"

She screamed in his face. "You son of a bitch!"

She stormed out of the room, sobbing loudly between stomped footsteps. I looked around the room. Mrs. Posner's face scrunched in outrage and disgust. Peter's face remained placid. Without a word, he left the room.

Mrs. Posner and I didn't say anything either. Our silence was replaced with the drone of news reporters and the endless clicks of the Regulator clock.

*** BREAK ***

I found Peter back at the Amiga, coding. He didn't look up.

"Are you going to call me a son of a bitch too?"

The metal chair squeaked as I sat down.

"What you said was technically right, but emotionally wrong."

"I'm not emotionally wrong."

We looked at each other.

"The same people who mourn for seven strangers stood silent when Father died."

"Really?"

Peter turned back to the screen and resumed coding.

"Even Darryl?"

Peter stopped typing, but he kept his eyes fixed on the screen.

I leaned towards him. "What was your father like?"

"He was a brilliant man. Intelligent. Talented in so many areas. More importantly, he was a man of principle. He won a dozen cases to prevent housing discrimination throughout Marin County. He battled an oil company that wanted to drill off the coast, right off Point Reyes. A spill, like the one in Santa Barbara, would have wiped out miles of coastline and killed numerous sea life. He faced off against their high-powered lawyers and won. He kept our beaches safe." He turned an angry scowl towards the dining room, where Mrs. Posner and Kathlynne were still watching news about that Space Shuttle. "When he died, they didn't say a word. It was like nothing happened. It was just another car wreck to them."

I spoke calmly to assure him. "People deal with tragedy in different ways. Mom was calm when the Army officers came to the door. I guess she accepted it was a possibility that Dad wasn't going to make it home, especially the way the war was going in '68. I was 6, almost 7 when he died. I didn't fully understand at the time. She tried to comfort and assure me as much as she could. But late at night, I could hear her sobbing. I did my share of sobbing too when I was old enough to understand."

He hung down his head.

"It might just take time, Peter. Maybe they just need time to process..."

He snapped his head towards me. His voice turned bitter.

"It's not that. It's the lies. The lies!"

"What lies?"

Peter sat mute.

"What did they say about your father? Why would they say such things?"

"It doesn't matter. They're lies! And I won't waste my breath repeating them!"

He stood up and strode hard out of the room.

CHAPTER TWENTY-SEVEN
November 2016

Wednesday morning. I sat at the kitchen table with my cup of tea and the *Daily News* spread out in front of me. The TV was on in the living room. We hadn't turned it off all night.

I had been through moments like this before, but this one felt different. It wasn't a tragedy, like the *Challenger* disaster, 9/11, or Sandy Hook. It wasn't even earth-shattering like the Berlin Wall coming down. It just felt weird.

Footsteps softly treaded behind me. I was surprised to see that Henry was up. He grabbed his coffee mug and put it in the Keurig machine.

I already knew the answer, but I still had to ask. "How was the party?"

"Great." He put in a pod and pressed hard on the handle. "We lost, and America elected a racist, alt-right, pussy-grabbing, Putin-loving narcissist. Most of us believe that in the next four years, we'll either be deported, imprisoned or dead. America will become a corrupt, repressive, climate-ravaged dystopian dictatorship right out of a YA novel. Outside of that, we had a wonderful time."

"Maybe it won't wind up that way."

"How can it not be that way? Look at us, Mom! What's going to happen to people like us?"

"A lot of things can happen to us that have nothing to do with who gets elected."

"Well, a lot of things could happen to us *because* of who got elected!"

The Keurig hissed and spat out a cup of coffee. Henry pulled out his mug.

*** BREAK ***

I didn't bother to listen to the radio on my way to work. I didn't even turn on the 80s Hits Channel on satellite.

A somber, off-balanced mood filled the halls of the office. Even Bob seemed unusually quiet. Warren noticed.

"Why are you so quiet, Bob? I thought you'd be wearing your 'Make America Great Again' cap and doing the happy Trump dance."

"I didn't think he'd actually get elected! Besides, did you read the email?"

"Email?" I sat down in my desk chair and looked through my inbox. My coworkers gathered behind me as I opened the message.

To our MHR Imaging employees in the United States:

We don't normally talk about politics at the workplace, but this election was indeed extraordinary. Now that the results are in, we're sure that many of you have questions about what changes may occur. What will happen to our development and testing centers in Mumbai, Shenzhen, Belfast, and Helsinki? What is the status of our H-1B employees? Will there be any changes in our healthcare? Will workplace protections for women, people of color, and LGBTQ employees remain?

We will certainly keep abreast of what rules and regulations come from the new administration. Rest assured that the company will do what is best for our customers, partners, and most importantly, you as MHR Imaging employees. Without you, there would be no MHR Imaging. Your hard work, dedication, and creativity have built our company to be a leader in our industry. We will make sure that your questions are answered as soon as possible, your needs are met, and your legal rights are protected.

In this spirit, we ask you to stay focused on your work. This election has divided our country, and we know that MHR Imaging employees have strong feelings on both sides. In a free society, we have a right to those feelings. At the workplace, however, it's important that we set these feelings aside and work together to serve our customers. Let professionalism and a desire to do your best work be your guide. The rancor and uncertainty of this election will pass. We will adapt and find new opportunities that a changing world offers us.

If you have any questions or concerns, we encourage you to discuss them with HR and to make use of our free Employee Assistance Program. Thank you for your patience, dedication, and service to MHR Imaging and its customers.

Deirdre Bugental
Senior Executive VP, Americas
MHR Imaging Corporation

The words at the bottom caught our attention.

"Deirdre Bugental?" Chris squinted at the screen. "Wasn't she Guacphix's CEO?"

I said, "Why would she write the email instead of Evan?"

Bob grumbled, "He's probably still partying. He claims that he and Trump are tight."

"Please," Warren spat out. "The only time he was even in the same room with Trump was at a performance of *Will Rogers Follies* on Broadway. That was back when Trump starting dating Marla Maples."

"Well..." I put my hands back on the keyboard. "Deirdre's right about one thing. The election's over. We might as well get back to work."

Bob, Warren, and Chris turned and started filing out of my cubicle. Then Tammy burst in.

"I can't believe that orange-faced prick won!"

*** BREAK ***

That was the last we saw of Tammy that morning. By mid-morning, the shock of the election had faded in the office. Talk about Trump and Clinton transitioned into the usual discussions about beta schedules, file check-ins, and bug reports. I checked my social media feeds during a bathroom break, and comments were still on full rage, complete with angry hashtags. But the world outside the phone was quietly accepting as if we had collectively shrugged our shoulders and gone on to the next problem.

At ten, I went to the weekly bug tracking meeting. Faisal from QA would run the meeting. Also attending were Kai, who was the project manager; Darius from Support; and Shoshana from Tech Comm. Tammy said she would attend the meetings to get familiar with our products. When I got there, Faisal wasn't there. Neither was Tammy.

Yvonne entered the conference room with her laptop tucked under her arm. She was also from QA.

"Sorry." She sat down and opened her laptop. She plugged in the HDMI cable for the overhead projector. "Faisal won't be able to attend the meeting today."

I knew I shouldn't pry, but I had to ask. "Is everything OK with him?"

She opened the bug list on the laptop. It appeared on the screen at the front of the room.

"His wife is visiting her parents in Qatar. Faisal is trying to make arrangements to get her back on an earlier flight. He's worried that if she leaves after January 20, she might not be able to get home."

The somber mood returned to the room.

Yvonne clicked open a window on the screen. "Our first bug is 642939..."

*** BREAK ***

It was almost two, and there was no sign from Tammy since that morning. I still had to remind her about my appointment.

Tammy's door was closed, but the lights inside her office were on. She was definitely there. I raised my fist to knock, but I heard sounds from the other side of the door. She was crying. Loud, distraught, full-throated sobbing. I lowered my hand.

I should have felt sympathetic. I've comforted my own children through whatever broke their hearts. But I found myself feeling something else, something that made me feel uncomfortable and ashamed, but also angry.

What right did this young white woman have to be upset about Trump getting elected?

How was she going to suffer? Was she going to get called "a six at best"? She'd still have a job. Trump hired women in positions of responsibility. He made one his campaign manager. She certainly wouldn't suffer because of her race. She was young and healthy enough that she wouldn't have to worry about healthcare. I assumed she didn't have any children, so she wouldn't have to worry about their education. Or if the planet would still be habitable for them and their children. Tammy would be fine under a Trump presidency. In fact, things would be great for her.

Tammy would never be called an illegal or have someone shout "Build the wall!" in her face. That's what might happen to me even though my family has lived here for generations, and my dad died for our country. Tammy would never have to worry about her husband getting stopped and frisked. Or her son getting shot and killed because a police officer got frightened. She would never have to see her daughter get denied critical medical care because an insurance company CEO needed to buy a new Bugatti Chiron.

Yet, I had to suck it up, be a professional, and get back to work even though I may soon get the worst news of my life.

I exhaled hard. I listened again. Tammy was now in dry heaves. I had no time for her grief. I had already told her I was leaving at two for Stacy's appointment. She said she put it on her calendar. I assumed she would remember.

*** BREAK ***

I went back to my desk to get my purse. Warren, Chris, and Bob were waiting for me.

"Is Tammy even here?" Chris grumbled.

I couldn't say anything. I exhaled hard through my nostrils.

Bob harrumphed. "Typical whiny liberal behavior. Her candidate lost so..."

"Hey!" Warren erupted, "I voted for Clinton!"

"You? I thought you had common sense, Warren!"

"I do have common sense, Bob! I don't spend my time in that right-wing Fox News echo chamber..."

"Echo chamber? You get all your news from the 'lame-stream media' and the 'Clinton News Network'..."

I hoped Chris wouldn't jump in too. He did.

"Bob, you voted for a vulgar, immoral..."

"Excuse me!" My shouting shocked everyone into silence. "I don't want to hear another word about this election. I'm about to learn if my daughter will die from cancer."

The men around me gasped. Eyes opened wide, gazing at me in shock. I realized how much I downplayed the seriousness of Stacy's condition.

Bob swallowed and spoke. "Laura, uh...we didn't know...We didn't know it was that bad. I'm so sorry..."

He lowered his head. His shoulders seemed to shake. The others stayed silent.

I stepped into my cubicle to get my purse from the drawer. I looked at the solemn faces around me. My lips trembled.

"I have to go."

*** BREAK ***

Dr. Kapoor turned the computer monitor towards Stacy and me. He used the mouse pointer to circle colored blotches within an outline of Stacy's body.

"You can see where the tumors have spread here, here, and here. The results of the biopsies confirmed what we had suspected. The cancer has spread to Stacy's lymphatic system."

Both Stacy and I sat quietly on the other side of the desk. I didn't feel any shock, numbness, or grief. Just a heightened awareness as we took in the information.

"We have to pursue a more aggressive treatment protocol. It's important that we stop the tumor growth now before it spreads further throughout her body."

I spoke calmly. "What do you recommend?"

"We will increase the dosage and frequency of chemotherapy and see what results we get. We are hoping to avoid hospitalization or surgery, but we cannot rule them out as options."

Stacy nodded. "When do we start?"

*** BREAK ***

Stacy and I didn't say a word all the way from the doctor's office to my CR-V. We said nothing when we got inside the car. When I reached for the Engine Start button, my hand froze. My finger shook. Waves and waves surged up my spine and crashed into my neck and shoulders.

Stacy reached over and wrapped her hand around mine. She set our hands on the console. We turned and looked into each others' eyes.

"Mom, I'm not afraid."

My face scrunched tight. My chest heaved. My whole body trembled. Tears burst out of me, burning my eyes and screaming from my throat.

Stacy's thin arms encircled my shoulders. I flipped up the armrest. I leaned towards her and drew her close, wrapping my arms around her. Feeling her ribs through her skin made the tears flow harder. Those tears poured out of every cell of my body. I cried, and cried, and cried, and cried as hard as a mother could. A mother who knew her baby might die.

CHAPTER TWENTY-EIGHT
February 1986

I couldn't imagine getting a worse piece of news.

Peter lifted his hands from the keyboard and set them on his lap. "With the changes we need to make to the code, including what Arnold sent us from his beta test, we can't load the program on a 512K Amiga."

Maria shifted uncomfortably in her seat.

Darryl grumbled, "What's that supposed to mean?"

"An Amiga can only be upgraded to 512 kilobytes of internal memory," I explained.

Peter added, "But you can use external expansion to install more RAM."

I turned to him. "How much more RAM do we need for our program?"

"The Amiga's RAM can be expanded to 8.5 megabytes, so how much do you want to use?"

I tensed. "So, we're expecting customers to pay all that money for additional RAM so they can use our program? Do you realize how much this is going to cost our customers?"

"So what?" Darryl groaned. "You're asking people to spend $2,000 on a computer and $295 on a camera just to use your stupid software. What's a few hundred more?"

Kathlynne stepped into the living room. "Like, seriously? All this money to produce photos that are nowhere as good as regular film. What's the sense of that?"

Peter argued, "But Arnold Hawthorne wants it."

"That's because he makes money selling pictures for people to jack off to," Kathlynne said. "Who else would use something like this? Would *you* spend this much to take pictures of your family?"

I answered casually, "Judge Posner certainly did. How much did he spend on that darkroom? He was willing to spend that much to develop his own pictures."

"Excuse me." Maria stood up and fled from the room.

We looked at her and then each other. Darryl seemed unusually tight-jawed, an expression of tension I had never seen from him before.

Then Peter spoke to me. "So, what do we do?"

I exhaled and thought for a moment.

"We have to find a way to fit PhotoLab in a 512K Amiga. If we require people to buy additional RAM, even customers like Hawthorne will balk."

"How can we do that?" Peter said.

"We may have to remove features..."

"We can't do that, Laura. We need all of those features!"

"Then we would have to find a way to load and unload program modules as needed. That would affect performance."

"We can't do that either."

"Then, what do we do, Peter?"

He stared at me in mute blankness.

"Peter, we have to compromise. Either we cut features, cut performance, or make the hardware requirements so great, no one will want to buy the product. What's it going to be?"

Peter's eyes darted side to side. He bolted from the chair.

"I don't know! You decide!"

He rushed out of the room.

*** BREAK ***

I waited for a while, hoping Peter would calm down and return to the living room. He didn't. I started looking around the house. He was nowhere to be found. I then glanced out the window into the backyard. It was pouring rain. The door to the shed was unlocked and partially opened. I grabbed my coat and went outside. When I stepped into the shed, I found Peter's shadows in the red darkroom lights. Outside the door, the rain continued in glassy streams, crackling as they hit the concrete walkway.

"Peter?"

He didn't turn around. I exhaled hard.

"I think we need to remove features from this release. We don't have the time to reengineer it to add and remove modules, and it would mean that Kathlynne would have to test the whole program all over again."

He still didn't turn around. I stepped towards him.

"This is just an initial release, Peter. If we find users are adding RAM, we can put those features back later."

He lowered his head. I walked close to him. I softened my voice.

"This program isn't going to bring your father back. You know that."

Finally, he turned around. Shadows obscured his face. "You must have loved high school."

I shrugged my shoulders. "It was just high school."

"Then why do you always wear those gym shorts?"

A chill seized my shoulders. I calmed myself down and let my body settle.

"They're comfortable. And I'm not into buying a lot of clothes."

"I hated high school."

He started pacing. The shadows shifted and deepened as he passed by a red light.

"High school was one giant stamping press. You were forced to conform, to fit in. You had to wear the right clothes, and have your hair the right length, and listen to the right bands, and watch the right movies, and take the right drugs, and use the right slang. You memorized history books full of lies, read authors who have been dead for centuries, and learned mathematical formulas you will never use outside the classroom. On Friday nights, you filed onto rickety metal bleachers where you pretended to care about other students, who you barely see in the hallway, as they wore ugly uniforms in garish school colors. You were supposed to cheer as they smashed into other students who happened to live in a different neighborhood from you. On Monday morning, you had to brag about what you did with some girl in the back seat of your parent's car on Saturday night."

"Is this why you're upset?"

His silence didn't answer my question.

"But what does this have to do with PhotoLab?"

"My time spent with Father in this darkroom was golden. The magic of turning strips of film into prints. The feeling..." His face beamed with excitement. "The feeling you get from those pictures, those faces, those...those..." He exhaled deeply. "It was the only thing that got me through high school."

"And that's why you can't compromise on the software."

He nodded.

My hands were getting cold, so I put them in my coat pockets.

"I'm not asking you to compromise on the important stuff. We just need to get this product out. We need to take your dreams and ideas and turn them into something people can see and use. Just like your father did with film and this darkroom, we can do it with computers. If we can make PhotoLab a reality, a real shippable product, that's the best way we can honor..."

The door flung open.

"What did I say about..."

"Mother!"

Mrs. Posner stepped in from the rain. Water dripped off her raincoat and beaded on her scarf. "I made it clear, Peter..."

I stepped towards her. "It's not his fault. I wanted to talk to him about..."

Her face tightened. "It would best if you both left here immediately."

I exhaled and headed towards the door. Mrs. Posner held out her arm to stop me.

"A gentleman called you."

*** BREAK ***

At first, it seemed strange that he would have me drive to the motel instead of meeting me at the Posner's house. In a way, it was for the best with all the weirdness I experienced that day.

I had a hard time seeing the road. It wasn't just from the heavy rain and the fog on my windshield. Hormones sloshed within me. My heart pounded. My crotch moistened.

I knew I was going to spend every day with him for the rest of our lives, but I wanted him in me right there and then.

*** BREAK ***

The instant he opened the motel room door, my lips pounced on his. Warm, wet, parting. I plunged my tongue in his mouth. I used my foot to slam the door behind me. I reached inside his Army jacket, running my hands down his t-shirt, fingering the contours of every muscle. Our lips parted for a second.

"Laura," he gasped.

I pressed my lips against him to silence him. I grabbed his belt, yanked out the end, and worked the buckle until it came undone. I reached for the top button of his jeans.

His lips managed to free themselves from mine. He gasped again, "Laura."

I kissed his cheeks, the side of his neck. I pulled down his zipper.

"Laura." His breathing got heavier. So did mine. I reached around to the back of his jeans and pulled them down with his briefs. My palms caressed his firm, sculpted buttocks on the way down.

"Laura? Laura."

He was only semi-firm, but I could fix that. I sunk to my knees and cradled his balls in my hand. I parted my lips.

"I reenlisted."

I froze. I let go of him and stood up.

"What did you say?"

"I reenlisted."

I stepped back from him. "That's why you wanted to see me?"

Greg sputtered and muttered.

"And when did you decide this?"

He continued to sputter and mutter.

"You couldn't wait to get out! You used to count the time to your discharge down to the second. What happened?"

He fumbled to coherency. "Well, it's—it's...My CO. He said if I finish my remaining college credits, he could get me into OCS. I wanted to be an officer. Now, I have the chance! You know I've never been good at a lot of things. The Army is the first thing I've found that I've been truly good at."

"What am I supposed to do?"

"Just like I said. We can leave California. We can make our lives an adventure!"

"So I'm supposed to pull up stakes here?"

"You were all about quitting that software job."

"I never said that! I said I want us to have a place of our own..."

"And we can, Laura! After I become an officer, we can be stationed in West Germany. It'll be great! We can explore a new country, experience a new culture, learn a new language, live in a new town."

A name popped into my head. "Freiburg."

"Yes, Freiburg's a wonderful town, and..."

"That's where she lives, isn't it?"

His mouth froze. He stiffened.

"That's where? C'mon, Laura, you really think that? I'd never!"

"All those postcards you sent me. They were all from Freiburg. Freiburg im Breisgau. Freiburg in the lovely state of Baden-Württemberg. Freiburg nestled at the foot of the Schwarzwald."

"So? I happened to like that town."

"For what? The wine?"

"C'mon, Laura! Why are you being like this? You're never like this!"

"I've never doubted you before!"

"You have no reason to doubt me now!"

"Then tell me the truth!"

I waited for an answer. His only reply was a drooping penis.

"Pull up your damn pants!"

"You pulled them down."

"Pull them up and tell me the truth!"

"All right!" His belt buckle jangled resentfully as he pulled up his underwear and jeans. He pulled up his zipper loudly, fastened his jeans button, buckled his belt, and said nothing.

I folded my arms. "Well?"

"The truth is..." He exhaled. "I love you, Laura."

"That's not an answer."

"That's the only answer you need. That's the only answer you needed before."

I bristled as I stared at him.

"I need a name, Greg. What's her name?"

"Does it matter?"

"Then I'm right! Aren't I, Greg?"

His already pale face grew paler, but blood rushed into my head.

"Greg!"

He jutted out his hands and shook them desperately towards me.

"Look, Laura. You've got to understand! It gets lonely out there. I was by myself. What was I supposed to do?"

"Wait! Like I did! For four fucking years!"

"It's not like you to swear!"

"It's not like you to lie!" The sniffs and tears came. "Ten years, Greg! We've been together ten years! We started going steady in ninth grade. I gave my body to you after the homecoming dance in junior year. And when you said that you were going into the Army to pay for school, I accepted it. Even though you could have wound up like my dad..."

I sobbed. I slapped my hands over my eyes so he couldn't see my tears. His hand touched my shoulder. I yanked away and flung my hands from my face.

"Don't touch me!"

He mumbled something like an apology.

"You expect me to go to West Germany, just so I can share you with some blond-haired, blue-eyed Aryan bitch whose dad was in Hitler Youth!"

"You won't. I promise!"

"You promise? After this, how can I trust any promise you give me?"

He sighed and lowered his head. He spoke at nearly a whisper. "I was afraid it would come to this."

Those faint words jolted me. My sobbing stopped. I stared directly at him. My eyes, though still stinging, saw him clearly.

"The truth be told, Laura, I did a lot of thinking since the last time I saw you, and..." He sighed again. "It's clear to me, and it should be clear to you that our lives are going in different directions. I can't fit into the life you want. And I can't expect you to give up your life to be a part of mine. I'm sorry."

I rubbed my hand over my nostrils.

"I wish you told me sooner." I sniffed. "I wish I hadn't wasted all this time."

"Laura, I don't know what to say."

"I do. Goodbye."

*** BREAK ***

By the time I pulled in front of the Posners' house, the rain subsided to a light and steady drizzle. I climbed up the stairs to the front porch, but I couldn't bring myself to go inside. I slumped down on the bench and stared at the steady crystal strings glowing under the street lights. I didn't turn my head when I heard the creak and slam of the screen door. I only turned my head when the footsteps stopped in front of me.

"I guess it's now my turn to go outside and see what's wrong."

I scooted over and let Peter sit next to me.

He looked at me. "Greg?"

"There's no more Greg."

"You had a fight?"

"We—had an understanding. I wasn't what he wanted."

"It may be for the best."

"They always say that."

"Perhaps because it's true."

My face tightened. "So, is it for the best that I wasted ten years on a man only to have him leave me for someone else?"

"People have the right to change their mind."

"Maybe Kathlynne was right about you…"

"But I'm not wrong, Laura."

I looked through my glasses, through his. His gray eyes seemed soft and reassuring.

"You deserve much better than him. You're intelligent—brilliant, in fact. You have a good heart. And, if I dare say so, you are beautiful."

I turned my face away so he couldn't see me blush. "Thank you."

"It's cold. We should come inside."

I turned back to him and took a long look at his rounded face. The unkempt blond hair. The thick glasses.

"May I ask you a personal question?"

Peter nodded.

"Have you ever been in love?"

Peter turned away and stared at the mist brightening the street lamp.

"I'm not the type women find dateable."

"You just haven't found the right woman."

"They always say that too."

I gave a small smile. "You're intelligent, sensitive, and dedicated. There's someone out there for you."

"I hope you're right."

"I'm not wrong either."

He smiled back at me. "I'm glad we had this talk."

"So am I. You are a good friend."

"And you're my amiga." He leaned over and kissed me. Just a quick peck on the cheek. I was OK with it. It was just a friendship kiss. And I needed friendship.

I stood up and stepped towards the door. It was too cold to stay outside.

He opened the door for me. "I have a possible fix for our memory problem…"

"It's been a long day. I think I'll turn in."

He patted me on the shoulder. "I understand."

*** BREAK ***

I had the longest, most restful sleep I've had in a while. This puzzled me at first. I had broken up with Greg. He was someone I had been with for ten years, and someone I had planned to spend the rest of my life with. Yet, I felt free and content. Like I was no longer tied to something that was never meant to be.

I guess what Peter said helped me feel better. People have the right to change their mind, and so did I.

When I opened my bedroom door, I saw Maria carrying the laundry basket. She walked stiffly and had a tight jaw. I remember what happened in the living room the day before. I stepped over to her.

"Are you OK?"

She set down the basket. Her eyes surveyed the hall. She grabbed my forearm, pulled me close, and whispered urgently, "Ten cuidado, amiga. He's just like his father."

CHAPTER TWENTY-NINE
November 2016

I didn't know how I got home from the doctor's office. I just found myself on the living room sofa. The TV was tuned to CNN. I didn't pay attention to what was on. I wasn't aware of anything until Kevin's arm was around my shoulders.

"Honey."

His deep voice was a beacon, telling me where to collapse into. He wrapped his arms around me, and I just wept. I could feel his tears on my shoulder.

"We should take work off tomorrow..."

"I can't." My voice cracked. "New boss and...damnit..." I cried some more. I finally caught a break from weeping. I exhaled hard and deep once, twice, three times until I could create a coherent thought. "Stacy will need someone with her. At least for the first few weeks."

"Henry can help. Where is he?"

For the first time that night, I heard the TV.

"Anti-Trump protests have broken out in several major cities, including New York, San Francisco, and Los Angeles..."

Kevin and I stared at the mass of people marching with signs and flags, filling streets and parks. We couldn't make out individual faces, even on our 4K big-screen TV. But we could sense that Henry had to be somewhere in that throng.

*** BREAK ***

I looked in on Stacy. She hadn't been awake since we came home from the doctor's office. I looked for the steady rise and fall to assure me she was breathing normally. I stepped out slowly and quietly closed the door. Kevin was standing in the hallway by the bedroom. I walked over to him.

"Any word from Henry?"

He shook his head. "He's not responding to text or calls."

"You don't think…"

"I've been following the news. No reports of violence or arrests."

"Then, why doesn't he…"

"I'm sure he'll be home soon." Kevin put his hands on my shoulder. "You should try to get some sleep."

"I'm not tired. Maybe if I check my email first…"

He nodded. "I'll meet you in bed."

He kissed me. I hugged him. He let go before I can start sobbing again.

I stumbled into the office. I wasn't much in the mood to check email either. I woke up my laptop anyway.

A Facebook Messenger notification from Greg appeared. I wanted to ignore it. I was in no mood to talk with him either. But I read it anyway.

> How is your daughter doing?

I planted my elbow on the desk, rested my forehead against my hand, and closed my eyes. I took several deep breaths. I fought an urge to cry and scream in frustration.

That night in that motel in San Rafael, I felt so hurt and betrayed. But it was the night when everything seemed clear. I wasn't meant to be with him, even after spending ten years together. So why did he come back into my life now? And why won't he tell me more about himself? What was he hiding?

I opened my eyes and stared at his notification. I didn't owe him an answer. I could ignore him and go to bed where Kevin's warm and comforting arms were waiting for me.

But I found myself typing.

> Not good. The cancer appears to have spread. She will need more aggressive chemotherapy. I'm scared.

As soon as I typed that last sentence, my pinky finger shifted over the Backspace key. I stared at that sentence for a moment. I moved my finger over to the Enter key and pressed it. I exhaled until I saw the animated dots.

I'm so sorry.

Another set of animated dots.

Do you want to get together and talk?

I responded quickly.

I'm needed here.

More animated dots.

What about Saturday after you see your mom?

I stared at the message. Why did he want to see me so much? To comfort me? And why would I need comfort from him when…
"Laura?"
I quickly turned around. Kevin stood in the doorway.
"I was wondering when you're coming to bed."
I looked at the screen for a moment, then looked at him. I got up from the desk chair and walked over to him. "Now. I'm tired."
"It has been a rough day." He put his arm around me.
I was tired. So tired that I didn't remember if I logged out of Facebook.

*** BREAK ***

When I went downstairs to make my morning tea and toast, I saw that Henry made it home. He left his tennis shoes in the hallway next to the small side table. When I got to the kitchen, he had his protest sign propped against a kitchen chair. I looked at it with dismay.
Feet shuffled on the tile behind me. I looked over my shoulder as Henry set his coffee cup in the Keurig machine. I looked at the sign again.
"Really?"
He glanced at the sign. "What's wrong with it?"
"'#NOTMYPRESIDENT'? A hashtag? Whatever happened to 'Make Love, Not War' and 'Peace on Earth, or Earth in Pieces'?"
"You know, Mom, it's 2016."
"What's that supposed to mean? We now chant in emoji?"

He stuck a pod in the Keurig machine and pressed the lever down hard. "I'm surprised you know what emoji are."

"Of course I know what emoji are. What do you mean by that?"

He turned around. The Keurig machine whistled and spat behind him.

"You live in the past, Mom. It's like time stopped for you when *Miami Vice* went off the air."

"What makes you think that?"

"You listen to your stupid eighties music all the time!"

"At least it can be called music. I don't know how to describe what you listen to. People cussing over oscillator noises?"

"We tell it like it is. Times are hard! And with Trump in charge, they're going to get harder!"

"You know, I'm getting tired of all this hand-wringing over Trump. We've had right-wing presidents before, you know. I lived through both Bushes. I lived through Nixon. I lived through Ford. Hell, I lived through Reagan."

"There you go again! Talking about the damn eighties!"

"The eighties were a scary time! At least Trump won't joke about bombing Russia in five minutes."

"Of course not. He'll tweet it."

"Henry, we've been through this before. We made it through then, and we'll make it through now."

"What if we don't this time? Things are different now, Mom!"

"Are they?"

"You think the past was so great! Like you wish you can hop in that time-traveling DeLorean and go back to 1985!"

"Did you even hear what I said? The eighties were a scary, difficult time! I wouldn't want to go back for a single minute!"

"But you'd sleep with your ex from then!"

"Excuse me!" Henry and I stared at each other. Neither one of us could believe what was just said. My voice rose. "Where did you get such a crazy..."

"I saw your laptop." His voice shook. "I went to look for you when I came home, but you went to bed. Your laptop was still on. I didn't want to look, but...How could you?"

"Henry! I can explain..."

He dashed up the stairs, leaving his mug and coffee in the Keurig machine.

*** BREAK ***

I headed straight up the stairs after him, but I didn't see Henry anywhere. He must have gone to his room.

I looked up and down the hall. Stacy must still be asleep. Kevin had to go to work early for his weekly conference call with their Stockholm office. I stood in the middle of the hall wondering what I could have messaged to Greg that made Henry so angry with me. That led me to the home office.

I woke up the laptop and started to fume. What right did Henry have to...no, what right did *I* have to reconnect with my ex? We broke up 30 years ago. I went on with my life, and he should have gone on with his. So, why would I even...

And that's when I looked at the Amiga again.

For years, I tried to forget about San Rafael. I tore up those memories and shredded the pieces. What if something happened there I needed to remember?

But I had no time to think about those things. I had to get to work.

I logged into my laptop. Facebook Messenger was the first thing on my screen. I found three messages I hadn't seen before. Greg sent them after I went to bed.

When I read them, I gasped.

*** BREAK ***

"Coming up next on the 80s Hits Channel, George Michael and 'I Want Your...'"

"I don't think so," I grumbled as I changed the channel.

"President Obama will meet President-Elect Trump at the White House this morning..."

I shut off the radio.

I had to deal with Greg somehow. If I didn't resolve that problem, anything I would say to Henry or Kevin would come off a typical phony-sounding denial.

First, I had to get through work.

*** BREAK ***

When I got to my desk, I messaged Greg on my phone.

Let's discuss over dinner tonight at Mamá Frieda's on Sherman

Way. 6:00? Ty.

I'd let Kevin know and tell him what I'm doing. If I explain everything, I'm sure he'd accept it. I was about to text him when Warren dashed into my cubicle.

"You better see Tammy quick. She's pissed."

*** BREAK ***

"Close the door."

The scrunched face and narrowed eyelids were the signs of an ass-chewing. But I found it hard to take them seriously when they came from a plump-cheeked, wrinkle-free, twenty-something kid. Still, I shut the door and sat down in the chair in front of her desk.

"A question came up yesterday afternoon regarding the Android graphic libraries you wrote. You weren't here to answer them. Where were you?"

"I told you: I had to leave at two o'clock yesterday for my daughter's appointment."

"I have no record of you telling me that."

I had to blink my eyes a few times. "Of course you have."

"I don't."

"Tammy, I told you last week. Right here in this office. In fact, it was a week ago today. I told you I was taking Friday the fourth off and had to leave at two yesterday."

"I have no record."

"I put it on my Outlook, and you said you'd put it on your—wait—How could you forget that meeting we had? I told you my daughter has cancer!"

"Your personal situation cannot impact your work schedules."

I was ready to explode. I needed to clamp my lips together and take some long, deep breaths through my nose before I dared to speak.

I was able to assume a calm, even tone. "When I told you my daughter had cancer, you were upset and sympathetic. Now, you're telling me, 'Your personal situation cannot impact your work schedules?'"

"That's true."

"And it hasn't, and it never will. My daughter may be dying, Tammy." I caught a quiver in my voice and suppressed it. "But I will do my job to the best of my abilities. I'm a professional..."

"And I'm not?"

I leaned forward. "Is there something going on that I should know about?"

"What makes you say that?"

"I don't understand your behavior towards me, Tammy..."

"Are you accusing me of being immature?"

I huffed in exasperation and held out both palms towards her. I took a deep breath and composed myself.

"Yesterday, you were clearly upset about something. You were so upset, you didn't attend a bug tracking meeting you asked to attend. And now, you seemed to have forgotten a meeting we had and time off you said you marked on your calendar..."

"And that makes me immature, doesn't it?"

"Tammy, if there's something going on..."

"There's nothing going on that concerns you!"

"But whatever it is, you're taking it out on me."

She sprung from her chair. "My boyfriend broke up with me, OK!"

"I'm sorry." I hoped I sounded sympathetic, even though I hated her taking out her anger on me.

But she didn't let up. "He said he didn't want to move to the Valley. He meant he didn't want to move with me!"

"I know how much it must hurt..."

"I'm going through a lot of shit right now, OK! I don't need any other problems!"

I took a deep breath. "If it would help, I will talk to the person who asked you about those Android libraries..."

"It was Deanna!"

My shoulders tensed. And they grew tighter as Tammy continued.

"How am I supposed to answer her question if the person who knows isn't here!"

I noticed a different tone in her voice.

"I'm supposed to be the one in charge of people with experience! I'm supposed to be on top of everything..."

"And because you broke up with your boyfriend, you weren't."

Tammy froze.

"I've known Deanna for years, Tammy. She's willing to wait to get the correct information. She's willing to accept an 'I don't know, but I'll find out and get back to you.'"

"That's not what she said! She told me I needed to calm down!"

"You do."

She didn't. Her face reddened. Her back stiffened. I had to find some way to calm her down before she exploded. Or fired me.

"Tammy, you're not the only one who's ever had to go back to work after something traumatic..."

"Great," she huffed. "Are you going to give me one of those, 'I'm older and wiser than you, you millennial dumbfuck' talks?"

"It happened when I was younger than you, Tammy. When I was 18, I worked as a bank teller. One day at work, I was robbed and tied up at gunpoint. But the next day, I put on my makeup and outfit and headed right back to..."

Tammy's face and demeanor instantly changed. She collapsed into her chair. She turned pale. Her eyes opened wide. Her lips trembled. Her voice shook.

"You were tied up? At gunpoint?"

I nodded. From the terror in her face, I could tell this wasn't just something she saw on TV or YouTube that upset her. This affected her viscerally. Personally. I looked at the teal sticker on her MacBook Pro. I understood. It all made sense.

I reached across her desk and put my hand on hers. I looked into her eyes.

"Tammy, let me tell you about something else that happened to me..."

CHAPTER THIRTY
February 1986

The code finished compiling. I double-clicked the PhotoLab icon and followed the steps Kathlynne wrote in her bug report.

> 1. Open PhotoLab Beta 14. 2. Click the pencil icon for the Pixel Edit tool. 3. Change the color to white. 4. Click a black pixel to change it to white. 5. Click the Contrast tool. 6. Change the contrast, and...

This time, the contrast changed correctly. No black screen. No blinking red rectangle. No Guru Meditation error.

I exhaled hard, slipped my fingers underneath my glasses, and rubbed my eyes. I had been up since three this morning to fix bugs before Arnold Hawthorne arrived.

Behind me, a click and the Westminster Chimes.

I turned my head towards the grandfather clock. Seven o'clock. I had to get to the shower.

*** BREAK ***

On the way up the stairs, I thought about all the things I had to cover with Arnold. He would want to discuss his concerns about file loading time. And the slow response of the zoom button. And the ship date. He said he would be ready to buy as soon as we shipped.

I reached the bathroom. I didn't knock or jiggle the handle to see if it was locked. I just opened the door. Fortunately, it was unoccupied.

How was I going to answer Arnold about the ship date? I shut the door behind me. We had to get the disk labels and packaging back from the printer, and Kathlynne had to finish reviewing my user manual. I pulled off my t-shirt and threw it on the floor. And the bugs. Kathlynne found six more this week. Two were Guru Meditation errors. I slipped off my gym shorts and panties. We couldn't ship with bugs that caused a system crash, but could we ship with the others?

I glanced at my naked torso in the mirror. It reminded me that Arnold wanted us to test with some nude photos he took.

I took off my glasses and set them on the sink. Then I cranked on the water and pulled up the knob to activate the showerhead. I stepped into the tub and pulled the curtain around it. The refreshing streams of water stilled my mind. I closed my eyes and let the warmness coat me. The water poured through my hair, down my face, and over my body. My shoulders settled. My neck unknotted. I relaxed.

Until I heard another stream of water outside the shower curtain.

I turned around. With my blurry vision, I could make out a vague rectangle of light through the steam and thick curtain. Did I leave the door unlocked?

I stepped to the end closest to the toilet. I kept the curtain tight around me as I peeked past the opening and focused as hard as my nearsightedness would allow. I gasped.

Darryl tucked it in his underwear and zipped up his slacks. He greeted me with a sly smile. "Don't you always lock the door?"

"Don't you know I was in the shower?"

"I did."

His eyes pierced through the curtain. I didn't know how much of me was visible, but he tried to take in every detail he could. I looked back at him. His belt was still unbuckled. The buckle jingled as he moved. The steam from the water increased, making it harder for me to see. I tried to look for his hands and what they were doing. They seemed to hover in front of his six-months-pregnant gut.

"I can see why he likes you."

I wanted to ask if he was talking about Peter, but I couldn't speak.

"He always gets what he wants. He asked for a girl programmer. I didn't think there was such a thing. At first, I thought it's because he's such a pussy he can't work with a man. But I figured it out."

He stepped towards me. His belt buckle jingled.

"He always gets what he wants. He's getting better than he deserves."

I could make out his head lowering toward his crotch. I pulled the curtain tighter around me. I trembled.

But Darryl fastened the button of his slacks and his belt buckle. He then looked straight at me.

"Don't use up all the hot water."

Footsteps and a shut door. I nearly doubled over when I exhaled.

*** BREAK ***

"The gentleman is here," Mrs. Posner announced with regal deportment.

Peter got up from his chair. He stepped towards the front door but stopped. He noticed that I was still seated.

"Aren't you coming to meet him?"

The squeak from the metal chair answered for me as I stood up.

I didn't say anything about what happened in the shower that morning. What could I say? And how could I trust what Darryl said was true? I'd been with the Posners for seven months. I felt comfortable with Peter for the most part. We had our moments. There were times I wondered if he had ulterior motives, or if he only wanted me around because I'm a woman. But each time, he showed me respect. If anything, Darryl did more to make me feel uncomfortable than Peter did.

Still, I found myself standing a foot away from Peter as we stood by the door.

The lock clicked. Mrs. Posner and Kathlynne stepped back as the door swung open. Peter moved next to me. Darryl was the first through the door. He wore the same slacks I saw in the shower. Then Arnold stepped in. He wore a sharp gray suit and a burgundy tie and carried a leather briefcase. A blend of cheerful "Welcome" and "Hello" surrounded him, but he reached for my hand first.

"Laura, I'm glad to see you again."

I shook his hand. "Likewise."

I saw Mrs. Posner's eager face. I figured I'd handle the introduction.

"This is Arnold Hawthorne, who we met at CES. Mr. Hawthorne, this is Mrs. Posner."

"Please, call me Hazel."

Peter and I exchanged puzzled looks. Especially with what happened next.

"Charmed." Arnold took her hand and kissed it like a Victorian gentleman. Did Mrs. Posner actually blush? Peter clearly grimaced.

"I'll leave you to your work." She spoke with an unusual coquettishness. "And I'll have Maria bring luncheon."

"Thank you." Arnold smiled and followed Peter, Darryl, and me into the living room. Was she checking out his butt?

I could tell from Peter's stiff walk that he was embarrassed by his mother's flirting. But Arnold's relaxed gait showed he enjoyed the whole affair. I wondered what Darryl thought, but I couldn't bear to look at him.

"It's a lovely place you have here," Arnold said. "I know a lot of businesses start in garages. It's rare to see one start in a beautiful place like this."

"Thank you." I had to reply because Peter still seemed too uncomfortable about his mother. If only she knew about Arnold's line of business.

Peter seemed to relax when he sat down in front of the Amiga. I figured I had to be the lady and get a chair for Arnold. I grabbed a side chair next to the sofa. A squeak came from the computer bench. Darryl had taken my seat.

I set the side chair at the other side of Peter. Arnold sat down and placed his briefcase on his lap. I took a step back and stood behind them.

"You said you wanted us to test some samples." Peter double-clicked the PhotoLab icon.

"I do, thank you." He took a seat and set the briefcase on his lap. "We've taken some photos with the beta you sent us. We wanted to see how they looked on your setup and go over some suggestions we have for your program."

"Perfect."

I watched as he flipped up the brass latches on his briefcase. He took out an unlabeled blue three-and-a-half-inch floppy. Then, his hand froze. He held up the disk like the hand that prompted us to insert the Kickstart and Workbench disks. He swiveled his head around left and right. He was looking for me. I kneeled into the space between Peter's chair and his so he could see me.

He gave me an apologetic glance. "I must tell you, this is a picture of one of our models. She's naked."

I smiled to assure him. "I don't mind."

Then Darryl burst out, "Of course not. She sees a naked woman every day!"

Darryl chuckled and squirmed out a dopey grin. The rest of us reacted to his attempt at a joke with silence.

Peter's expression was hard to figure out. Was he embarrassed to hear me talked about that way? Just like he was embarrassed to see his mom flirt?

Arnold cleared his throat and set the disk next to the Amiga keyboard. Peter picked up the disk and inserted it into the external drive. He selected the Open command. When the file selector appeared, he found the file on the external drive. The floppy disk grunted away as the picture emerged on the screen.

I stared at the black-and-white picture with a professional detachment. Arnold did too since he saw that woman in the unpixelated flesh when he took that picture. Peter's eyes widened in a way that made me uncomfortable. I didn't dare look at Darryl's reaction.

I exhaled and turned to Arnold. "What do you think?"

"It looks like you made some improvements. The image loads faster than at CES."

"That feature is one of the things we've been working on. What do you think about the quality?"

"It's a little dark. Do you think we can adjust the brightness?"

"Let's try contrast first." I couldn't reach the mouse, so I turned to Peter. "Can you increase the contrast?"

His eyes remained focused on the pixels that formed the woman's nipples.

"Peter?"

He jolted. His hand fumbled for the mouse. The red pointer trembled on its way to the Contrast slider.

My shoulders and neck tightened. I had never seen this side of Peter. Even when he commented about my kneecaps and said I was beautiful, there was something innocent and awkward about it. But this? And how are we going to deal with all the other photos Arnold would want us to look at? And all the other potential customers in that business?

I found myself looking at Darryl. He flashed me a "told you so" smile.

My head turned stiffly as I watched Peter click on the contrast slider. He nudged it one setting at a time as the woman's figure became more distinct.

"Now, let's try brightness," My voice had gotten tighter.

A click. A few nudges of a slider. The shadows made the woman look more comely.

Arnold leaned back in the chair. "You realize what you're doing, right?"

I glanced at Peter and Darryl. Who knew what those minds were thinking?

"You're creating art."

I realized that Arnold was directing his comments towards me. I turned towards him and listened.

"Think about the classical sculptures from Greece, Rome, and the Renaissance. How they fashioned nudes from marble, carefully chiseling until every muscle and contour of skin looked natural and beautiful. Now, we're doing this with pixels. It's not just for self-gratification, Laura. This is a celebration of the human body. At last, we have the tools to do it justice on a computer."

I nodded, but I wasn't sure Peter felt the same way. Darryl surely didn't.

Arnold turned to me. "So, it looks like you're close to releasing. Do you have a ship date…"

PBUM-TSCEEE.

We turned around quickly. Maria stood there, her hands and face trembling. The serving tray by her feet, covered with broken china, splattered tea and separated sandwiches. Her eyes darted side to side, and she ran out of the room sobbing.

Peter's expression turned sour. Darryl seemed ready to explode. Arnold looked grave.

"I'm sorry. I know some people have a hard time with these type of…"

"It's all right," I assured him. I turned to Peter. "Why don't you, Darryl, Kathlynne, and your mother take Arnold to lunch? I'll take care of things here."

"I think that's a wonderful idea," Arnold chimed in. "I've never been to this part of the Bay Area. It seems charming."

I managed a smile to assure them. Peter's face maintained a sour silence, but he finally nodded. Darryl's face relaxed.

Arnold stood up. "Shall we?"

Peter nodded and got up slowly. The metal chair squeaked as Darryl stood. I remained kneeling by the bench and watched them walk around the debris of their intended lunch.

*** BREAK ***

I should clean up the mess so that Maria didn't get in trouble, but it was more important that I find out if she was OK. Something about that picture must have really bothered her. She didn't seem to have that delicate of a disposition to be that shocked by the image of a naked woman. Or maybe she picked up the vibe from Peter and Darryl.

How did she feel about them? And how did they feel about her? All this time with the Posners, and there was so much I didn't know. Or was afraid to ask.

I looked around the house, but I couldn't find Maria anywhere.

I stepped to a window overlooking the backyard. The rain had stopped for a few days, but puddles remained in the part of the lawn where we put the pool in the summer. Dark clouds from the west threatened again.

That was when I noticed the shed door was open. I grabbed my coat and headed towards to the shed. Mrs. Posner wasn't around to stop me.

When I approached the door, I heard sobbing. I peered inside. The lights were white instead of red. I didn't think that darkroom had regular light bulbs. I found Maria crouched by some cabinets at the end of the darkroom. I rushed over to her and knelt beside her. I wrapped my arm around her.

"Maria! What's wrong?"

She muttered rapidly and tearfully, "No puedo...no puedo decir..."

I cupped her face in my palm and turned her towards me. Her reddened eyes darted side to side. I gazed into those eyes and spoke softly.

"Maria, you can tell me."

She turned away. I gently turned her face back towards mine.

"We're alone. You're safe with me. Please tell me."

She pulled away from me and shifted to a drawer at the end of the cabinet. The old track groaned as she slid it open. She pulled out several 8 x 10 photographs on glossy paper. She stared at me intensely as she handed them to me.

The second I looked down, I gasped. My stomach knotted. Blood fled from my face. I looked at the frightened eyes in the photographs and then turned to Maria's red-ringed eyes.

"The pictures," she murmured, "They weren't the worst part."

The photos fell from my hands.

"Who did this to you?"

She looked away. "No puedo..."

"No," I said firmly. "Tell me. Who did this to you?"

She started sobbing.

"Maria?"

"He said he would take care of me. He said he would keep me safe. I would never have to go back to Mexico. He would pay me well. I would have money to send to my family. He would teach me English. I would go to school. All...All I had to do was..."

She cried uncontrollably, painfully. I wrapped my arms tight around her. Her whole body shook against mine. I kissed her on her forehead. Rage boiled inside me. I was grateful Judge Posner was dead. I hate to think how I'd react if I saw him alive.

Maria's sobbing subsided, but she still sniffed as she pulled away from me. She picked up the photos—those hideous, horrifying photos—put them back in the drawer, and closed it. She struggled to her feet. I stood up and steadied her.

Her voice rasped. "I should clean up the mess..."

I shook my head. "I'll do it..."

"No. It is my job. It is my fault. I will clean it up."

I held her still.

"Maria, there must be something I can do."

"There is nothing you can do."

"Then what can I do for you?"

Her eyes, still watery, stared directly into mine. "Ten ciudado, amiga."

*** BREAK ***

From the living room, the clinks and scrapes as Maria cleaned up the broken china and food. From the dining room, the steady ticks of the Regulator clock. And I found myself in between, pacing around between the door and the stairs.

I stopped and picked up the brass figurine of the goddess Diana with her quiver of arrows, the deer, and the dent on the side of her head. A symbol of feminine power. But I felt powerless and trapped. How could I continue to work here, knowing what I know? Maria warned me to be careful, but of what?

From the other side of the door, I heard laughing. I put down the figurine and rushed towards the living room. "Maria, they're..."

But Maria was already gone. So were the serving tray, broken dishes, and the food. Perhaps that's what Judge Posner did to her. Made her invisible.

The door creaked open. Laughter blew in. Mrs. Posner led the group into the living room.

"A luncheon out was a splendid idea, Laura." Her smile narrowed. "I hope Maria is all right."

I nodded and carefully formulated a response. "She was feeling a little ill. She'll be OK."

Peter stepped towards his mother. "I guess Laura and I can continue the testing with Arnold…"

Mrs. Posner raised her hand to stop him. "Laura must be famished. She must have something to eat."

"But Mother…"

"Peter, I insist. You must be hungry, aren't you, Laura?"

I certainly didn't feel hungry, not with all the eyes staring at me. Especially Darryl's.

Arnold grinned. "I have no problem waiting until Laura has had lunch."

"Splendid!" Mrs. Posner's forced cheeriness made me nervous. So did the way she cupped my elbow. "Then come!"

*** BREAK ***

Mrs. Posner rushed me towards the kitchen. She let go of my elbow once we entered. I went to the kitchen counter. She continued to the counter on the opposite corner. I found myself staring at her.

"Go on, Laura. Help yourself."

I opened a cupboard and took down a plate. But as I turned towards the refrigerator, Mrs. Posner was still there.

"You are a fortunate young woman. You know that, Laura."

I set the plate on the counter.

"You are intelligent, talented, and strong. You let nothing prevent you from pursuing what's important to you. You are quite capable of making your own way in the world." She brought her hands together and interlocked her fingers. "Things were different when I was your age. If a woman desired money or any type of decent life at all, she had to marry into it. That was why I married Mr. Posner. I didn't marry him for love. I certainly didn't marry him for his looks or, let's say, certain manly qualities. But he provided me with wealth, a comfortable home, children, and anything I asked for. Mr. Posner had his, well, peculiarities. He loved that photo studio. He would spend all day there if he could."

She unlocked her fingers and let her hands fall to her sides. I stepped towards her and looked into her eyes.

"You knew."

"Not for the longest time. Darryl was the one who brought it to my attention."

I looked down. My brain started swirling.

"When I found out, I discussed the situation with Mr. Posner right away. Of course, something had to be done."

Her precise, clinical tone made me shudder even more. I tried lifting my head again, but I couldn't look into her eyes.

"You called the police?"

"Before I had the opportunity...well, let's just say a more honorable circumstance came about."

"The crash? He killed himself?"

"The sheriffs never determined the cause of the accident. It was simply a coincidence. A tragic coincidence. But I will say that it saved him from public disgrace and an undoubtedly horrible incarceration."

Sickness came over me. Cold, numbing. My body trembled. I felt like my bowels would let loose. I took several deep breaths, all while Mrs. Posner stared at me. I finally gathered enough strength to turn away.

"I better...I better go back to work with Arnold and Peter."

"What about your luncheon, Laura?"

"I'm not hungry right now."

*** BREAK ***

"Everyone on the floor! Now!"

The voice was different from the man who forced me on the floor. There were more than one. Screams surrounded me. No further gunshots. But all I could see was the thin beige industrial carpet in front of my face.

The man above me pulled my wrists tightly together. Stickiness pressed against my skin. A scraping noise as the stickiness wrapped around my wrists.

An itch pricked the right side of my forehead. A tiny, persistent itch that I couldn't scratch. I rubbed my face on the matted carpet, but the itch wouldn't stop! I tried rubbing it some more, but a rough hand clasped against my forehead. Duct tape pressed hard against my lips. The itch grew. I wanted to scream, but the tape sealed my lips shut. I couldn't speak! I couldn't breathe!

*** BREAK ***

I gasped.

Once again, I found myself in bed, face-down on my pillow with my hands behind my back. My heart pounded. I unlocked my hands, scrambled to the window, and flung it open. A blast of coldness cut through my t-shirt and gym shorts all the way into my skin. After the shock of cold passed, I breathed in every bit of air.

The rain had returned. It fell hard and crackled on the concrete below. Beyond it, the cars on the freeway whooshed and sloshed by.

"Uhh! Uhh! Not so fucking hard! Uhhh! Ahhhh!"

I shut the window and latched it. My head tilted towards the window. The cold damp glass against my forehead. My breath fogged the inside of the window as raindrops streaked outside.

I had to get out.

How could I stay there? How could I stay there with everything that happened?

How did Darryl find out? And did Peter know? He adored his father. Perhaps he didn't know. Or knew, but couldn't accept it. Or...

If what Darryl said was true about his father, was he also telling me the truth about Peter? Could I still trust Peter? I turned down a real programming job with a decent salary at a legitimate company because I thought Peter respected me. But what if Darryl is right? And Maria? Didn't she warn me about him too?

We were so close to finishing PhotoLab, and Arnold seemed pleased with what we created. It really is a great program. But what did we create it for? What if people used it the same way Judge Posner used his darkroom? Computers could do lots of incredible things, things we never imagined. But some of them could be evil. Maybe a lot of them. Was I creating a monster?

And what really did happen to Judge Posner? This couldn't have been an accident. Did he kill himself? Or did somebody kill him? And why was Maria still here after everything that happened to her? Was she a prisoner in this house? Was I?

I had to get out. The house was closing in on me. Nothing would be open at this time of night except a 7-Eleven. But a short drive would clear my head. I opened my closet...No. If I got dressed, it would look like I was leaving them, and who knows what they'd do. I might get soaked and cold in my t-shirt and gym shorts, but the Civic had a good heater. I got my purse out of the closet and made sure my car keys and wallet were there. I went to the drawer, got my case with Grandma's pearls, and slipped them into my purse. I froze. Why did I do that? I was coming back after the drive. Or should I?

In six hours or so, I could be back home in Reseda. Even if I left everything behind, at least I would be safe. But what would happen to Maria?

And Kathlynne? Both of them deserve better than they have. They're intelligent and fast learners. They shouldn't be prisoners of their pasts or this house.

And Peter? Even with what Darryl and Maria said, he really wasn't that bad. Or at least he hasn't done anything bad to me.

And that Amiga. Would I ever get a chance to use a computer like that again? I couldn't afford my own, not with all the expenses I incurred in the Bay Area and the Posners' small salary. I couldn't justify getting a new computer when I already had a Commodore 64 at home. Still, I'd miss the Amiga.

In a way, I'd miss the Posners. I had gotten used to this house, and its antique furnishings, and Mrs. Posner's fastidious manners. I could even stomach Darryl at times. We did create something great with PhotoLab. We did it together. We were a team, a family.

But a very sick one.

I really needed that drive, even if I didn't know where I was headed.

I slipped on my sandals and slung my purse over my shoulder. I crept down the stairs, trying not to make a sound. I set my purse on a table by the front door, ready to get out my car keys.

*** BREAK ***

"Thank goodness you're up."

Peter took my hand. I found myself pulled into the living room. He grabbed me by both shoulders with a strength I didn't think he had. His eyes were filled with unusual excitement.

"I have a brilliant idea!" His voice punctuated with deep breaths. "It will amaze Arnold..."

"Arnold already likes the product. He's ready to buy as soon as we release it."

"I know, but we need to do one more test."

"What?"

With his hands still clasped around my shoulders, he walked me to the metal chair and forced me down on it. The chair let out a loud shriek. He let go of me and stepped towards the Amiga. I found the camera staring at me.

"Come on, Peter. We have enough pictures of me. Why do we need..."

"Take off your shirt."

"Excuse me?"

"Take off your shirt." He jerked his head in an upward arc to gesture how he wanted me to remove it.

"You can't be serious."

"You said you'd play model for me."

"But not that way!" I stood up. "What do you want from me?"

"I want one shot."

"For what?" I backed away from the chair. "You don't need another photo of me. You don't need a shot of me topless. We just need to fix the bugs Kathlynne found, get the labels back from the printer, and..."

"We need to show Arnold what we can do..."

"He knows what our product can do." I glanced at Peter. I then turned my head towards the opening of the living room and focused on my purse and car keys by the front door. "I have to do a quick errand. Excuse me."

I strode towards the opening. Peter's hand clasped my forearm. He put his other arm around my back and clasped my other shoulder. He turned me back towards the Amiga.

"What are you doing?"

He didn't answer me until I was back in front of the chair. He let go and faced me. "Listen, Laura, you and I—we are close, so close..."

"To what?"

"To finishing PhotoLab, of course."

I cocked my head. His face squeezed with puzzlement.

"Laura, what's wrong?"

"What's wrong with you?" I stepped away from him. "I've never seen you like this before."

"You don't know how important this program is to me."

"It's important to me too."

"Then take off your shirt!"

"Why? Give me one good reason why?"

"I need it—I mean, we need it. We need it for Arnold..."

"He doesn't need it."

"We need a picture..."

"Peter..."

"Laura? Just one picture. Please?"

I took another step back. "Peter, why did your brother hire me?"

"I needed a programmer."

"A woman programmer?"

He glanced off to the side. "I...I thought...well, you know..."

"I'd wind up having sex with you?"

"Laura! Who do you think I am!"

"I don't know, Peter!"

He took a step towards me. I took a step back. And when he waved his pleading hands towards me, I took another step back.

"Laura, I depend on you! I need you! If it weren't for you, PhotoLab would be nothing! I would be nothing!"

"If you value me so much, drop your request."

"Laura, I just need a picture!"

"Peter!"

"Please!"

"No!"

Peter stood stunned, mute, frozen in place. I should have run away, but I just found myself staring at him. It was like the first time I saw him. Disheveled light blond hair, white t-shirt, and baggy sweat pants, aviator glasses. A man I didn't know.

"Peter, I'm going to do my errand. By the time I get back, I hope you've thought about how you've acted, and you won't do it again."

I turned around. Footsteps followed me. I swung back towards him.

"Peter!"

"Laura, I need you!"

I gave a quick glance over my shoulder. I was in the middle of the living room. It was probably another 10 to 15 feet to the door. My Civic was parked on the street. I'd have to run out on rain-slicked porch steps in my sandals and pray I won't slip. Maybe someone will hear by then.

"Peter, I'm going to do my errand now. If you have feelings for me, we can talk about it. We can talk about it when I come back…"

I walked calmly out of the living room. He rushed past me and placed himself between me and the front door.

"Peter!"

I hoped my raised voice would attract someone's attention. But Kathlynne was having screaming sex with Darryl. Mrs. Posner, her bedroom was way in the upstairs corner. Maria, if she could hear, she would be too scared to do anything. After what Judge Posner did to her, I wouldn't blame her.

I took a deep breath. I tried to keep my voice calm even as my shoulders trembled.

"Peter. I'm doing a quick errand. I'll be back in a few minutes. You think over what you said, and then we'll talk when I get back."

I stepped toward the door. He stepped in front of me, blocking it.

"Peter!"

I gave a quick glance around. No one else was there.

"Stop this, Peter…"

"But Laura…"

"Peter!"

His voice quivered. "I just want a picture…"

"Like your father's?"

The words blurted out of me. And I regretted them the moment his desperate expression turned into a scowl.

I stood in place. "You know what he did."

"Lies! Wretched lies!"

"They're not lies, Peter! I saw the pictures!"

He nostrils flared. His shoulders rose and fell with deepening breaths. But I was too outraged to be intimidated.

"How old was Maria when he took them? How old was she when he molested her? Fifteen? Fourteen? Thirteen? She was just a girl, Peter! A girl who couldn't speak out! A girl who couldn't fight back! Your father exploited her, Peter! For years!"

"She's an illegal alien!"

"She's a human being! And so are you! But your father, what he did, he was a monster!"

"My father was not a monster! That's a lie!"

"He may have been a good father to you. He may have defended people's rights. He may have protected the environment. He may have done many, many good things. But that doesn't excuse what he did to Maria. What he did was evil! That's what made him a monster!"

"My father was not a monster! My father was not an evil man!"

"What he did was wrong!"

"He did what he was entitled to do."

I gasped. Peter looked straight at me.

"My father worked hard. He did good things. Why couldn't he have what he wanted?"

A jolt of cold ran through my body as I stared at him.

"You're just like your father, aren't you?"

He took a step forward. I backed up.

"I want you, Laura. I've always wanted you. Now that soldier boy is gone…"

He took another step towards me. I took another step back. My heart pounded. My whole body trembled.

"Peter, please..."

He wouldn't stop advancing. I couldn't stop retreating. I gave a quick and urgent glance up the stairwell. Why won't somebody come?

The small of my back bumped against something. Metal clattered. Without thinking, my body spun around, grasping something in my hand. It was the figurine of Diana.

I held it up high, brandishing it for Peter to see.

"Back off, Peter! I don't want to hurt you, but I will defend myself."

"Don't do this to me," he cried. "You're my amiga! I need you!"

"No. You need to be a better man than your father."

"Laura!"

I shook the metal figurine at him. "Get away from me!"

"Laura!"

"Get away!"

"Laura!"

"Peter!"

"Don't leave me, my amiga!"

He lunged towards me, arms open wide. On impulse, my arm flung up and swung down. Resistance. Something stopped my arm. The figurine flew out of my hand. It clattered on the floor.

I wanted to scream, but I couldn't.

Peter continued towards me, but his head slumped down. His right hand grabbed for my glasses and pulled them off my face. Everything blurred around me. His forehead landed at my waist. Warm liquid seeped into my t-shirt and gym shorts. It continued as his head rubbed down my leg until he collapsed at my feet.

My body convulsed. My breathing shallowed. But I had to find my glasses. I looked down and tried to pick them out from the blur on the floor. I pulled my feet away from Peter and found my glasses next to him. I was afraid to pick them up in fear he would wake up and grab me. But he was motionless. Did I kill him? I couldn't see clearly enough and was too afraid to check. I scooped up my glasses and put them on as best as I could. He must have bent the frames. Everything waved between clarity, blurs, and double vision.

Peter remained motionless. His breathing slowed. Was he dying? His forehead had a red, glistening gash. His blood smeared on me, staining my t-shirt, gym shorts, left thigh, and sandals.

I looked up the stairwell. They were all there, looking down at me. Darryl and Kathleen gasped. Maria covered her mouth and trembled. Mrs. Posner leaned over the railing.

"Leave. Now."

*** BREAK ***

I grabbed my purse and keys and ran out the door. The rain came down hard, soaked through my clothes, and smeared Peter's blood down my leg and feet. A temple popped out from behind my left ear. My vision was doubled and thrown out-of-focus again, worsened by fogged and rain-spotted lenses. But I didn't need to see or think. Somehow, I got in my Civic and started the ignition. Without looking, I shifted the transmission to drive and hit the accelerator.

HONK.

I stomped on the brake. Headlights flashed by me. I couldn't wait to see if any other cars were coming. I just pulled out and kept driving. My head pounded, "Go south. Go south."

I turned a corner. Then another. I didn't know where I was going. I just had to leave. Leave the Posners. Leave San Rafael. Leave the Bay Area. Leave. Leave as fast as I could.

Ahead of me, green signs with white text big enough for me to see in the haze, rain, and my out-of-focus vision.

101 South
San Francisco Oakland
Freeway Entrance

Blurry and doubled red taillights, white headlights surrounded me. I followed them up the ramp.

The lights spread out. Darkness ahead of me. My windshield blanketed by rain. I turned on the wipers. I then realized I hadn't turned my headlights on. I turned the knob. White brightness streaked with rain. The black outlines of the hills of Marin against the gray of fog and rainclouds. I kept one eye on the rearview mirror, looking for police lights and sirens. Nothing but the headlights of cars behind me.

My hands gripped the steering wheel to keep them from shaking. Windows fogged. My body shivered from my wet clothes, hair, arms, and legs. I had to turn on the defrosters and the rear wiper. The hatchback window was again clear enough to see through the rear view mirror. Still, nothing but headlights.

WHUUUUAH-WHUUUUAH.

My body locked in place.

WHUUUUAH-WHUUUUAH.

What do I do? Move to the right and let them pass? Pull over and stop? I can't outrun them in this car. What do I do?

WHUUUUAH-WHUUUUAH.

The siren grew louder.

What do I say? Will they believe me? Was I wrong? What really happened? What did I really do?

WHUUUUAH-WHUUUUAH.

My car swayed as something large whooshed by me.

The siren faded as a fire truck rushed ahead.

I started breathing again. My breaths were deep and even, but they became shallow and broken. The shallow and broken breaths turned into sobs. My tears came hard, as hard as the rain outside. But I straightened my glasses and kept my eyes on the small patch of highway lit ahead of me. I had to keep driving. I had to get the Posners and San Rafael far behind me as fast as I could.

*** BREAK ***

The drive was a complete blur. I vaguely remember stopping to get gas. Some trucker said, "You tell me who did this to you, and I'll kill the motherfucker." But I didn't know if Peter was already dead, killed by my own hand.

Why did Mrs. Posner tell me to leave? Why didn't she send the police after me? Did they know what Peter did? If so, why didn't they stop him? Maria warned me about Peter. So did Darryl. Why didn't they stop him? Why did they let me go through this?

Will they forgive me for what I did to Peter?

Tears welled up again. But I had to take a deep breath and keep my eyes on the road.

By the time dawn broke, the San Fernando Valley sprawled out in front of me, glistening in the growing light. But only one thing could make me feel safe, seeing my house on Vanalden Avenue.

"Laura?"

Mom was in her business suit. She was about to get into her Accord to go to work. She slammed the car door shut and rushed towards me. I collapsed in her arms and wept.

*** BREAK ***

My eyes opened to a blur.

My posters were there. So were my yearbooks, certificates, and plaques. And my Commodore 64. I felt the familiar comfort of my bed and soft flannel pajamas. But nothing was right. I was home, but I had left too much behind in San Rafael. More than just my lime green Bermuda shorts and CSUN sweatshirt.

My hand fumbled on the nightstand for my glasses. I could only place them over my eyes and hook the good temple over my right ear. When my vision cleared, I found Mom standing by the side of my bed. She smiled.

"We'll get those fixed today."

My face scrunched tight. My chest heaved. My whole body trembled. But I had no more tears left to cry.

Mom sat down at the side of my bed. She reached out her hands. I clasped them.

"What I am going to do, Mom?"

"What we always do, Laura. We go back to work."

She leaned over and kissed my forehead.

*** BREAK ***

"Thank you for calling West Valley Savings and Loan. To whom may I direct your call?"

The ringing of telephones. The clacking of typewriters and keyboards. The chatter in hallways. The beige cubicle walls and gray industrial carpeting. Water coolers and coffee pots. Copiers and fax machines. It felt good to be back in a normal office again. I felt normal too. I wore my grandma's pearls with a new navy blue dress blouse, and black slacks Mom bought me. I decided I would never work anywhere that required me to wear a dress, skirt, or shorts.

But when I got to the air-conditioned computer lab with its white tile floor, it didn't seem normal. The IBM System/370 was still there, but everything else was gone. Just gray outlines where the punch card reader and terminals used to be.

I stepped outside the lab and walked towards adjacent glass-enclosed room with rows of computer benches. A man leaned over an open IBM PC.

He must have been new, because I hadn't seen him before, and Mom never mentioned him. I entered the room and walked towards him to get a closer look. My attention was drawn more to the man than the computer. The tailored light blue dress shirt fit well on his trim body. His strong hand flexed as he used the socket driver to remove the slot cover. His skin was a rich brown. After ten years of alabaster and freckles, melanin enticed me. Especially when he looked up and smiled.

"Oh, hi." His voice was deep and friendly.

"Hi." I brushed my hair behind my ear. "I was wondering what happened to all the punch card machines."

"They're replacing them with PCs."

I smiled. "So we finally decided to join the 1980s."

I looked down at the box with the add-in board still in its protective plastic bag. I picked up the user manual. "An AST card."

"An AST-3270 card with coax connector and 3278 terminal emulation software."

"EBCDIC support?"

"And ASCII-to-EBCDIC conversion."

I nodded. He moved closer to me and looked into my eyes.

"You must be Laura Rodriguez."

I chuckled a little. "I must be."

"You're a legend around here. Everyone knows your name."

"I'd like to know yours."

"Kevin." He held out his hand. "Kevin Hamilton."

"I'm happy to be working with you, Kevin Hamilton."

I reached out my hand and shook his. His skin felt good against mine.

*** BREAK ***

When I came home late from work one day, I found several boxes in the entryway.

"Mom?"

She had changed into a t-shirt and jeans. She looked down at the boxes.

"UPS left them on the doorstep. I brought them in. Some were very heavy."

I glanced down at the return address. My jaw tightened. Mom folded her arms.

"At least those horrible Posners had the decency to send your things back."

"But I didn't have that many things there. Did I?"

Mom stared at me in puzzlement. I picked up each box. The first one wasn't too heavy. Things seemed to shift around. This might have been my clothes. The same with the other box. The next box seemed unusually large and heavy. I looked up at Mom.

"Do you have a…"

"Here." She grabbed her keys from the side table. "Use my house key."

I dragged the key along the tape and pulled the flaps apart. A thin layer of foam pellets concealed what looked like another box. I brushed the pellets out of the box.

"Oh, no. Oh, God, no."

I picked up and shook the other boxes. I found another heavy box, slightly smaller than the one I just opened. I dragged the key quickly down the tape and ripped the flaps apart. I clawed out the foam pellets. I gasped.

"Laura?"

I dug my hands into the pellets and pulled out a glossy cardboard box. I set it next to the shipping box.

Mom gasped. "Oh, dear Lord."

The top of the box had the logo and picture of a Commodore Amiga.

Mom knelt next to me. My heart pounded. My hand shook as I flipped open the cardboard latch. I opened the top of the box. On top of the foam packaging was a piece of paper folded in thirds.

Mom wrapped her arm around me. I stared at that paper, too afraid to open it.

"Read it," she urged.

I swallowed hard and picked up the paper. When I opened it, some things fell out. I didn't pay attention to them. I just stared at the dot-matrix printing and writing that could have only been done by one person.

21 February 1986

Dearest Laura,

I've never been good with words, and there are no words that could adequately express how terrible I feel about what happened. I am deeply sorry. This was completely my fault. I know that you can't forgive me, and you shouldn't. I know you will never come back to finish PhotoLab, and I don't expect you to. You are intelligent and talented, and you deserve to have success in an established company. You deserved better than what I did to you.

As you would gather from my correspondence, I did recover from the blow you gave me. I suffered a gash and a slight concussion, but I was released from the hospital. Although I may regain my physical health, the damage I've done will never be repaired. I hope the following may at least ameliorate some of the harm I have done.

First, we have packaged and shipped to you all of your clothes and other belongings you had at our house.

Second, I don't recall how much we already paid you, but I asked Mother to send you the full remuneration we promised you of $10,000 in the check enclosed herein.

I looked down. A check hung off the edge of the box. I remembered something else falling out. I turned to Mom. She was looking at a newspaper clipping and trembling.

"Laura."

She handed me a newspaper clipping. I set down Peter's letter and looked at it. It was dated February 23, 1986. A glance at the headline made every muscle seize.

Judge's Son Killed in Wreck

I looked at Mom. With a twitching mouth and loud sniff, she urged me to read on.

MENDOCINO - Peter Issac Posner, son of late Marin County Judge Roland Abraham Posner, was killed in a car accident off Highway 128 in Mendocino County. In a tragic coincidence, his vehicle, a 1985 Pontiac Fiero, was found in the same ravine where his father was killed in a similar accident in 1984. According to the Mendocino County Sheriff's Department, the accident happened sometime late Friday night, possibly related to heavy rains that hit the area...

It wasn't an accident. It wasn't a tragic coincidence, as Mrs. Posner and the newspaper put it. My eyes shifted from the newspaper clipping to the dot-matrix printed paper. What Peter wrote was a suicide note. And I had to read the rest of it. I set down the newspaper. I struggled to keep my hands steady as I picked his letter up again.

Third and lastly, I give you my Amiga.

I gasped. I shuddered. Mom put her arm around me. Her touch steadied me.

> You understood this machine better than me. Without you, PhotoLab would have never gone as far as it did. But I want you to use it to create something that matters to you. Create something that is pure and positive. You saw what the Amiga could do. Make it do something good in the world.

PBUM.
A teardrop fell on the paper.

> I saw how you lifted up everyone around me. You saw things in Maria and Kathlynne that they didn't see in themselves. You saw things in me too. You made me a better programmer, and you tried to make me a better person. I know that I disappointed you. But this wasn't your fault, but mine. You were right; I was just like my father. I needed to be a better man than him, but I knew I could not. My only course was to seek an honorable resolution, just like he did.
> Don't get me wrong: I love life. I love life so much that I cannot live it with disgrace. It is better to face the eternal unconscious void than to face years of the constant pain of ignominy. But if what the church teaches is true, I hope Jesus forgives me for my sins and how I prevented myself from committing any others.

My hands trembled. Mom put a hand on mine to steady it.

> You are a wonderful person, Laura. I know that someday you will find a man who honors, appreciates, and respects you. A man who will give you the freedom to succeed and be the best programmer and the best woman you can be. I hope that what happened here in this house and what happened between us that night will become a distant and faded memory. But if you ever choose to remember, please recall, and I mean it in its purest and more honorable sense, you were my amiga.

> With highest regards,
> Peter

I straightened my glasses and stared at those dot-matrix printed words. Waves and waves surged up my spine and crashed into my neck and shoulders. Anger, then grief. Grief, then anger. A shock I'd never felt before. When it was all too much, I collapsed on the Amiga box, burying my face in my arms. I sobbed. I sobbed harder than I ever had before. Mom clutched me tightly. Her body heaved against mine with every one of her tears.

CHAPTER THIRTY-ONE
November 2016

"So you're the one!"

The wide eyes. The urgent tone. The speed at which she got up from her chair and dashed around the desk. She was almost out the door when she ordered, "Come on!"

I followed her, not knowing where I was going or what was going to happen when I got there. Tammy must have known about my time in San Rafael. How did she? And what were the consequences of me telling her more about it?

She took me to Dean's old office. She called out to the person in the office. "It's like you told me! She's the one!"

She stepped aside to bid me to enter. I didn't know what trouble I was getting into, but I took a quiet breath and walked into the office. A woman sat behind the desk. She looked like someone I knew before, but I couldn't quite place her. The face was somewhat recognizable, but the tailored navy blue suit threw me off somehow.

She turned to Tammy. "Would you please excuse us?"

The voice sounded familiar.

Tammy nodded and left the office, closing the door behind her.

The woman smiled. "Laura?"

I gasped.

"Maria?"

I looked at her face again. The face I last saw 30 years ago when I struck Peter. That trembling face with the covered mouth.

But now that face broke into a smile. She rushed from behind her desk. I rushed towards her. Our arms clasped. Joyful mutterings. Tight, swaying hugs. She looked at me, her eyes glistening.

"You look great, Laura!"

"So do you."

"When I found out you are working here, I had to take this job!"

She seemed far different from when I knew her in San Rafael. Her accent was mostly gone, but I could hear remnants in how she pronounced some words. Her eyes had crow's feet. The most notable difference was her joy and enthusiasm. She wasn't that scared and damaged young woman I saw at the Posners. I could tell that she was free.

I exhaled hard and broke out into a smile. "We have a lot of catching up to do."

*** BREAK ***

We sat back down and showed each other family photos on our phones. Her husband Patrick works for JPL in Pasadena. His college roommate is an oncologist. I told her about Stacy. She offered to put me in touch with him. Her oldest daughter is studying pre-law. Her youngest is on the swim team in high school, and she wants to pursue a career in music. I told her about Henry wanting to be a DJ. I showed her photos of Kevin, and she told me I was lucky to have such a handsome husband.

The time came when we had to talk about San Rafael. The office became quiet as she leaned back in her desk chair.

"You know about Peter."

"I got his letter and the newspaper clipping."

She nodded. "Darryl, he put your stuff together."

I sat silently for a moment, trying to picture what must have been like in that house after Peter's suicide. I then spoke hesitantly.

"Then what happened?"

Maria stroked her chin and rocked in her chair for a moment.

"Kathlynne broke up with Darryl just after you left. She moved to Santa Clara and got a job with a software company. Last I heard, she finished college and got a director's job at Apple."

"And Darryl?"

"He got involved with some shady real estate deal. It was a big scandal in Marin for a while. The trial was on TV. I could not watch it. I was busy with my first software job. Well, the first one since I worked with you."

"What about Mrs. Posner?"

Maria sat quietly for a moment.

"You see, Mrs. Posner and I, we had an agreement. After her husband…" She exhaled hard. "She promised she would help me become an American citizen and put me through college. She promised that to keep me from going to the police. That's why I stayed. But she did nothing. There was always some reason, some delay. When she got Peter the Amiga and started that business, everything with me was put on hold."

I shuddered. I thought I was helping Maria by getting her involved in PhotoLab? Did I make things worse for her?

She stared at my face. She must have sensed my shame.

"You were not to blame, Laura. When Mrs. Posner saw how much I was helping you, how much I could learn and do, she started respecting me. After Peter died, she started paying for my college. And when President Reagan signed the Amnesty Act, she helped me get my citizenship."

"Where is she now?"

"She died in 2003."

"I'm sorry to hear that."

She nodded. "We reconnected before she passed. She was alone. Darryl went to prison for his part of the scandal. After he got out, well, he was out of the picture. She did not even know where he was. She asked me to help her sell that house on Irwin Street. I used my share of the money to start my own company. That house is now an office building. A startup that makes smartphone apps has its headquarters there. Can you believe that?"

I nodded and let out a small smile.

"Before she died, she asked me to do her a favor." Maria turned her desk chair to a desk drawer and leaned down to open it. "She said if I were to ever see you again, I should give you this."

She pulled something out of the drawer and placed it in my hands. I stared at it. It was the brass figurine of Diana. I ran my finger over the large dent.

"She knew you were defending yourself. Just as she once had to with her husband."

I looked up.

"Did Mrs. Posner ever tell you why she bought it?"

I shook my head.

"It was on a trip to Italy. She felt ashamed for what her life had become. She bought it as a reminder to stay strong. Then you came into our lives."

Maria sniffed softly.

"She told me how much she admired you. How you were able to do what is important to you when she could not. How you lifted up everyone around you. Even her. You are the only person she would give that to. She felt you were strong enough to have it."

Maria's face relaxed.

"When I sold my company, I wanted to go back to work. I guess I was driving my husband and daughters crazy staying at home." She chuckled. "I worked for Dean McKinnon when I was starting off in software design. When he told me he was retiring, he asked if I would be interested in the job. Then, he told me about you..."

Our eyes met.

KNOCK-KNOCK.

Maria nodded, and I opened the door.

Tammy popped her head into the doorway. "I'm sorry, but I'm...um..."

Maria glanced at her watch. "I'm sorry. I guess we lost track of the time."

"No problem," Tammy chimed.

Maria gave me a smile and a whispered, "We will talk more later."

*** BREAK ***

Tammy glanced at the figurine in my hand.

"That's my favorite of the Greek and Roman gods. My therapist suggested I make her my patronus."

She stopped. I turned to her. She seemed near tears.

"I didn't mean to interrupt you with Maria, but I couldn't wait, and...I'm sorry." She lowered her head. "I did have your time off on my calendar. I was so upset about the breakup..." She sighed. "I'm really sorry."

I put my hand on her shoulder. "It's OK."

"It's not. I feel like an unprofessional shit."

"You made a mistake, that's all. But if I could give you a piece of advice, it is unprofessional to say *shit* in an office."

I smiled, but she didn't smile back.

"Tammy, do you get intimidated by people like me?"

"Well, um, I..." Finally, she nodded. "Yeah. Yeah, I do. Sometimes, I worry people don't take me seriously because I'm young. I mean, look at us. I'm young enough to be your daughter."

"I may be old enough to be your mother, but you're old enough to be my manager."

She looked up at me.

"I know how hard it is starting out, Tammy. If you ever need someone to talk to, including about what happened to you, I'm here, and I'll respect your privacy."

"I'd really appreciate it." She smiled. "Maria says you bring the best out in people. She's right."

We walked side-by-side towards our part of the building. She turned to me. "I have some ideas on how we can modernize our core graphic libraries. Can I get your feedback on them?"

"Of course, Tammy."

CHAPTER THIRTY-TWO
November 2016

I had the radio turned off as I drove from work to the restaurant in Reseda. I was still processing what happened at work. Now, I had to deal with my ex, the one I broke up with in 1986.

Everything reminded me of 1986. The figurine of Diana that sat in my console. The buildings I drove past. Stores and restaurants had new names and bright coats of paint, but they looked like places I went to with my friends after school. And they still had that old movie theater, abandoned for nearly 30 years. I couldn't go into the heart of Reseda without remembering something that isn't around anymore.

I didn't recall what the restaurant was called before it became Mamá Frieda. I just knew that the place would be packed Thursday night for their special kosher tacos. So packed, I wouldn't feel alone with Greg. Fortunately, he came early and got a seat for us. He waved at me as I weaved through the tables.

"I'm glad you came." Greg smiled as I sat down.

"The tacos here are amazing."

"And they have their taco night on Thursdays instead of Tuesdays like everyone else. Brilliant idea."

I smiled and nodded.

"I got that message you sent me this afternoon," he said. "The one about the veterans' support group."

"I'm glad. My coworker passed it along. He'd be happy to help you."

He seemed puzzled. "Why did you send it?"

"Because I said I would. When we went to that Vietnamese place. You remember?"

"Oh."

The waiter came. "Can I start you off with something to drink?"

"Just water for me, please," I said. "And I think we're ready to order."

Both the waiter and I looked at Greg. He nodded. "Yes, we're ready. I'll have the three taco plate and a Diet Coke."

"Ma'am?"

"Just a taco a la carte, please."

"Certainly. It will be right up."

Greg's forehead furrowed. "I thought you like this place."

"I'll have something with the family later." I straightened my back. "You've never told me about your family."

"I want to talk about you." He leaned forward. "You're really scared about your daughter."

"I am." I unfurled the napkin and set it on my lap. "When we got the diagnosis three months ago, it was terrifying enough. A few years ago, one of my coworkers had leukemia. She died after nine months. And now to hear Stacy's cancer has spread..."

I exhaled hard. I didn't allow myself to cry in front of Greg.

"She's my child. I gave birth to her. I'd like to see her finish college, start a family, hold her children."

I looked away.

"You know, if you need me, Laura, I'm here for you."

I felt warmness. I looked down at the table. Greg was holding my hand.

"Your tacos." Greg let go of me as the waiter set down our plates. "Be careful, my friends. They're hot."

"Thank you," I whispered.

Greg picked up his fork and dug into the rice and beans. Steam came up as he brought the forkful to his mouth. Greg set down his fork and picked up one of his tacos. The crunch of the shell and the glimmer of the spicy salsa on the top of the shredded beef usually made my mouth water.

But I wasn't hungry, especially with what I had to tell Greg next.

"I'm worried about my son too."

Greg finished chewing. "You mean, the one who quit that Google job and moved back to be a DJ?"

"Yes."

Greg took another bite of taco.

"He saw your messages."

He kept chewing and finished the rest of the taco. I waited for him to finish eating to answer, but he picked up another taco.

"My son now thinks I'm being disloyal to my husband by meeting with you."

Greg set the uneaten taco back on the plate. He wiped his fingers on the napkin.

"Is he right?"

I blinked several times. "Excuse me?"

His chair creaked as he leaned forward.

"Laura, are you happy? Really?"

"No. I'm not happy because I'm going through a hard time. I'm not happy because my daughter is sick, and my son is having a career crisis, and..."

"You wish things were different, don't you?"

"What are you saying, Greg?"

He stared at me for a moment and then looked into my eyes.

"Do you ever regret the choices you made?"

"No! Of course not!"

He hung down his head. "I do."

"But Greg, those were *your* choices! *You* wanted to reenlist..."

"That's what I thought I wanted..."

"You said wanted to be an officer. You said the Army was the first thing you've found that you were truly good at. I remember that. What happened?"

"After OCS, I was stationed in Georgia. Then, Kentucky."

"What about that girl in Germany? The one in...what's the name of that town?"

"She wouldn't move. I never saw her again."

"You must have met someone else."

"A few."

"Did you get married? Do you have children?"

"Sandy. I met her in Georgia. It was sort of a rush thing. She was one of those old-fashioned Southern belles who wouldn't have sex without a ring. Then, I was transferred to Kentucky. I got involved with Lucille. We had a son, Jeremiah. She gave birth to him when I was in Iraq. He never saw me when I could run." He exhaled hard. "Things weren't the same between us when I came home. There were a couple others until I met Constanza. I thought we really had it made. We had a boy and a girl, Dean and Carly.

But…" Another hard exhale. "I didn't realize how broken I was until they left."

"So, what did you do?"

"I went to look for you."

My throat tightened.

"Laura, the time we had together, it was the only time when things were right."

"And you walked away from it."

"But you broke up with me."

"Because of what you did."

"And I regret it."

"Greg, you can't reboot your life. There are no take-backs and do-overs. You make your choices and live with them!"

"I can't. Not anymore."

"I'm not giving up my life to fix yours."

"Your life is broken too."

"My life is broken, but it's my life. I own it. I own every decision I've made. Yes, my life is hell right now, but it's my hell. I built it myself, down to the last chunk of brimstone. And I wouldn't want it any other way."

"But you can change it, Laura! It's not too late for us…"

"It is."

He sighed and looked down at his plate. I shook my head.

"I don't believe this, Greg. You seriously thought I'd drop everything? For you? You wasted 10 years of my life. I'm not throwing away the past 30."

He looked up at me with intense eyes. "You don't know how desperate…"

I stared back at him. "You need help!"

"I need you." His mouth quivered.

I saw the owner of the restaurant, a middle-aged woman who walked with a cane. I called out to her as she passed by. "Excuse me, but may I please have the check for my taco?"

"Of course." She spoke with a soft slur.

Greg stared at me. I folded my arms. He then looked off to the distance.

"What the hell was I thinking?"

I kept my arms tightly folded. He sighed and lowered his head.

"I'm sorry, Laura. It was wrong for me to put you in this spot. I—I don't know what to say."

"I do. Goodbye."

The woman with the cane handed me the check.

"Thank you. I'll pay for it up front."

The woman continued on her way.

I glanced at Greg. "Just promise me you'll get help."

He kept his head lowered and said nothing.

The chair groaned against the tile floor as I pushed away from the table. I got up and walked away without giving Greg another look.

*** BREAK ***

I felt a tremendous sense of release. Everything that happened 30 years ago, all the things I wanted to forget, they finally fell into place. It became so clear. What happened in San Rafael set me on the road I had to travel. If it weren't for Greg and the Posners, I wouldn't have the life I had today with Kevin, Henry, and Stacy. And if I could survive and grow from what happened then, I could deal with whatever happens next.

I turned on the radio.

"We have some REM and 'It's the End of the World' on the 80s Hits..."

I tapped the button to change to FM.

"Bruno Mars is up next with '24K Magic'..."

I leaned back in my seat. A smile spread across my face as the thump of twenty-first-century music filled my 2015 Honda CR-V.

*** BREAK ***

I set the figurine of Diana on the small side table next to the stairs. It belonged there.

My stomach grumbled. I was sorry I didn't have that taco at Mamá Freida. I figured I'd ask Kevin and the kids if they wanted me to order delivery. When I got to the kitchen, I found Henry at the table, busily texting.

He looked up. "I got a gig at an anti-Trump protest."

"That's good." I pulled a chair around the table and sat next to him.

"I thought you don't care about politics."

"I care about you. What matters to you matters to me."

He looked at me. "Dad said you were going to deal with your ex."

"I did. He's not going to cause us problems anymore."

"Why'd you even talk to him?"

"It can be good to see people you knew and remember old times."

"What if there are things you don't want to remember?"

I held Henry's hand. "What are you trying to forget?"

"Lisa."

"What happened?"

He exhaled hard twice. Whatever it was, it must have bad. So bad it made him leave everything behind. Just like I did when I fled from the Posners.

"We were at our apartment. I had some work to do in the office, and Lisa was hanging out with her white friends in the living room. I could hear them talk from where I was sitting. And they started joking. They called Lisa and me 'Kimye,' just like Kim Kardashian and Kanye West."

"I know what 'Kimye' means." I grimaced because I knew where this story was headed.

"So, you know how white people talk when they want to imitate us? They were doing that. So was Lisa." He looked down. His facial muscles twitched. "And then...Lisa...she called me a..." He exhaled hard.

I leaned closer to him. "Did you call her out about that?"

He nodded. "That's when she admitted it. She said, 'I thought it'd be cool to date a brutha.' She didn't love me for me."

I put my arm around his shoulders. "I'm so sorry."

He hung down his head. "I just wanted her to love me, the way you and Dad did."

"We still do."

He looked up at me. I looked directly at him.

"But Henry, just because you broke up with Lisa, it didn't mean you had to quit Google."

"When I took the job in the first place, I was wondering if I was doing the right thing."

"But I thought that was what you wanted. I thought you wanted to be a computer programmer. You did so well in it at school."

"Programming's all right, but I *love* music. You know that."

I nodded.

"You know how much I loved playing in marching band, singing in choir, and performing in musicals. And remember when I played bass in that band with Cathy, Kris, and Angel?"

"You did such a wonderful cover of 'Sweet Love' by Anita Baker for our anniversary. I still remember it."

He gave a small smile.

"But I thought music was just a side thing for you. You wanted a programming career."

"I wanted to get paid. You know how it is. But when I started working..." He sighed. "It's like every day, I was just waiting for six o'clock to roll around so I could get out of there. After I broke up with Lisa, I realized I wasn't being true to myself. This career wasn't right for me. It's not who I am. And if people are going to hate me for who I am, why I am pretending to be something I'm not?"

"But if you were that unhappy, why didn't you tell us?"

"I thought you and Dad would be disappointed in me."

"Henry, we want you to be happy. We want you to live a life that fulfills you. We want you to have a career that supports you financially but also gives you a reason to wake up in the morning. You know that music is a hard business to break into. Maybe you can find a way to make a good living and still do what you love."

"How do you do that? How *did you* do that?"

I gave my shoulders a small shrug. "Trial and error."

"That's it?"

I nodded. He scrunched his face.

"I thought you'd know. What did you learn from your past?"

"How to adapt and endure. Henry, no one knows what the future has in store. I didn't know then, and I don't know now. No one knows the outcome of our choices, no matter how well we think them through. All I know is that we have to carry on, no matter what happens next. We can't hold on to the past or run away from the consequences of our actions. We can't give up when things get too hard or too scary. All we can do is live."

He nodded. I put both my arms around his shoulders.

"Henry, just know that I love you very much. And Dad and I will always be there for you. Whatever happens, we'll always have each other."

"Laura!"

Kevin called from upstairs. Henry and I let go. He slipped his phone into his pocket, and we both rushed to the foot of the stairs. Kevin looked down from the top.

"Stacy needs help!"

*** BREAK ***

Henry and I sprinted to the top of the stairs. The door to the home office was open. Kevin nodded towards it. Henry and I rushed in.

We found Stacy seated in front of the Amiga.

"Mom, I want to see your old computer. Can you please show me how to use it?"

I caught my breath. My muscles relaxed. I noticed how well Stacy was sitting in the desk chair. Her back was straight, and her arms relaxed. She still looked too thin, but she seemed stronger.

"Of course, honey."

I stepped behind the chair and put my arm around her as I showed her how to boot the Amiga. Her hand seemed firm as she inserted the Kickstart disk, pressed the button to eject it, and inserted the Workbench disk. Her eyes opened wide as the white-and-orange icons appeared against the blue screen.

"Can you show me the program you worked on?"

"Sure." I reached for a disk with "PhotoLab Beta 15" in my handwriting on a label. It was the last version I worked on before I fled from the Posners.

"Insert this disk in the external drive." I handed her the disk.

I showed Stacy how to open the program. When it appeared on the screen, I realized that I hadn't seen it in 30 years. I was surprised when that old low-res camera made our image appear on the screen. Stacy leaned back in the chair.

"It looks like my photo app!" She looked up at me. "Just like the one on my phone."

She picked up her phone and opened its photo app. I looked at her phone and then looked at the Amiga. With the black-and-white image floating from the camera and Maria's white shutter-release button, the Amiga looked like the grandmother of Stacy's smartphone. I just kept staring at the Amiga and our software in amazement.

Stacy gave a small chuckle. "I bet you took the first selfie ever!"

I looked at the pile of disks. One had the label "Photo - CES January 1986."

"Excuse me," I whispered to Stacy. I ejected the Workbench disk from the internal drive and inserted the disk. Then, I reached over to the mouse and used it to open the file on the disk. The drive grunted and groaned until the image appeared. I stepped back and smiled. "There. My first selfie."

"Whoa!" Henry gasped.

Stacy stared at the picture and then looked up at me. "Mom, you looked so young. And beautiful!"

A smile broke across my face.

Henry shook my shoulder. "Mom, you invented the photo app!"

"Others did."

"But if you stayed and finished the program..."

"I wouldn't have met your dad and had you and Stacy."

Henry smiled at me. I turned to Kevin. He gave me a loving look I hadn't seen in a while.

Stacy's voice rose in excitement. "Can we take a picture?"

"Of course!" I reached for the mouse. I closed my 1986 picture and used the commands to start a new picture. Our 2016 faces floated on the screen. I let go of the mouse. "We have to get in really close."

We scrunched in together, pressing our faces to each other, fitting in as much of ourselves as we could on that antique low-res camera.

"When you're ready, Stacy, click the white button."

"OK, Mom." She chimed, "Smile!"

Stacy clicked. Code I wrote 30 years ago made the canvas turn white and bright for a fraction of a second, just like the flash on a camera. And there was my family, rendered in black-and-white pixels on a computer built before my children were born. We remained close together, staring at that image.

Kevin's voice trembled with awe. "We should save that."

I fished through the disks until I found an unlabeled one. "We will."

I ejected the disk with my CES photo and inserted the new disk. A few clicks of the mouse and I saved the image. I wasn't sure if it actually saved, so I swiped up the Workbench screen, eliciting "Wow!" and "I didn't know you could do that!" from my family. I double-clicked the icon for the disk. The image file was in the window. But what did it put down as the date?

"Excuse me, Stacy."

She scooted the desk chair away from the Amiga. I opened the CLI window and entered "LIST DF1:". The listing included our file with a timestamp of 10-Nov-16.

Now, I found myself blown away.

Henry turned to me. "What else can the Amiga do?"

Kevin's voice rose in excitement. "We should play that game. The one we always used to play."

My smile turned into a mischievous grin. "You mean, the one I always beat you at?"

"Yeah," Stacy beamed. "Let's see it!"

"All right." I fished through the disks. One caught my attention. "First, I have to show you the bouncing ball."

"I heard about that!" Henry shivered with excitement. "That's one of the most famous computer graphics demos ever!"

"Now, you can see and hear it." I ejected the disk with our picture and inserted the demo disk. I double-clicked the icon.

PBUM. PBUM-PBUM.

"Whoa!"

PBUM-PBUM. PBUM. PBUM-PBUM-PBUM.

Our eyes stayed fixed on the screen as that 3-D white-and-red checkered ball bounced against a gray background with a purple grid.

PBUM-PBUM. PBUM-PBUM. PBUM-PBUM-PBUM.

Henry seemed especially interested in the bouncing ball. "I wonder how they handle the collision detection and synchronize the video with the audio."

"I could show you the source code."

He smiled in a way I hadn't seen it in a while. "That would be so cool!"

I nodded.

PBUM-PBUM-PBUM. PBUM. PBUM-PBUM.

I stepped back and let Stacy scoot back in front of the Amiga. Kevin leaned over and kissed me. I kissed him back. In that kiss, I felt a spark between us that had been missing for a while. He put his arm around me. I rested my head on his cheek and let the warmth flow between us.

Together, we watched our children play with the Amiga with the same wonder and excitement I had a long time ago.

This novel may have one name on the cover, but it couldn't have been created without the work of a number of people. I appreciate the help of the following:

Reagan Rothe and the team at Black Rose Writing for taking a chance on this book and helping it take shape.

NaNoWriMo for inspiring me to dedicate time every day during November 2016, even during Black Friday sales, to commit this story to words.

The online Amiga community who continues to support and use this computer. Their videos, articles, and tales of recapping motherboards and dealing with leaking batteries refreshed my memory and provided helpful in-depth information.

My mentors Darlene Loiler and Robert Oliphant who gave me the inspiration and tools to write.

My family for their love and support.

Finally, Jay Miner, Robert J. Mical, David Needle, Dave Morse, and the others who brought this wonderful computer to the world.

NOTE FROM THE AUTHOR

Word-of-mouth is crucial for any author to succeed. If you enjoyed the book, please leave a review online—anywhere you are able. Even if it's just a sentence or two. It would make all the difference and would be very much appreciated.

Thanks!
Matthew

ABOUT THE AUTHOR

Amiga is inspired by Matthew Arnold Stern's experiences in the computer industry in the 1980s as a technical writer and computer journalist. He earned awards for his writing and public speaking, including Distinguished Toastmaster and an Award of Excellence from the International Online Communications Competition. He grew up in the San Fernando Valley and graduated Summa Cum Laude from California State University, Northridge. He is married with two children, a granddaughter, and lots of cats.

Thank you so much for reading one of our **Women's Fiction** novels.

If you enjoyed the experience, please check out our recommended title for your next great read!

The Apple of My Eye by Mary Ellen Bramwell

"A mature love story with an intense plot. This book has something important to say." –William O. Shakespeare, Professor of English, Brigham Young University

View other Black Rose Writing titles at www.blackrosewriting.com/books and use promo code **PRINT** to receive a **20% discount** when purchasing.

www.ingramcontent.com/pod-product-compliance
Lightning Source LLC
Chambersburg PA
CBHW011133100726
47898CB00009B/2963